Jane Austen stole my boyfriend

Cora Harrison worked as a head teacher before writing her first novel. She has since published twenty-six historical novels for children and many books for adults. Cora lives on a farm near the Burren in the west of Ireland.

Also by Cora Harrison

I Was Jane Austen's Best Friend

CORA HARRISON

Illustrated by Susan Hellard

MACMILLAN

First published 2011 by Macmillan Children's Books

This edition published 2012 by Macmillan Children's Books
a division of Macmillan Publishers Limited
20 New Wharf Road, London N1 9RR
Basingstoke and Oxford
Associated companies throughout the world
www.panmacmillan.com

ISBN 978-0-330-50954-1

1 3 5 7 9 8 6 4 2

A CIP catalogue record for this book is available from
the British Library.

Printed and bound by CPI Group (UK) Ltd, Croydon CR0 4YY

*This book is dedicated to Rachel Petty,
editor, enthusiast, Jane Austen fan,
my companion and adviser through this
speculative excursion into the girlhood of
Jane and her cousin, Jenny (Jane) Cooper.*

MY JOURNAL
Monday, 11 April 1791

'I hate Jane Austen! I really hate her!'

I stop. I know that voice.

'Oh, Lavinia, Mama says that Jane Austen is just a vulgar, husband-hunting, affected little minx. She says you are to take no notice of her.'

I know that voice too.

It's Lavinia and Caroline Thorpe. I remember them well from the time when Jane and I were at boarding school at Southampton. They made my life a misery there. I can still hear them chanting, 'Look at Jenny Cooper's muslin – it looks like a rag.' 'Jenny Cooper has the snub nose of a servant girl, she's such a little dwarf, isn't she?'; or else, to the owner of the school, 'Mrs Cawley, Jenny Cooper has broken a school rule!'

And now here they are at the Assembly Rooms at Basingstoke.

I hesitate at the door of the ladies' cloakroom. One curl has come loose from its knot at the back of my head during the hectic pace of the Boulanger dance, but it will have to stay like that. I can't go in there and face the two Misses Thorpe. I turn to go, but then something stops me and I turn back. Before my courage ebbs away I burst through the door, say to them icily, 'Jane Austen is my best friend; I'll thank you not to gossip about her.'

I push past them and examine myself in the glass, trying to appear calm. I pretend to look at myself, but I can see them sneering, shrugging their shoulders as if I am not worth a reply. I carefully pin up the stray curl, and then decide to leave it lying there on my neck – it looks nice, I think. I half turn and with my head over my shoulder survey my gown, pure white and sprigged with dainty silver flowers. The train is beautiful. A hundred tiny deep blue beads have been sewn to it and they twinkle in the candlelight. I smooth my long white gloves, making sure that they fit snugly over the elbow, and then I sweep past the two Thorpe girls without another glance. As I close the door behind them I hear Caroline say, 'Anyway, we're going to Bath for the season; he's bound to be there.' She raises her voice a little and says, 'And the Austens and their beggarly cousin won't be there to interfere.'

When I get back to the Assembly Rooms the new dance has not yet been called, but Jane is already hand in hand with Newton. No wonder Lavinia is so upset. The Honourable Newton Wallop is the second son of the Earl of Portsmouth and it's rumoured that he will be the heir to the Portsmouth estates as the eldest son, John, is strange and, according to Jane, it is feared that he is a lunatic. Newton has been a pupil at Mr Austen's house at Steventon, and he and Jane seem great friends, joking and laughing. They've been dancing together for most of the evening.

'Your very humble servant, ma'am,' says Newton, and Jane replies in very affected tones, 'La, sir, pray do not be such a tease.' And then she laughs as Newton reminds her of the time that she and he made an apple-pie bed for Jane's prim sister, Cassandra. Lavinia would be furious if she could hear how friendly they sound.

I don't waste any more thoughts on Lavinia. I can see Thomas coming towards me. I don't push my way through the crowd to join him. I just stand and look at him.

Captain Thomas Williams, the youngest captain in the navy — brave, handsome and noble . . . and in love with me! Tall — taller than most people at the ball; broad shoulders; black hair gleaming like a blackbird's wing under the candlelight from the chandeliers above; dark brown eyes, so piercing and yet . . . I think back to the little damp woodland and the bluebells and tiny forget-me-nots at our feet and how those eyes were so soft and pleading then. And still I can't believe that he has asked me to marry him.

He has reached me now.

'You look so beautiful,' he murmurs in my ear, and I smile and know that whether my curls are pinned up tidily or escaping down the nape of my neck, it makes no difference to him. He loves me as I am and no matter what I do or say. We go and stand beside Newton and Jane.

'Oh la, sir, you make me blush,' she is saying to him, and Newton instantly responds with a deep bow and says loudly, 'Madam, your beauty overwhelms me. No poor words of mine are enough to describe you.'

'Dearest Newton . . .' Jane begins in a very lofty way, her voice so loud that several people turn to listen to her, and then she spoils it by hissing, 'You're on the wrong side, Newton. You are such a ninny. Go and stand beside Jenny. Quick, the music is starting.'

I smile at Newton as he joins me. He's quite handsome – not handsome in the same manly way as my Thomas, but he is large-eyed, curly-haired and fresh-faced. He stretches out his hand to Jane, and Thomas takes my hand and we whirl around as the last dance of the evening begins.

I can see Lavinia and Caroline Thorpe now. Neither is dancing. They are standing in front of their mama and Lavinia is half twisted towards her, saying something. I can guess what. When she turns back her face is full of rage, eyes narrowed as she looks at Jane.

'Jane,' I whisper, 'look at Lavinia Thorpe, over there by the fireplace. She's furious with you.'

Jane looks over her shoulder, a lightning look, but that is enough for someone with Jane's quick wits.

Newton dances back and Jane puts up her hand to hold his. She smiles sweetly into his face and drops a demure curtsy and then they are off dancing rather closer than is usual, both of them laughing as the two rows of dancers clap them energetically.

'Jane,' I say when we are back in our bedroom at Steventon, 'I think that you have made an enemy.'

'Don't care,' she says, carefully hanging up her ball gown.

'She'll gossip about you,' I say, hanging my gown beside hers.

'Who cares about Lavinia Thorpe?' Jane's voice is scornful as she sits on the stool in front of our little looking glass and begins to take the pins from her curls.

'Not me,' I say, taking up the hairbrush. I will brush her hair a hundred times and then she will do the same for me. I don't care about Lavinia Thorpe either. All I can think of now is that my uncle, Mr Austen, will be coming back from Oxford tomorrow and that Thomas will ask for my hand in marriage.

And then we will live happily forever after.

Wednesday, 13 April 1791

It's my birthday today. I'm seventeen years old.

And I am in love with the most wonderful man in the world.

And he is in love with me too – he wants to marry me.

I'm trying to draw him, to do justice to his tall figure, his broad shoulders, his dark hair and his lovely brown eyes, but I am crying so hard that my tears splash down and spoil my drawing.

Because we cannot be married. The match has been forbidden.

And to think that my own brother, the only near relation I have left in the world, should have done this to me. I know that it is his horrible wife, Augusta, who has prompted him, but he didn't have to obey her in that cowardly way that he always does. If only my mother were still alive, she would not have allowed it to happen.

I look across the room at the figure of my cousin and best friend, Jane; the curtains of her bed are drawn back, but she is still asleep. Not surprisingly really, as it must be very early in the morning. There are no noises to show that anyone in the house is up. The birdsong sounds as if it's not much past dawn. Jane has a smile on her lips. Just before she fell asleep her last words were: 'I'm definitely going to put your dreadful sister-in-law into a book. People will laugh at her in the years to come. You just wait.'

No doubt she is now dreaming of the great novel she is going to write.

Or is she dreaming of the Honourable Newton Wallop and what fun it was to snatch him from Lavinia Thorpe?

No, it's probably her novel – writing is more important to Jane than anything.

I have to smile a bit at the memory of all the ridiculous things that Jane writes about this Augusta who is going to feature in her novel, but then my tears well up again. Soon I will run out of dry handkerchiefs, so I try hard to stop.

And I will stop!

I'm not going to allow this to happen.

Thomas and I will get married just as we planned.

I will go to live in his house on the Isle of Wight and walk through the forget-me-not woods with him.

It's good for me to get angry. It makes me feel that I can change things.

All I have to do to feel furious is think of what happened between Thomas and my stupid brother, Edward-John, and his wife, Augusta, who has hated me from the moment that my mama died and she had to 'welcome' me into their house.

I must try to write down everything that was said, and not said . . .

Mr Austen, my very kind uncle, had suffered a heavy cold while staying with his eldest son, James, in Oxford and was still not very well, I think, when he arrived off the early-morning coach on Tuesday morning. He looked pale and tired, and when Thomas asked him for the favour of an interview in his study he seemed more resigned than curious. I saw my aunt, Mrs Austen, look up with an air of sharp interest, and now I wish so much that she had joined her husband from the start. If she had, perhaps Edward-John would not have been involved so quickly.

But she didn't, and Jane and I were left gripping hands under the table until Mrs Austen said abruptly, 'Come on, Jane; help your sister to clear off the breakfast things. Jenny, you look in a dream — a bit of housework will bring you down to earth, won't it, Cassandra?' But Mrs Austen did not look annoyed. She flashed an amused look at her eldest daughter to invite her to join in the joke and then patted me reassuringly on the arm when I went to take her plate.

At that moment Mr Austen's head popped around the door, looking flustered.

'Edward-John,' he said in his hesitant manner, 'perhaps you should come into my study and have a word with Captain Williams.'

'Certainly.' Edward-John got to his feet in a stately manner and Augusta immediately followed him from the room. Mr Austen shut the door firmly behind them without glancing at his wife, who compressed her lips angrily and then tried to smile reassuringly at me.

'Papa won't allow Edward-John to say no,' whispered Jane to me, but I said nothing in reply. I was very fond of Mr Austen, but if Edward-John and Augusta, especially Augusta, were against this marriage, I feared there was not much chance of Mr Austen changing their minds.

The three of us had finished clearing the table. Jane was vigorously sweeping the oak-boarded floor, while Mrs Austen, instead of going off to the dairy as usual, set about rubbing the copper kettle to a high shine. Mr Austen's pupils had been sent to the schoolroom to start on their lessons by themselves and I had begun, nervously, to polish the sideboard when Thomas came to the doorway.

'Jenny, could you come here for a minute?' he said. His voice was tight with anger. I went towards him, putting my hand in his. Suddenly I felt cold. Behind me I heard Mrs Austen get to her feet, dropping the copper kettle with a thud back on to the hob by the fireplace. She said nothing but followed us both, and Jane squeezed in beside her.

Mr Austen's study was a small one. He was seated behind the desk, with Edward-John standing beside him, and Augusta had arranged her lace flounces across the only other chair in the room. Mrs Austen did not give her a glance as she placed herself on the window seat. Jane perched on her father's library steps, and Thomas, still keeping hold of my hand, drew my arm through his own and faced my uncle and brother across the desk.

'I don't see what this has to do with Jenny and Jane,' began Augusta. Even she did not have the courage to say it had nothing to do with Mrs Austen.

'I disagree with you, ma'am,' said Thomas. I had never heard his voice so hard. 'I think Jenny's future is very much her business.'

'Miss Cooper,' said Augusta, trying to make her reproof of his familiarity with my name sound jolly, but Thomas did not reply. He did not even look at her. He pressed my arm close to his ribs and turned to Edward-John.

'Perhaps, sir, you would be good enough to explain to your sister why you have refused my offer of marriage,' he said, and he sounded as though he spoke through gritted teeth.

Edward-John gulped a bit. He wasn't used to dealing with naval officers like Thomas, who had a note of authority in every word that he spoke.

'My sister,' he said with an attempt at bluster, 'doesn't need any explanation of an action that I, as her sole guardian, take for her good.'

'Jenny knows,' said Augusta sweetly, 'we just want the best for her.'

Thomas squeezed my arm again and this gave me courage to speak up for myself.

'The best thing for me,' I said boldly, 'is to be allowed to marry Captain Williams. That is what I want to do and that is what will make me happy.'

I saw with some compassion the slightly ashamed look that Mr Austen gave me. I understood and was sorry for him.

'Oh, Jenny dear . . .' Augusta affected a tone that I supposed was meant to be motherly, but still sounded spiteful. 'Believe me, we just want the best for you. You are so young, just sixteen years old!'

'She's seventeen tomorrow,' said Jane. 'And then she'll be in her eighteenth year,' she added, earning herself an angry glance from Augusta.

I took a deep breath. It was ridiculous, but I was so afraid of Edward-John and Augusta. I think that, between them both, they had broken my spirit after my mother died. While I lived in their house in Bristol, I had been like a little mouse, just whispering replies and silently agreeing to everything that was proposed. It was only when I had become best friends with Jane — when I had learned from her to be independent and to think for myself — that I had begun to question whether Edward-John and his wife Augusta really were devoted to my interests. Augusta hates me; I know that. She hates me and she doesn't want anything good to happen to me.

Suddenly I was angry.

'I want to marry Thomas.' It all came out in a bit of a rush, but I made sure that my voice sounded clear and strong. Thomas pressed my arm again. I almost felt as though we were one person, standing up there in front of the hostile presence of Edward-John and Augusta.

'Come now, let us be reasonable. What are Captain Williams's prospects?' Mrs Austen sounded unusually conciliatory. Usually she gave her opinion in a very forthright manner. She was my mother's only sister, and if she could not change Edward-John's mind, then no one could. However, in her usual alert fashion, she had sized up Augusta and there was a note of caution in her voice.

Thomas turned to her gratefully. 'My prospects are good, ma'am,' he said respectfully. 'As you know, I am a captain in the Royal Navy; my yearly salary is five hundred pounds. In addition I have been privileged by being entrusted with various commissions from the East India Trading Company, and these have proved very lucrative indeed to me.'

Even Augusta looked a little impressed at that. The Austens had remote connections with Warren Hastings, the director of the East India Company, and everyone knew that Warren Hastings was almost as rich as the King of England himself.

'And,' continued Thomas, pressing home his advantage, 'since I understand that Jenny's mother left her fifty pounds a year until she turns twenty-one, this money can be invested for her in diamond mines in the East Indies and I can guarantee to double and treble its value within a few years.'

And that, as Jane said afterwards, was his mistake. He should never have mentioned the fifty pounds. Augusta hates me, but she quite likes having that extra fifty pounds a year – very little of which is spent on me!

'I could see those boiled-gooseberry eyes of hers pop out even further than usual,' said Jane when we were talking about it in our bedroom. 'It was obvious that she was thinking about how much she would lose if you were married. Edward-John would have to hand over your property to your husband then. That's the law.' Jane as usual knew everything about marriage.

'It will, of course, be put into a trust for Jenny, or for her children, if that is what she wants,' continued Thomas, a little puzzled by the silence in the room. 'And there will no doubt be another war with France any moment now . . .' He stopped.

Mrs Austen immediately chipped in. 'Of course, you have already won so many rich prizes in the last war, haven't you? My son Frank told me all about it. And I understand that you have a good property in the Isle of Wight, which has been handsomely furnished.'

I looked around the room. Edward-John was standing there, his mouth slightly open and a frown knitting his black eyebrows. I knew the expression on his face: it was envy. He didn't like to hear of another man being richer than he was. Augusta had pursed her lips and was doing her best to look like a concerned mother. Mr Austen looked uncomfortable, but Mrs Austen just sat there beaming, a broad smile of approval lighting up her weather-beaten face.

Thomas noticed this as soon as I did and he immediately addressed himself to her. 'What do you think, ma'am?' he enquired. 'Do you think that your late sister, Jenny's mother, would have approved of this match for her daughter?'

'I'm certain that she would.' Mrs Austen's voice rose to its highest pitch to drown out something that Augusta was saying. 'My sister Jane would always want the best thing for her daughter's happiness.'

'My dear,' said Mr Austen tentatively, 'I don't feel that we can interfere. Edward-John—'

'Stuff and nonsense!' Mrs Austen interrupted, the light of battle in her faded blue eyes. 'As if I should not have the liberty of giving my opinion on this important matter for my only niece! Edward-John, I'm sure, will be guided by the experience of his aunt – as indeed his poor mother would have wished.'

'After all, there can be no reason for him to want to retain Jenny since she no longer lives with them . . .' put in Jane with an innocent air.

'Jane!' exclaimed Mrs Austen automatically, but not being a woman to disdain any weapon, she hastily added, 'Not that there isn't sense in what she says. You were happy to leave Jenny with us for the next few years, so why do you now wish to prevent her making this very advantageous marriage, Edward-John? It wouldn't be anything to do with retaining her legacy for your own use for another four years, would it?'

Edward-John flushed an unpleasant blotchy shade of red, but Augusta was made of sterner stuff. She rose to her feet, her flounced gown sweeping around her.

'After that insult, I fear that we must leave this house immediately,' she said in her loud, bullying tone of voice. 'Pray, sir,' she addressed herself to Mr Austen, 'send a boy to summon a post-chaise; we will take the midday stagecoach back to Bristol.'

'Not so fast!' Thomas leaned across the desk, his face coming close to Edward-John who flinched, drew back and gave a sideways look at his wife. 'You haven't given me any sensible reason for turning down my suit. You haven't made any enquiry into my character or my prospects. You didn't even want to bother asking Jenny whether she would be happy with me. I cannot take this rejection. What if we waited another six months before announcing any engagement? Would that change your opinion?'

'Captain Williams,' said Augusta sweetly, 'I'm sure that you naval gentlemen are used to having your own way, but I must assure you that my husband and I are quite certain about this matter and nothing you can say will make any difference to us. Jenny is far too young to get engaged and certainly too young to get married. I don't feel that any girl of less than twenty-one should be married, and I will not countenance a long engagement which would spoil her prospects for a better match. The answer is no, Captain Williams.'

She sounded quite certain as she said that final 'no'. My heart sank. Of course, Augusta herself was in her middle twenties when she married Edward-John, and since everything Augusta does is always perfect, then of course no other girls should be married earlier than that. A feeling of panic rose inside me and I turned back to Thomas, who had made an impatient movement.

'I wasn't speaking to you, ma'am.' Thomas dropped my hand and strode across the room to stand behind the desk, deliberately interposing his broad back between Augusta and her husband. Bending down a little, he gazed intently into Edward-John's eyes. His own, I could see, were black with anger, and I wasn't surprised when Edward-John, never the bravest of men, looked away. Thomas persisted though.

'Mr Cooper, please listen to me for a moment.' His voice had a note of heavy formality in it, and despite himself Edward-John looked back at him. 'I have asked you for the honour of your sister's hand. I am a man of good character, of a reasonable fortune and with good prospects. You can ask anyone. Ask the Earl of Portsmouth. Ask my uncle, Admiral Williams. I'm not demanding an immediate answer, though I would have hoped to get one this morning. What I am asking now is that you will consider the matter and let me know what you think as soon as possible. I would like to have this matter settled before I embark on my next voyage to the East Indies.'

I'm not sure whether Edward-John really was considering the matter, or whether he was too afraid of Thomas to give a direct refusal, but he definitely looked ill at ease, trying to avoid everyone's eye and saying nothing.

Augusta, however, was not to be defeated. Now she boldly pushed her way past Mr Austen and took her husband's arm.

'Come, Edward-John,' she said coldly. 'I'm sure you feel that we have been insulted enough in this house. We will wait outside until the post-chaise is summoned. Pray, Mr Austen, ask a servant to fetch it and to bring down our travelling bags.'

She turned on Thomas.

'Believe me, Captain Williams, we are acting for the best for all concerned here. Jenny, poor girl, has problems and would not make a suitable wife for you. I speak only for your own good, Jenny, but I must say that you have no grace of manner, no true politeness, no accomplishments worth having — these perhaps could have been compensated for by good looks, if you possessed them, but alas!'

And then she escorted her husband from the room and left everyone staring at each other. Mrs Austen was looking furious and Mr Austen distressed, but Jane burst into a loud infectious laugh and Thomas joined in. I laughed too and a broad grin creased Mrs Austen's face. Somehow at that moment I left the last vestige of my fear of Augusta behind and saw her for what she was: a concentrated ball of spite and malice.

Once they had gone, the day was not unhappy. Thomas was very certain that they would change their minds. He said immediately that he would get his uncle, the admiral, to write to them. And Lady Portsmouth . . . And Warren Hastings for good measure . . . He was so sure this would succeed that I began to cheer up a little and to forget all that I knew of Augusta's stubborn character. After church, Mrs Austen suggested that I take Captain Williams for a walk, and she gave Mr Austen a stern look when he tried to say something. I'm sure that my uncle felt that I should be chaperoned since no engagement was going to be allowed, but Mrs Austen, like Thomas, was determined that my story was going to have a happy ending.

'Hold my hand,' said Thomas softly as we passed through the gate and into the field beside Steventon parsonage. The sun was out and it lit up the pale yellow of the cowslips among the blades of new grass.

'If only you didn't have to go tomorrow,' I said as I boldly gave him my hand. I shouldn't have done really – we were not even properly engaged. Still, I didn't care. I turned a smiling face towards him. I would pretend that all was well and that my brother was pleased to hear of my engagement and that everything was being planned for our marriage next year.

'Tell me about your ship,' I said, bending down and touching an early bluebell under the hazel bushes in the hedgerow.

'Have you ever been in a ship?' He asked the question with a smile and didn't seem surprised when I shook my head.

'One day you'll come on a voyage with me,' he promised. 'I'll make them fit up a snug little cabin for you just near the front mast and you can sit there and do your sewing.'

'I'd prefer to be out on deck with you,' I said boldly. 'I would love that. I've seen the sea at Bristol. That's just a port, but I can just imagine how wonderful it would be if there was nothing but sea and sky.'

Thomas looked at me and smiled. 'Wouldn't you be frightened of the sea?' he asked tenderly. 'Not even in a storm?'

I thought about that. But then I shook my head. 'No, I wouldn't, not if you were there.'

'Jenny,' he said, looking at me intently, 'I'll always be there, I'll always look after you and I'll never allow you to be scared again.'

'Not even of Augusta?' But I laughed as I said it. Somehow, standing there with him in the clear April sunshine with his arm around my waist and watching the young calves race up and down the field, it seemed as if not even Augusta could be a threat to our happiness.

'Certainly not of Augusta. She's just a low-bred piece of nonsense. What possessed your brother to marry her? We will count ourselves as engaged, won't we? Even if it has to be in secret . . .'

'A secret engagement,' I murmured. It seemed very romantic. I remember thinking that if only I could keep the way I felt in that moment within me, then I wouldn't care whether the engagement was secret or whether the whole world knew of my happiness.

Now it is time for breakfast. Before I dress and go downstairs there is just enough time to write of what happened this morning. I had already put my journal away when I heard a creak of the stairs and then a soft footstep outside the door. I put my wrapper around me and ran to the door. There was no one there, but lying on the ground was a lovely bunch of forget-me-nots and a small box wrapped in gold paper. I picked up the little forget-me-nots and tucked the bunch into the lace of my nightgown so that they would lie against my heart.

And then, without my even knowing what I was going to do, I ran down the stairs.

The front door had just closed cautiously. I flew down the hall, my bare feet making no noise, and opened the door. He had started to walk across the gravel when he saw me. In a moment he was back. He snatched me up from the cold, hard stone.

I was in his arms. Held against his broad chest.

And he was saying things . . .

Incoherent statements of love and endearment . . .

'My darling, my darling, my darling . . .' He must have said that forty times.

And I was trying to reply as he kissed the tears from my cheek as they fell.

It seemed only a second but yet almost like hours before he finally put me down.

The forget-me-nots fell out from the lace on my nightgown and on to the step. He snatched them up, put them to his lips and then gave them back to me, opened the door and gently put me inside.

And then he was gone and I was left holding the limp bunch of forget-me-nots that had been crushed between us when he kissed me.

And I have never been so happy or so miserable in my life, standing on the stone floor of the hall and remembering his last words, muttered in a hoarse whisper.

'Keep these, my darling; they will be the symbol of our love.'

Wednesday afternoon, 13 April

Everyone was very nice to me at breakfast time. There was a chorus of 'Happy Birthday' when I came into the parlour wearing the beautiful little gold cross studded with tiny seed pearls that Thomas had left for me in the little box. The delicate forget-me-nots had been pressed. I would keep them forever.

All the family gave me presents. Mr Austen gave me a book of poems from his library, Mrs Austen a lovely little box for keeping letters in, young Charles gave me a drawing of my donkey that he had done himself, Jane gave me a purse she had netted and Cassandra a small needle holder made from neatly embroidered pieces of cloth. Frank had whittled a ring stand for me from a piece of cherry wood (congratulating me on being the same age as him now) and his older brother Henry (who was back from university) a coloured transparency of Tintern Abbey to put on my window. There was going to be a cake and perhaps even some whipped syllabub for supper tonight – all to be a big surprise, Jane told me in a whisper. I think that everyone had prepared for a celebration of my engagement as well as my birthday.

Jane is doing her level best to amuse me and to take

my mind off my troubles. This morning, after we had each brushed the other's hair for the usual one hundred strokes, she took out her writing desk from the drawer, dipped her quill into the ink pot and immediately began writing. It's amazing how fast she writes her stories. It's very different writing down things that have happened – I only have to remember and to write the interesting bits, but she has to invent, and yet she does it so quickly.

And this is what she wrote:

Augusta Cooper would have been considered to be a raving beauty had not she possessed two of the most ugly pale green eyes that anyone could have imagined. Her nose was good, though it would have been better if it were precisely halved in size. Her mouth would have smiled sweetly except that it was permanently locked into a downturned expression by a scowl that made horses bolt when they saw it. She was madly in love with a handsome young naval captain, but alas, he preferred another!

'Stick it into your journal,' advised Jane. 'And then draw a picture of Augusta beside it and that should cheer you up every time you look at it. That woman is so madly jealous of you that she would do anything to spoil your happiness. Now let's go up to Deane Gate Inn and meet Eliza. She's coming on the stagecoach

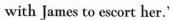

with James to escort her.'

James, of course, was coming for the grand performance of the play *The Rivals* (James had written a prologue) that we had all been rehearsing for ages. Eliza was his principal actress – bound to be the star of the play.

Eliza de Feuillide was Jane's cousin, Mr Austen's niece. She had been born in India, spent her early years in England, then as a very young girl had been taken to France and invited to dances in the court of Louis XVI and his queen, Marie Antoinette. She had met a French aristocrat, the Comte of Feuillide, and had married him. She lived in London with her mother and her little boy now as France was so dangerous with talk of revolution, but her husband visited her from time to time.

Some people, Jane had told me, whispered that Eliza was actually the natural daughter of the great Warren Hastings, the Governor-General of India. Whatever her birth, Eliza is incredibly sophisticated and worldly and Jane and I both love her. She gave us such good advice when we were both going to our first ball and got us ready, using her Indian shampoos –

something to wash our hair with – and some gorgeous soaps and bath oils.

The two of us were walking up the steep hill between Steventon, where Jane's home was, and Deane Gate Inn, where the stagecoach stopped, and I was just asking Jane what she thought Eliza would say when she heard of Thomas's proposal when we heard a shout from behind us and Henry came racing up the hill after us, his long legs covering the ground quickly.

Henry is Jane's favourite brother – though I think that I like Frank the best. It seems strange to me now that when I met Henry first I fell in love with him and his bright hazel-coloured eyes. I don't think that he was in love with me though, just flirting. Still, we are good friends now and Thomas likes him.

'Hang on a minute,' he said, pretending to pant. 'I'll come with you; knowing Eliza, there will probably be a hatbox or parasol that she needs someone to carry for her.'

'James will be there,' said Jane, but she was pleased to have Henry. I was a bit sorry because I was looking forward to talking to Eliza about Thomas and I didn't think that I could do that while Henry was there.

The Austens, however, are a very close family and Henry seems to have decided to treat me like a sister now that he knows it no good flirting with me.

'Poor Jenny,' he said. 'What a shame! I would have thought that your brother would have found Captain Williams a good match. What's the problem? I asked

Father but he was very tight-lipped with me and forbade me to discuss the matter.'

I wondered how he knew that Thomas had proposed, but Henry just laughed at me and told me that all the signs were pretty obvious.

'You should have asked Mama; she would probably have told you,' said Jane.

'I was going to, but then I thought I would come and ask you instead.' Henry turned an interested face from one to the other of us, his dark eyebrows slightly raised.

I told Jane to tell him, and she made a great story out of it. Even I had to laugh a little at her description of Augusta's face when Mrs Austen asked Edward-John whether he was thinking about my legacy.

'And of course he will have the use of that until you are twenty-one. Sharp old Mama!' Henry gave a long, low whistle.

I told him that I thought his father was a bit upset about it all.

'He gaped like a fish when Mama said that about Edward-John wanting to hold on to you for the sake of your legacy,' put in Jane with a grin. 'Dear Papa, he can never bear to think badly of anyone.'

'You'll have to marry a lord, Jenny,' said Henry. 'That would be the only thing that would compensate Edward-John for the loss of your fortune.'

I told him that Jane was the one to marry a lord; that I would be happy with my captain from the navy. 'And won't Lavinia be jealous,' I said to Jane, and we both giggled so much that Henry heard the noise of the galloping horses before we did.

Eliza and James were the only passengers on the stage-coach when it drew up in Deane Gate Inn yard. James, Jane's eldest brother, jumped out, and before he greeted us he carefully handed out Eliza, who looked even smaller than usual standing between her two tall young cousins.

'Jane! Jenny!'
She kissed us both, before standing on her toes and giving Henry a quick peck on the cheek.

'Oh, but Pug!' she exclaimed. 'I've left my darling Pug. James, get Pug out immediately and let him meet his cousins.'

With a slight grimace James dived back into the carriage and emerged, rather red in the face, with the smallest and ugliest dog I have ever seen. James looked so funny holding him that I found it hard to keep a smile from my face and Henry laughed aloud.

'Suits you, James,' he said mockingly. 'The latest accessory for an Oxford fellow – one pug.'

'Here,' said James impatiently, thrusting the pug into his sister's arms.

'Oh, he's sweet,' she crooned, and Eliza beamed with satisfaction.

'I've got James to write some additional lines in the play. Pug will act in it too. I'm sure that Mrs Malaprop would have had a pug.'

Jane opened her mouth to say something and then gave a hasty glance at James and shut it again. Eliza was busy giving instructions about hatboxes and the two young men were quite busy. We were all loaded up by the time we followed the post-chaise down the hill to Deane, and I whispered to Jane not to say anything to Eliza for the moment. I didn't really want my love affairs discussed in front of James. He was never as friendly to me as his brothers and sisters were.

Mr Austen was delighted to see Eliza; she was the daughter of his only sister and he was very fond of her. Mrs Austen too was in very good humour, though she looked rather dubiously at 'Puggy'. She and Eliza enjoyed each other's wit and jokes were soon flying.

Jane and I went upstairs to write our weekly letter to George, Jane's handicapped brother, who was now boarded with a family some distance away. Since George could not read, the letter was mostly pictures, which I had to draw, as Jane was not good with the pencil. I drew a picture of Pug and then one of the stagecoach with Eliza and James getting out of it. George was always interested in stagecoaches, and he would like this.

'Let's go along and help Eliza to unpack,' said Jane when we had finished and folded over the piece of paper and stuck it down with a blob of scarlet sealing wax.

Eliza welcomed us with open arms. 'Come in, come in, *mes petites*,' she said, as usual mixing up bits of French with bits of English. 'And, Jenny, tell me all. What is happening with your *amours*?'

'You tell it,' I said to Jane.

'In one word,' interrupted Eliza, 'did he propose, the gallant captain, *hein*?'

'Well,' said Jane dramatically, 'first there was a lovers' quarrel. Jenny wrote to him saying that she never wanted to see him again. And then Captain Williams revealed himself to be a hero. You just can't imagine, Eliza.'

I walked over to the window while Jane told Eliza the whole story of the misunderstanding between Thomas and myself and about his heroism at the stage-coach robbery. He did sound so magnificent!

'So . . .' breathed Eliza. 'Come and tell me, Jenny, *chérie*. Did he propose?'

I came back over and sat on the bed beside her and she kindly put her pug on my knee. I must say that it made things easier to be patting the comic little dog

while I told the sad story about Edward-John's refusal of the offer of marriage.

Eliza drew in a deep breath and nodded her head
solemnly. 'This needs thinking of,' she said. 'I will
talk to *mon cher oncle* about this. There are legal steps
which could be taken. If your legacy were to be taken
out of Edward-John's hands and placed in your uncle's
since you are now living with him, then the objections
might disappear. I have a lawyer, who is very much
in love with me, who may be able to help in this matter. I shall see him when I go to Bath.'

Jane looked at me and I looked at her. A little thrill
of excitement passed through us. We could read each
other's thoughts in our eyes. Neither of us believed
that this lawyer could do anything – after all, my
brother was my guardian. It was the mention of Bath
that was exciting. We had considered asking Mrs Austen to take us to Bath, but to go with Eliza would be
such fun. Jane clasped her hands together.

'Oh, Eliza, would you take us to Bath, Jenny and
myself? Oh, please – we'd be no trouble to you.'

Eliza pursed her lips and looked a little concerned.

'And we'd take care of Pug for you,' persisted Jane.

Eliza laughed. 'It's not that you will be any trouble
to me, Jane, *ma chérie*. It's just that I fear your mother
may not trust me with you two. But *nous verrons*.
Let us concentrate on the play now. You help me to
unpack and then we must go out into the barn. James
is eager for the rehearsal.'

Thursday, 14 April 1791

Jane was awake before me and was leaning over my bed when I opened my eyes. Her face was very near to mine, her hazel eyes sparkling and her dark curly hair still neatly tied in two plaits. She gave me quite a start.

'I know what you must do, you and your gallant captain.' She sounded the way she always does when some elaborate story has got hold of her mind.

'What?' I asked sleepily.

'You'll have to go to Gretna Green!'

'Where?' I stared at her stupidly.

'Wake up, Jenny,' said Jane impatiently. 'You must know where Gretna Green is. Haven't you read about it in novels? Don't you know that once you reach the border between England and Scotland you can get married without asking permission of any parent or guardian? A blacksmith at Gretna Green can marry you. I thought of trying it myself so that I will have the experience for my novels, but now if you do it, I shall go with you as a sort of chaperone and not have the bother of making up my mind whom to marry.'

I rubbed the sleep from my eyes, sat up and told her that I didn't think that Thomas would like that and that I couldn't imagine him doing something like going to Gretna Green. 'He's more likely to fight it out with Edward-John,' I added.

'A duel!' Jane's eyes sparkled with excitement.

'Pistols at dawn! Or swords! I definitely think swords. They would be much more romantic.'

I asked her whom she would go to Gretna Green with if she were going to make a runaway marriage (partly to distract her from the idea of a duel – I didn't want to even think about that).

'I think Newton Wallop would be the most fun,' pronounced Jane. 'Anyway, he is the son of an earl and I do want to make a splendid match.' And then she added thoughtfully, 'The elopement might even be gossiped about at court, and what more could a girl want?'

I got out of bed and shivering a little began to wash with the cold water in the basin on the washstand. Now that we were almost to Easter, Mrs Austen had declared that fires in the bedroom were an extravagance so instead of picking a can of nice hot water from the hob by the fire, we had to wash in cold.

While I was washing, Jane scribbled vigorously on a piece of paper, her quill dipping rapidly in and out of the ink pot, and she was shaking sand over the result by the time that I dried myself.

'Listen to this,' she said. 'You can stick it in your journal afterwards. It's another few words for my Augusta story. I think it will be my best novel by the time I have finished. Augusta will be a clergyman's wife and my heroine will despise her. I think I will call my heroine "Emma". I like that name. It seems cool and clever, somehow.'

I pulled on my stockings while she read it out. When she had finished she gave it to me to stick it into my journal. I must say that I think she is very clever. I don't know how she gets these ideas.

"Dearest Augusta," said Belinda to her sister-in-law, "how often have I wished that I possessed as little personal beauty as you do; that my figure were as inelegant, my face as unlovely and my appearance as unpleasing as yours is."

It was short, but it did make me giggle. I don't think I would ever have the courage to say something like that to the real Augusta.

'A letter for you, Jenny,' said Frank as Jane and I came into breakfast. He had already been up to Deane Gate Inn for the letters delivered there every morning by the mail coach and was busily distributing them. He put the sealed and folded sheet of paper by my plate and then moved on to give Henry his numerous letters.

I'm sure my face showed my thoughts when I saw the square firm handwriting on the outside of the sheet. I couldn't believe that I had got a letter from Thomas already. He must have written almost as soon as he arrived back at Southampton.

'Jenny, my dear,' said Mr Austen quietly. 'Please give your letter to your aunt.'

I stared at him. I could not believe it. He, so gentle, so slow to interfere, was actually asking me to give my beloved letter to Mrs Austen. I made no move to obey, just held my precious letter clenched within my hand. Mrs Austen stared stonily ahead with an air that said plainly: this is nothing to do with me.

'My dear,' Mr Austen got to his feet, 'I think you and I should just have a quick word with Jenny. Go on with your meal, the rest of you. No, Jane, you stay there.'

His voice was unusually firm for him, and to my surprise Mrs Austen, usually the one in authority in the household, got to her feet as meekly as I did and followed him into his study at the back of the house.

'Dearest Jenny,' he said affectionately, taking me by the hand when I had closed the door to the study. 'Try to understand. Although we love you as we love our own children, we have to remember that your mother left your brother as your guardian, not us. Now your brother has declared that he will not countenance an engagement between you and Captain Williams and that means that you must not correspond or meet with the captain – except as a friend of the family of course. Will you promise me that you will not do this while you are under my roof?'

I thought for a moment and then I told him that I would obey his orders. He looked a little surprised at that, almost as if he were half sorry that he was not able to use all of his prepared arguments.

'And will you agree to your aunt opening this letter and judging whether it is a suitable letter for a young girl in your position to receive?'

Without a word I handed it to my aunt, who looked annoyed at her husband's scruples. Nevertheless, she was probably curious, because she broke the seal and opened it quite quickly, spreading out the page.

A tiny forget-me-not slid out and I picked it up quickly before anyone else could touch it. Mr Austen was looking out of the window in a slightly embarrassed way and did not see the flower, but Mrs Austen gave a quick grin. She scanned the letter quickly and then handed it to me.

'Perfectly correct in every way,' she said. 'Read it aloud to your uncle, Jenny.'

So I read aloud in a colourless voice, the letter in one hand and the forget-me-not clutched in the other:

Dear Jenny,

I hope you are well and that your rehearsals for the play are going successfully. I had a good ride back to Southampton and arrived earlier than I had expected. The ship needs much work and I will be busy all day checking supplies.

Yours etc.

Thomas

I folded the letter and returned it meekly to my aunt, who briskly handed it back to me.

'Well, well . . . well, that all seems satisfactory. My dear, perhaps I'll leave you to speak with Jenny.' Mr Austen shot off back to his breakfast.

'Hmm,' said Mrs Austen when he had gone. 'That's a clever young man of yours, my dear. He guessed that your uncle would have these scruples. That's gentle-men for you, Jenny. Your uncle is the best of men, but when he puts his foot down about something, well, we might as well give in as waste our time trying to change his mind. I suppose the message is in the forget-me-not, is that it?'

When I looked back Mrs Austen was pursing her lips in a satisfied manner.

'He's a nice young man,' she said. She seemed to think for a minute and then said, avoiding my gaze, 'Jane liked him, didn't she, Jenny? I suppose there is nothing wrong in Jane writing to him and giving him news of you?'

I nodded. I was about to say that I had thought of that idea also, but then I decided that was enough. There was a gleam in my aunt's eyes which warned me to say no more.

She looked at me with satisfaction and pushed the curls away from my face, patting my cheek gently. 'You're so like your poor mother,' she said with a burst of emotion. 'She was such a pretty girl. I don't know why she married Dr Cooper. Your brother is the image of him.' And then she kissed me quickly and we went back to the breakfast parlour. As I slid into my seat beside Jane her eyes scrutinized me and I smiled blandly and helped myself to breakfast.

Friday, 15 April 1791

Today was such fun. At last the great day of the performance of the play had arrived. Mr Austen's pupils will be going home for their Easter holiday tomorrow, so this is the final opportunity to have all the cast together. Even James, who is so fussy, just can't have any more rehearsals.

But before I write about that I must write about the letter.

After I had finished writing in my journal yesterday evening, I said to Jane that I wished that I could write a long letter to Thomas, but I had promised Mr Austen not to – and Thomas could not really write to Jane or everyone would want to know where her letter came from. And then I suddenly got a good idea and thought of Harry Digweed, the boy who lives next door to the Austens.

The Digweeds lived in an ancient manor house next door to Steventon church. Harry was the second son, a quiet, friendly boy with a nice smile but not much to say for himself. He spent a lot of time at Steventon parsonage and he and Frank were always discussing shooting, hunting, horses and dogs. I had a feeling that he was rather fond of Jane. He seemed to watch her often when he thought he was unobserved and he laughed uproariously at any joke that she made.

I asked Jane whether she thought Harry could keep a secret.

'I should think so,' said Jane after a moment's thought. 'I always trusted him. I used to tell him all my secrets. You know what children are like with their little private affairs!' And Jane sighed in an elderly fashion.

'You see,' I said to her, 'I was thinking that if I could get Thomas to send a letter to Harry Digweed and to put a cross or some mark like that on the outside, then he could bring it over here to me.'

'Better still, bring the letters secretly by dead of night to the hollow yew tree outside the church,' said Jane dramatically. 'Do you remember how Cassandra and Tom Fowle used to use that as a letter box? They've given it up now that they've become officially engaged; I've looked a few times and there never is anything there. We could use that now, and it's so near to the Digweeds' house it would be quite convenient for Harry.'

'And if we could get Harry Digweed to send your letters to Thomas, then no one in this household need be involved.' I was getting enthusiastic about this idea. It was so much better than my first idea, of asking Frank to post them and to collect the letters from Thomas and give them secretly to Jane and to post my replies. I would hate to get Frank involved in something of which his father disapproved.

'You'll have to play your part cleverly, Jane,' I warned. 'You must make Harry Digweed think that he is doing a great favour to you. He's fond of you.'

'Ye . . . es,' said Jane thoughtfully. 'I'll have to think out a "girl in distress" storyline.' She stared unseeingly out of the window for a few minutes and then said rapidly, 'You have appealed to me to help you, and all I could think of was to go to this friend of my youth, my dear Harry Digweed. The thought of his manly profile, of his blond hair and his blue eyes made my knees feel weak. He was the one, the only one, that I knew I could trust. One who could be a friend to weak girls . . . a brave, handsome, gentle, perfect knight.'

'Don't overdo it,' I advised, though I couldn't help laughing.

'No, just a touch of a quaver in the voice, just a hesitating gesture towards putting a hand on his sleeve – halted abruptly, of course . . . Leave it to me. I can manage Harry.'

'Poor boy,' I said laughing, but I didn't care really. All I cared about was being in touch with my lovely Thomas and to have him able to write letters to me that could freely show what was in his heart.

'Let's write the first letter now. What do you want to say? Or do you want to write it yourself?'

I told her that I had given my word to her father not to write any letters while I was under his roof so I wanted to keep my promise. I think she was quite relieved at that because she got out the paper and trimmed a new quill very enthusiastically.

'Just leave it to me,' she advised. 'I'll tell him all

about how you wander the house as a pale as a ghost; how you start and blush when anyone mentions something to do with the navy, like ships, or the sea, or even the colour blue.'

I begged her not to be so dramatic, that Thomas would think she was just laughing at us, but she assured me it would be a perfect letter.

I went to the window and waited while she was writing, and when she had finished she read it to me:

Dear Captain Williams,

Jenny is in a sad way without you. She has been forced by evil powers to agree not to communicate with you so I write to give you news of her. She asks me to tell you that she is even more in love with you than she was yesterday and that her love doubles with every passing hour. Your image is in her mind constantly and today at breakfast she passed the tea cosy to my mother when she was asked for the butter. Could love go further?

Your faithful friend,

Jane Austen

PS Please write to Jenny, but address the letter to Mr Harry Digweed at Steventon Manor and draw a small anchor on the outside of the letter, just under his name.

Jane was quite proud of her letter and I had to acknowledge that the idea of the anchor was a good one. I wished that I could write my own letter though. There were so many things that I wanted to say, and I definitely would not have mentioned the episode with the tea cosy.

After breakfast Jane and I walked up the lane towards the church, and when we were almost at the manor we met Harry and his dog, a lovely friendly black pointer, who wagged her tail enthusiastically at the sight of Jane.

'Oh, Harry,' said Jane dramatically, clasping her hands, 'we are in such trouble, and we come to you for help.'

'What's the matter, Jane?' he gasped. He really is very sweet.

'I hate to ask you to do this, Harry, but would you swear never to tell anyone about this matter?'

'What matter?' He looked so bewildered that I felt I should explain. However, I kept silent. He must be used to Jane's manner; he has known her all his life.

'We need your help, Harry. True love must find a way. Tell me that you will help us in this affair of the heart.'

'Love?' queried Harry. Now he flushed slightly, and this time I could not help intervening.

'Jane's talking about me, Mr Digweed,' I said in a dignified way.

Jane shot me a look that said you're spoiling

everything, but I didn't care. I didn't want Harry to be confused. I explained to him what we wanted him to do and he nodded agreeably.

'Yes, of course, yes, of course, no problem,' he kept saying. 'Yes, that's no problem, Miss Jenny. No, no trouble at all. I'll take this letter now and give it in at Deane Gate Inn before the mail coach comes. I'm going that way in any case. And if a letter comes back, I'll stick it into the old hollow yew tree.'

Then he blushed a little as he said, 'Do you remember, Jane, when we were young and you made Frank and myself play a game with you there? You were supposed to be a new bride – I remember you had a small tablecloth around your shoulders. Frank was your wicked husband who has only married you for your estates, and I was a passing woodman who hears your piteous cries and rescues you just before you expired.' He laughed at the memory and Jane laughed also, though I had a feeling that she didn't remember.

I was impressed at how well Harry recalled all the details. 'Marrying for your estates' and 'your piteous cries' and '. . . expired' all sounded just like Jane. It was as if he had kept her words in his mind all through those years. I turned to go back, and Jane joined me instantly, saying over her shoulder, 'We'll see you later on at the play, Harry.'

I couldn't help feeling sorry for Harry, so I lingered a little and petted his dog and forced Jane to wait so that we could all walk down the path together. She was a bit shy of him now, which probably meant that she had realized the significance of his little story. For Jane, she was very silent until after we parted from him at the gates of the parsonage and she waited for a moment, watching him as he jumped the bank into the field and then strode up the hill, followed by his obedient dog.

'He looks like a knight from the tales of King Arthur,' I told her, watching the way that the sun lit up his golden hair.

'I thought you preferred dark-haired men,' said Jane abruptly, and then she ran on into the house. I followed her thoughtfully into the parlour. Was she thinking of Newton? I wondered.

We were supposed to do what lessons we could think of – Mrs Austen was too busy making up end-of-term laundry bills for the pupils to give us even her usual vague directions – but we mostly discussed the best way of getting Mrs Austen to allow us to go to Bath with Eliza.

'We'll ask her after the play,' decided Jane. 'She'll be in a very good mood then. She does enjoy plays.'

Neither of us even thought of Mr Austen. We were so used to his agreeing to anything that was proposed by his womenfolk.

The play was supposed to start at three o'clock — dinner was early and rushed. As soon as it was finished everyone went over to the barn. The boys dressed there and Cassandra, Jane and I grabbed our gowns and took them back to our rooms. Eliza had brought her own gown — no one had seen it yet, but it was something that she had worn ten years ago when she was a girl at the court of Versailles.

My gown and Cassandra's had both belonged to Mrs Austen when she was young. Mine was a beautiful shade of blue and had panniers on either side, holding out the skirt. I have drawn a picture of it here. It felt so strange to be wearing it — it was almost like having two baskets, one at either side of my waist, underneath my skirt. That makes it sound silly, but I felt quite elegant in it. Jane, as a maid, was dressed quite plainly, with a gown of striped dimity and a huge mob cap covering her curls. I was a bit

myself

Jane

sorry that she wasn't more elegant-looking, especially since Newton Wallop was playing the part of James's servant, but Jane didn't seem to mind; she was dancing around the room, repeating funny lines from her part.

Eliza was late in coming over for the play, and James was sending frantic messages by Charles, and I didn't actually see her until she strode on to the stage, pointing at Cassandra and declaiming:

'*There, Sir Anthony, there sits the deliberate simpleton who wants to disgrace her family, and lavish herself on a fellow not worth a shilling.*'

I felt Tom Fowle, Cassandra's penniless fiancé, shake with silent laughter at my side as we waited in the wings, but I was too fascinated by Eliza's gown to take much notice of him.

I could well imagine her dancing in front of the King and Queen of France in this magnificent outfit. Her gown, like my own, had panniers, but poor Mrs Austen had never possessed anything like this creation of a bodice and petticoat of pale green lutestring (I think it is called that – a sort of glossy silk fabric anyway), all covered with a transparent gown of silver gauze – and the petticoat and sleeves were puckered up and tied with silk ribbons and small silk violets. Her dark hair was heavily powdered to a silver colour and rose so high on her head that I suspected that she had a small cushion embedded in it.

A huge burst of clapping rang out after she had said her first words. The audience of the neighbouring families – the Digweeds, the Terrys, the Chutes and the Lefroys – all obviously knew Eliza and were expecting fun from her.

I had never seen her act so well. '*You thought, miss!*' she shrieked at Cassandra. '*I don't know any business you have to think at all – thought does not become a young woman!*'

And then, advising Cassandra to '*illiterate*' the thought of her beloved from her mind, she had everyone on stage roaring with laughter. Whenever she pronounced the wrong word, like substituting '*illiterate*' for '*obliterate*', she put such emphasis on it that even the dullest and sleepiest audience could not fail to get the joke.

James was splendid as Sir Anthony, and Mr Austen almost fell off his chair from laughing when he thundered magnificently:

'*Objection! – Let the boy object if he dare! – No, no, Mrs Malaprop, Jack knows that the least demur from any son of mine puts me in a frenzy directly.*

My process was always very simple – in their young-er days, 'twas "Jack, do this"; – if he demurred, I knocked him down – and if he grumbled at that, I just knocked him down again.'

When Eliza said in her best Mrs Malaprop fashion: '*Nothing is so conciliating to young people as sever-ity . . .*' she gave a lovely artistic pause at the wrong word '*conciliating*' and at that very second Jane, with a quick flash of a grin, jumped forward and tickled Pug, who gave a loud shrill bark.

I was standing beside Harry Digweed (who had the task of opening and closing the curtains) when she did that, and he was laughing so much that I thought the audience would hear him. But there was little danger of that. The audience, also, was roaring with laugh-ter, and William Chute gave a loud '*toot, toot*' in imi-tation of a hunting horn, and that made Pug bark even more hysterically.

I wished that Thomas could have been present to see me act as Julia, the girl who stays faithful to her lover, despite any objections.

I didn't really have to act – I just pretended that Henry, who played the part of Faulkland, was really Thomas and when I said lines like: '*I never can be happy in your absence*' I was saying the words to him. Afterwards Jane said that she could hear them ring with such sincerity she thought I was quite good enough to act in Covent Garden, or in the Theatre Royal in Bath (Jane will always exaggerate!), and when I spoke the last lines of the play and talked about '. . . *hearts that deserve happiness being united at last*' the thunder of applause was so loud that a barn owl, who had slept through all the many practices and throughout the whole play, suddenly woke up, swooped down over the heads of the actors and the audience, and flew blinking into the sunlight.

'Bravo, bravo!' called Mrs Austen. And then everyone was on their feet, clapping and stamping and shouting congratulations.

Harry and Charles pulled the curtains open and closed so many times that we all began to feel dizzy as we bowed and waved and smiled – again and again and again.

And then it was all over. The actors were all kissing and hugging each other in delight with themselves and with each other. Everybody admired Eliza's wonderful gown, and James didn't say a word about her arriving so late that she almost spoiled his play. In fact, he was the first to kiss her!

And then, just as everyone was streaming out into the sunshine, laughing and talking, echoing lines from the play, I saw Jane slip back on to the stage. I couldn't hear what she said, but I saw her hug Harry and I think I saw her kiss him on the cheek.

Luckily Mrs Austen had already hurried off to see to supper. She would have died of horror to see Jane do something like that. I thought it was nice of her though. Otherwise, Harry might have felt a bit left out.

Saturday, 16 April 1791

I know it is far too early to hear from Thomas, but I still persuaded Jane to go for a walk by the church-yard, and I glanced, just casually, into the darkness of the hollow yew tree, but of course it was empty so we went back to the house. The pupils begin their holidays today and they have been thundering up and down the wooden stairs all the morning hauling down their trunks and their leather travelling bags.

This is what Mr Austen's farm cart, piled high with their luggage, looked like:

After dinner we all walked up to Deane Gate Inn to see them off. As they were all clambering on to the stagecoach, Mrs Austen warned Gilbert East not to be late back after Easter – apparently at the beginning of last term he stayed at home after term began because there were some balls in his neighbourhood – and Gilbert pulled out of his pocket the poem she had written to him then and he read it aloud. Everyone laughed, and Mrs Austen blew them all a kiss and only laughed also when Jane did the same.

When we went back to the house I asked Mrs Austen about the poem she wrote to summon Gilbert back, and she produced a rough copy. Here are a few lines from it:

> That you dance very well
> All beholders can tell
> For lightly and nimbly you tread;
> But, pray, is it meet
> To indulge thus your feet
> And neglect all the while your
> poor head?

I had not realized that Mrs Austen was a writer of poetry. Jane must have inherited her gift from her mother.

Sunday, 17 April 1791

Today was a quiet day. Eliza didn't come down at all. After church in the morning, the boys all disappeared to the houses of various friends and neighbours, and Cassandra, Jane and myself went for a walk. Cassandra did most of the talking – we heard a lot about her beloved Tom Fowle and how, when we come back from Bath, Cassandra is going to stay for a week with his family in Berkshire. Cassandra, like me, can think only of when she will be able to be married – when Tom gets a parish from his rich relation, Lord Craven. That will not be for years and years, but it doesn't stop Cassandra, who is very domesticated, from planning her bridal meal.

Tonight, while I am wondering what else to put into my journal from this dull day, I was thinking about Cassandra. I feel sorry for her. After all, I am not as badly off as she is. At the worst I only have to wait another four years till I am twenty-one and can be married. Tom Fowle won't be able to support Cassandra for another five or six years at least.

Monday, 18 April 1791

And now it is all settled. As Eliza had guessed, Mrs Austen was not keen to let us go to Bath under her niece's care. However, she decided that she would have a short rest from all the housekeeping and dairy making and spend a couple of weeks with her brother, James Leigh-Perrot, and his wife at Bath. And that she would take us with her. Poor Cassandra is going to stay to look after the household affairs. Now we are busy washing and ironing and getting everything ready for a three-week stay in Bath, and we are leaving in two days' time!

I asked Jane what was going to happen about my letters from Thomas, and she said that we would ask Harry to send them to Eliza at her Bath address.

I wish I could see Thomas before he sets out for the East Indies. It seems very unfair that I should not be able to.

I asked Jane, jokingly of course, whether she thought I could ride as far as Southampton on my donkey and Jane was full of wild ideas.

'Let us borrow the fare from Bath to Bristol from Eliza,' she said in her usual dramatic way. 'When we get to Bristol we will hide until Augusta goes out and then steal into the house and take some banknotes from her desk drawer. You could use these to buy a seat on the stagecoach to Southampton. If you took plenty of banknotes, you could put up in a respectable inn.'

I asked her what we would do if Augusta returned and discovered us, and Jane had a prompt answer for that. She quickly produced her novel *Love and Freindship* (Jane never could spell 'friend') and read aloud from it and then gave me the rough copy to stick in my journal as an example of how I could behave in Edward-John and Augusta's house in Bristol.

Just as the lovely Sophia was removing the fifth banknote from the drawer to her own purse she was suddenly and impertinently interrupted by the entrance of Macdonald. Sophia instantly put on a most forbidding look and darting an angry frown at the intruder, demanded in a haughty tone of voice to know wherefore her retirement was thus insolently broken in upon. And when he persisted, 'Wretch,' she exclaimed (hastily replacing the banknote in the drawer), 'how darest thou accuse me of an Act of which the bare idea makest me blush.'

This cheered me up a little, and I thought about what Eliza had said of speaking to the lawyer (who was so in love with her) at Bath.

We went to find Eliza, who was out in the garden. James had brought out so many cushions that he had almost made a bed for her and she was reclining on them, propped up against an elm tree, her little pug on her lap, as James read aloud from the magazine called

The Loiterer which he and Henry edited and tried to sell to the students at Oxford.

Eliza, I think, was bored, because her eyes lit up at the sight of us, and in her usual dramatic manner she said, 'Dearest James, how lovely of you to enter-tain me. But I must not keep you any longer. You are like all men; you want to be out hunting and shoot-ing. Sit down, *mes petites*, sit and keep me company. Here, Jenny dear, you hold Pug. Why the sad face?' she enquired after James had bowed and strode back across the lawn. Even his back expressed acute annoy-ance with us. He had been enjoying himself, reading to Eliza.

Still, Mrs Austen will be obliged to us. She was hinting to James this morning that he should go and call upon Anne Mathew, the daughter of the wealthy General Mathew. She would be a good match for him, and Mrs Austen is very keen on the idea (according to

Cassandra) and doesn't think it matters that Anne is six years older than James. His mother wouldn't want him to waste his time flirting with a married cousin.

I stroked Pug and didn't reply, and Jane said, 'She's upset at not having heard from Thomas.'

'But, *chérie*, it is only a few days, you are not *raisonnable*.' Eliza rolled each letter *r* in the back of her throat in the French style. I wish that I could speak French — it seems such a romantic language.

'Aunt Leigh-Perrot had time to reply,' I said dolefully. I had gone three times to the hollow tree, but there had been nothing there. And then Jane had gone over to the manor house to see Harry and he had been most upset that we thought he had not bothered to deliver the letter.

'I'll take it over no matter what — even if I am in the middle of sowing turnips,' he said, according to Jane — who didn't think he showed much romantic taste in mentioning turnips in the same sentence as love letters.

'But there is a difference,' cried Eliza. 'Your aunt is an old lady who has nothing to do in her life other than to write letters. The good captain, ah, now that is a different matter. He is busy, shouting orders, standing on his ship deck . . . La, la, I do not know, but I'm sure a thousand things must occupy him. How can he sit down and write a pretty love letter when his men are standing by, waiting for him to shout, "Lower ze boat, my hearties."?'

I had to laugh at that, especially as Eliza made no effort to copy a sailor-like voice but pronounced the words in the refined tones of a Parisian lady.

'I know why you haven't heard from him,' exclaimed Jane when we were reluctantly responding to Mrs Austen's shouts from the open window.

'Why?' I asked. Jane had stopped in the middle of the gravel sweep in front of the door and was staring at me with serious eyes.

'He's been taken prisoner by French brigands, of course.' She looked quite satisfied by that explanation and shook her head when I pointed out that England was no longer at war with France.

'Once a brigand, always a brigand,' she said wisely. 'We should write and find out his news – and tell him ours.'

She raced upstairs, seized a pen, sharpened it to a fine point, trimmed the feathered end carefully and took a piece of scrap writing paper from her desk.

Then she folded the paper in four, wrote the address, scattered some sand on it, opened it out, turned it over and wrote the message on the inside in her most elegant hand. Then she refolded the paper, melted the end of a wax stick, dropped a blob to seal the letter, told me to stick the copy into my journal and then jumped up. 'Let's go and see Harry,' she said enthusiastically. 'I bet he will ride straight up to Deane with it. That will be in Southampton by tomorrow morning.'

Jane's letter to Thomas:

Captain Thomas Williams
H M S Bonaventure
Southampton Docks
Southampton.
(To be opened by his second-in-command in the event
of the above captain's unavoidable absence)

Miss Jane Austen presents her compliments
to Captain Thomas Williams and begs to inform
him that she and her cousin Miss Cooper will be
visiting the city of Bath in three days' time for a
period of three weeks.

However, previous arrangements for
correspondence should be adhered to. Send all post
to Mr Harry Digweed, Steventon Manor,
Steventon, Hampshire.

Tuesday, 19 April 1791

It's very early in the morning and I am writing in my journal before the others are awake. Everything is ready for our journey to Bath. The post-chaise will call for our bags and trunks and then, at Deane Gate Inn, only a short walk up the road, we will get on the coach and start on our journey to Bath.

Jane is very excited about it, but I am not. I wish now I could stay on in Steventon and keep inspecting that hollow tree to see whether Thomas has remembered me. Everything is so uncertain for me. I feel that I am in danger of going back to being the very insecure, worried girl that I was before I came to Steventon.

Perhaps Thomas doesn't love me any more. That thought keeps coming into my mind. Perhaps he has found another girl whose parents are very pleased at the idea of a match between their daughter and the handsome naval officer with his own property in the Isle of Wight and his uncle, the admiral.

After all, my brother has turned him down. When he got back to Southampton, Thomas must have thought of that. He must feel very angry.

Tuesday night, 19 April

By six o'clock in the evening we had been travelling for hours. The journey across the Salisbury Plain was long and tedious. Eliza entertained us in the early part by telling us about an undercover agent — a *rrrrevolutionary* who took part in storming the Bastille. She told us some hair-raising stories of this daring individual who even swam through the murky waters of the River Seine in Paris, with his pistol clenched between his teeth. Although Eliza's husband is an aristocrat, she seems to find this '*rrrrevolutionary*' undercover agent very attractive, and Jane's eyes were sparkling with excitement. Mrs Austen fell asleep in the middle of the story and then Eliza dozed off, but Jane and I discussed the undercover agent for a long time. We planned a book about him, with Jane writing the story and me providing the sketches.

After we finished discussing this I began to feel sleepy, and even Jane started to yawn. Everyone woke up suddenly at Andover when the coach stopped. A stout woman got in and sat next to me, squeezing us both up against the window. Jane started to have a little fun.

'Mama,' she said in a penetrating whisper, 'did you hear what the ostler said about the highwaymen?'

Mrs Austen gave her an annoyed glance. 'Don't be silly, Jane. I heard nothing of the sort.'

'Dear Mama,' confided Jane in a whisper, supposedly meant for my ear, but definitely aimed at my fat neighbour. 'She doesn't wish to frighten us, but I know that she has stowed her diamond necklace in her left boot.'

Poor Mrs Austen! I doubt that she ever owned a diamond necklace, but if she had I fancy it would have been long sold to buy a couple of Alderney cows. She would get more satisfaction from supplying her large household with milk, cream and butter than in flaunting a diamond necklace to impress her neighbours.

The fat lady, however, immediately got to her feet and shouted out of the window to the driver to hand in her small travelling bag to her.

That was a nuisance, as the four horses had to be pulled up and the bag retrieved from the luggage basket at the back of the coach, but it was very funny to watch the fat lady, her side turned firmly towards us, rummaging in her bag and stowing things into secret pockets inside her travelling cloak and poking something else down into her boots.

'Terrible times, ma'am,' she said to Eliza, as Mrs Austen had firmly shut her eyes to distance herself from her embarrassing daughter.

'*Terrrrible*,' said Eliza, giving the word its French pronunciation. 'You would not believe the scenes that I have witnessed. The mob! The riots! The burnings!'

'What?!' screamed the lady. 'In Andover!'

'Doesn't seem possible, does it,' commented Jane gravely. Eliza, by the look on her face, was trying not to laugh.

Mrs Austen opened one weary eye, looked from Eliza's animated face to Jane's, and then closed it again. I think she had decided to disown us all.

'These people are animals,' pronounced the stout lady.

'*Oh la*, the *paysans*! The . . . how you say it? The peasants — they say they are starving!' was Eliza's next contribution.

I thought that would put a stop to the conversation, but the stout lady was just getting into her stride.

'Animals, that's what I call them, greedy animals. Always wanting more. Never content with what was plenty for their fathers and their grandfathers before them. I could tell you such a story . . .'

'What's that?' asked Jane sharply, sticking her head out of the coach window. 'Not a highwayman, I hope!'

'What!' screamed our travelling companion and she also put her head out of her window.

'We are being followed, ' announced Jane, pulling her head in. 'No, really. I've been listening to the sound of horse hoofs for the past five minutes. They've been getting nearer and nearer.'

'Coachman, there's a man following us!' The scream was enough to rouse the whole neighbourhood and we were now passing through a town.

'We're at Devizes now,' said Mrs Austen calmly, opening her eyes. 'Did I ever tell you that I stopped at this very inn on the day of my wedding? Myself and Mr Austen rode all the way from Bath to Devizes and then on to Steventon, did you know? I was married in a red riding habit and jumped on to the horse straight after the ceremony. Did I tell you about that?'

'Yes,' said Jane bluntly, and Eliza smiled faintly and peered hopefully from the window. For someone so easily bored as Eliza, a highwayman seemed a better prospect than the thousandth repetition of Mrs Austen's story of her honeymoon ride and of the fate of her red riding gown . . .

I felt a little worried though. Who was this man who was following us?

The coach now swung sharply to the right, toppling the stout lady over on to me, and me on to Jane. We were entering the inn yard. The ostlers were running forward to catch the reins of the four horses, hens scattered with indignant squawks and the landlady came out with a welcoming face and a clean white apron, but there was no fuss, no exclamations of horror . . .

'It's Harry Digweed,' whispered Jane, sticking her

bonnet into mine, the deep rims making a private little screen between us and the others in the coach. 'He must have a letter for you!'

I looked at her wide-eyed, but Mrs Austen had already pushed open the coach door and was clambering heavily out.

'Harry Digweed!' she exclaimed. 'What in the world are you doing here?'

'Hallo, ma'am, this is a surprise,' said Harry in such artificial tones that I was sure that Mrs Austen must suspect something. 'I'm on my way to Bristol to see about some new seed for my father.' He laboured on with his prepared speech and then turned to us with relief. 'Had a good trip?' he asked. His words seemed directed at Jane, but his eyes were on me, and they were so full of meaning that I blushed a little.

'Are you staying the night, Harry? You must join us for supper, mustn't he, Mama? We'll go with you while you see to the stabling of your horse. It will be good to get moving after sitting in that coach for six hours.'

'That is a good idea.' He said each word separately like a child learning to read. It was a good job that James had not given him a part in the play. He certainly couldn't act.

Once in the stable, though, he relaxed. I rather admired the easy way that he gave instructions about his horse to the ostler and how he gave the horse an affectionate pat as it was being led away. I saw Jane smiling — a small, private smile. She put a hand on his arm as we stood there in the warm-smelling dimness of the inn stables. Harry beamed his gorgeous smile down at her . . .

'Here's your letter, Miss Jenny,' he said. He had my letter carefully carried inside his inner pocket and he had even put a piece of stiff cardboard with it so that it wouldn't be crumpled.

'Oh, Harry, you don't know how grateful I am to you.' In my excitement at the appearance of Thomas's letter with the neatly drawn anchor on it, I called him Harry, just as Jane did.

'URGENT', read Jane over my shoulder.

'That's why I thought I should ride after you,' explained Harry. I felt like kissing him. I turned slightly aside, broke the wax seal and unfolded the sheet of paper. I expected to find a long letter and I could hear Jane engage Harry in conversation.

But the letter had only six words on it. I've stuck it in here.

> See you at Bath.
> Assembly Rooms on Friday.

And tomorrow is Thursday!

But why didn't he say something loving? I still worry that he might have decided that it was too much trouble to marry me. Perhaps instead of Jane's brigands, he had been captured by a beautiful girl — I could just picture her, very tall, with an aquiline nose and glossy black hair.

I showed it to Jane, looking at her doubtfully, ready to see her make a face at the lack of expressions of love, but she hugged me.

'Oh, I just adore Thomas,' she breathed. 'He is such a man of action.'

I laughed then. I was being stupid, and straight away I put the tall, raven-haired, aquiline-nosed girl out of my mind. Thomas was just in a hurry; perhaps there were men standing there by him, waiting for his orders while he scribbled the note. The important thing was that he was coming to Bath.

'We'll be in Bath by tonight, Harry,' said Jane. 'What do you think about that?'

'Wish I was going on a holiday,' said Harry. There was something almost lonely in his voice and I felt sorry for him.

Harry is such a nice young man. He has a kind face, already bronzed with the sun, blue eyes the colour of the cornflowers that will soon speckle the fields of wheat, his blond hair well-brushed back from his tanned forehead. I thought that he and Jane looked a lovely couple standing there side by side – she so dark-haired and lively, he so blond and dependable.

'Couldn't you come to Bath for a few days, Harry?' I asked impulsively. Again I had called him Harry, but I didn't care. I thought of him almost as one of my cousins.

'Why don't you?' Jane supported me, but in a calm,

slightly indifferent manner. 'When does your father expect you back?'

Harry blushed at that innocent question. I suspect that he had just gone off as soon as the letter arrived, leaving a message for his father.

'Oh, I . . . I don't think he would care,' he stuttered after a minute. 'In our house one or other of the four of us boys is always missing. I've done my share of the work this spring. I've been working as hard as any of the labourers. The lambs are all born, the seed has been sown . . . this is a quiet time for us now until the hay is ready for cutting.'

'Where would you stay?' I was so full of gratitude to Harry for actually riding all the way after us that I wanted to help. How terrible it would be if I had not got Thomas's letter and had not known that he wanted to meet me.

'Well, I know the landlord at the Greyhound Inn; he's very interested in farming and always glad of a chat; he'd give me a bed for a night or two, I dare say.' Harry sounded cheerful and I smiled encouragingly at him. It occurred to me that I had never seen Harry at the Assembly Rooms at Basingstoke, although he was often at the Austens' place and always joined in the dancing there.

'And you'll come to the Assembly Rooms on Friday, won't you, Harry?'

Jane had said nothing, which was not like her, but she was smiling so I thought that was enough. 'Come, let's go and have supper now.' And once I saw that they both followed me obediently I made sure not to glance over my shoulder at them. Jane was different with Harry to the way that she was with Tom Chute or Newton Wallop, I thought as I made my way into the inn. With Newton and Tom, she flirted continuously, but with Harry she did not say much. As soon as we entered the inn, she abandoned him and went over to Eliza, signalling me to follow her with a quick jerk of her head.

'Show your letter to Eliza, Jenny,' she murmured. I cast a quick glance at Mrs Austen, who was telling Harry that we were about to have a supper of a neck of venison, but with no oyster sauce, which she would have preferred. While she was in full flow I took the letter from my reticule.

Eliza's eyes widened as she read the few words. '*La, la*, what a man this captain is, *n'est-ce pas*?' She sighed heavily. 'Such a man, *mes petites*, such a man I could have loved in my youth. He does not sit back, does he? Say nothing, Jenny dear. Your aunt is not against this match, but she has to pretend to obey her husband. Leave it all to me. It will be my idea, and I will be getting up a little party to go to the Assembly Rooms on Friday – after all, I have my cousin, Philadelphia Walters, coming to stay with me and I must entertain her, *n'est-ce pas*? You will be very surprised to see your captain on Friday, Jenny, *ma chérie*, will you not?'

And then Eliza took out her fan and waved away the every-day smells of farmyard poultry and sweating horses and set it in the position of 'if only I were free . . .' Jane and I, remembering Eliza's lessons on how to send messages with a fan, found it hard to stop giggling.

After our meal, when Jane was chatting to Harry on the window seat and her mother was dozing by the fire, I whispered to Eliza my guess about Harry being fond of Jane. She gave him one perfunctory glance and then shook her head. 'No prospects,' she whispered back. 'I know the family: a good family, birth and breeding, but there is no money there. He's not even the eldest son. What money there is will go to John, the eldest brother. He is to inherit his uncle's fortune.'

I hate the way everything comes down to money. Why can't people live their lives and fall in love, without money always coming into it?

That night when we were going to bed in the inn I told Jane how grateful I was to Harry and how wonderful it was of him to just ride after us as soon as the letter arrived. Then, very carefully, I asked her what she felt about him.

Jane opened her eyes very wide. 'But I adore him!'

she exclaimed. I was not fooled. This was Jane acting the part of a romantic heroine.

'Do you like him as well as you like Tom Chute or Newton Wallop or any of the other boys that you dance with?' I asked.

Jane didn't answer immediately. There was a shout of laughter from the taproom in the inn downstairs and a creak on the stairs outside our room, which sounded like Mrs Austen and Eliza making their way into the room beyond ours. I wondered where Harry was sleeping. He had been very quiet during supper, and both Mrs Austen and Eliza had given up trying to talk to him and had busied themselves gossiping about the Prince of Wales and about the King. Judging by the giggles we heard outside our door, Eliza was still relaying the latest stories about the prince to her aunt.

I tried again. 'Could you imagine marrying him?' I asked.

'He's different,' said Jane eventually.

I didn't rush her. I remembered all the times that Jane had allowed me to think about things and eventually to bring out my feelings. Her eyes were on the fire and I waited patiently until she turned towards me.

'I'd like something romantic,' she said thoughtfully. 'I think that my ideal man would be someone like that French revolutionary Eliza was telling us about. Very daring, very dashing. Involved in undercover missions. Or else . . . someone rescuing an innocent maiden from the clutches of a dastardly baronet. Galloping after them on his noble black stallion.'

'Sounds like something out of a novel.' I laughed, but Jane shook her head.

'Look at yourself, Jenny,' she pointed out. 'Your love affair with Captain Williams was so romantic. There you were, in terrible danger, alone, and he protected you. You think you will never meet again and then he turns up at the Assembly Rooms at Basingstoke. He dances with you; you fall in love with him. You meet again at the Portsmouths' ball. You are even more in love. He comes to visit you. Then there is a misunderstanding. You write him an angry letter. He comes to see you and behaves like a hero, rescuing us all. And then you learn that he is blameless. He offers marriage and you accept.'

I was smiling to myself, thinking about how very romantic the story between myself and Thomas sounded. And then I felt selfish for thinking of myself and I looked at Jane who had been silent for a moment, and I tried to smile at her. She didn't smile back. She looked more serious than usual.

'That's what I call a romantic story, Jenny,' she said. 'I've known Harry Digweed since I was a baby in short frocks. I've known him all my life. Nothing remotely romantic has ever happened between us. I don't really think that I can fall in love with him now.'

She stopped for a moment, running the comb

through her hair absent-mindedly and staring at her reflection in the mirror. 'I'd like to marry a man who is a hero, a man who loves me wildly, passionately, who would gallop through a raging torrent to be at my side, a man that I adore and worship.'

'But you like Harry, don't you?' I was beginning to feel out of my depth. 'Or perhaps Newton is the one. Could you imagine marrying Newton?'

Jane looked unsure. 'He is the son of an earl, of course. We can't forget that, can we? Earls are romantic. They come into all the novels.'

'Well, marry him, then. He seems to like you a lot. You and he are always chattering and you make the same kinds of jokes. It would be so exciting if you married him, Jane. What would Lavinia say?'

'His hair *is* a bit long,' said Jane doubtfully, pursing up her lips, 'and a bit too curly. Perhaps I should marry a man with blond hair, since my hair is dark. Heaven forbid that I should be mistaken for my husband.' She looked shocked at that thought.

'Well, Harry, then,' I said. 'He's blond.'

'Yes, he is,' agreed Jane. 'But you couldn't call him very romantic, could you? Can you imagine him fighting a duel with pistols at dawn? Or rescuing a maiden from a watery grave?'

'Frank says that Harry is a very good swimmer and a very good shot,' I pointed out. 'And you do like him, don't you?'

'Yes, I like him . . .' Jane hesitated and then she got

up and stretched. She had a wicked grin on her face. 'I was thinking that if he would kiss me, I might be able to decide. What do you think? Should I ask him to kiss me?'

I thought about that; I felt a bit horrified.

'Jane,' I said, 'I don't really think that you can ask a man to kiss you. You might ruin your reputation. I think that you must wait for him to kiss you of his own accord. And . . .' I could hear my voice sounding doubtful as I continued. It was usually Jane who was the expert on love affairs. However, I finished by saying, 'Properly speaking, he should offer to marry you before he kisses you.'

'The trouble is that Harry is so accustomed to my telling him what to do,' confessed Jane. 'I don't think that he will suddenly rush up to me and kiss me unless I tell him to.'

'Do you think that he would make a suitable husband though?' I was beginning to regret that I had got myself involved in this affair. Jane was right; it didn't seem very romantic.

'I feel . . . I feel . . . that I won't know until I kiss him,' said Jane lightly, looking at me with big innocent eyes. I was quite taken aback and told her firmly that I was sure that she couldn't kiss a man until she was sure that she loved him, but Jane just smiled mischievously and asked me what it felt like when Thomas kissed me. I told her that I couldn't describe it, but that I knew I loved him even before he kissed me.

'What about Newton, then?' I asked.

Jane's face changed and she put on a yearning look.

'Oh, Newton is just so gorgeous, with his hand-some face and lovely long curly hair,' she said. 'I do declare that I feel weak at the knees when I think of . . .' She stopped and then added mischievously, '. . . his fortune.'

And then she got into bed and I said no more.

I'm really not sure what to think.

Thursday, 2I April I79I

Yesterday was spent travelling and we arrived very late. When I woke up, for a moment I hardly knew where I was as I lay there squinting against the bright light. And then, instead of the chirping of swallows and the two-tone call of the cuckoo, I heard the clip-clop of horseshoes on the paved road outside. My first thought was for Thomas – I am going to see him tomorrow! I jumped out of bed.

'Wake up, Jane,' I said urgently.

There was no answer, and I looked behind Jane's curtains to see whether she was still asleep but there was no one there. She must have dressed earlier and gone downstairs.

At that moment there was a tap on the door and in came the chambermaid with a can of hot water.

'Good morning, Miss Jenny,' she said with a quick bob of a curtsy. 'I'm Rosalie. Here is your hot water.'

'Do you know where Miss Jane is, Rosalie?' I felt rather grand as I took the can from her.

'Lord, miss, no. Isn't she still in bed?' She seemed a bit shocked when she peered behind the curtains, but by now I guessed that Jane had got up early, washed in cold water and had gone downstairs, or even outside. I told Rosalie not to worry as Jane had probably gone to talk to my uncle.

When I came down to the breakfast parlour, however, there was no one there. Then I heard Jane's laugh floating up the stairs from the kitchen. For a minute I hesitated. I wasn't sure that my uncle and aunt would like me going down there, but then I thought there would be no harm in it.

Jane was sitting on the kitchen windowsill chatting happily to Franklin, the black servant of the Leigh-Perrots. He looked a bit embarrassed when he saw me and said that he had to go and see about the breakfast. So Jane and I walked back up to the hallway and Jane opened the front door and we looked down at the busy street where every kind of vehicle – gigs, barouches, landaus, even a mail coach – seemed either to be going up the hill towards the London road or else down the hill towards the centre of Bath.

'Let's go for a walk and see if we can find Queen's Square,' said Jane. 'We'll give Eliza a surprise. I bet she is still in bed.'

'Better not – it will be breakfast in a few minutes,'

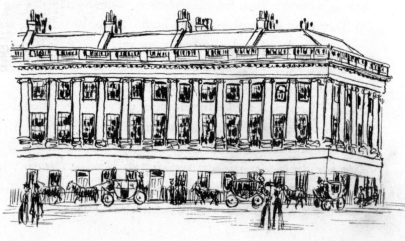

I said with a backwards glance to where maids and a footman and Franklin, of course, were tripping to and fro with dishes and trays.

'Come on, girls,' called our uncle from the stairs. 'Look at them, Franklin! They can't wait to get out to see Bath. They don't even want their breakfast.'

'Bath is a fine city for two beautiful young ladies,' said Franklin. 'They will be the belles of the ball, Mr Leigh-Perrot, won't they?'

'And you've been invited to a party tonight,' said Uncle Leigh-Perrot. 'Friends of ours, the Forsters, are giving a party for their granddaughter who has just left school.'

Mrs Austen and Mrs Leigh-Perrot were whispering together on the window seat when we came into the breakfast parlour. They stopped as soon as they saw us. Mrs Austen looked out of the window in a careless way, but Mrs Leigh-Perrot narrowed her eyes and surveyed me from the tip of my shoes to the knot of curls on the top of my head. And then she smiled broadly — like a crocodile that has seen something tasty, remarked Jane afterwards when we went upstairs after breakfast to fetch our parasols before walking to the Pump Room with our uncle.

Bath is so beautiful, I thought, as Jane and I, with our uncle between us, walked down through the fine streets, which were lined with buildings made of honey-coloured stone. Our uncle was very kind to us, leading us down Gay Street and pointing out Queen's Square, with its fine houses surrounding a lawn and trees in the centre. The blinds were still firmly drawn in the upper windows of number 13, and we guessed that Eliza was still sleeping.

Then we went down Milsom Street, where we were shown all the fine shops, with windows full of gowns and charming bonnets behind bow-fronted glass. Our uncle expected us to spend a long time looking at these, but Jane seemed anxious to press on and kept asking how far the Pump Room was and trying to get him to walk a little faster.

The Pump Room was down near the splendid abbey. The heavy wooden doors were set wide open and we passed between the two sets of stone columns and went into a huge room, full of people even at this early time of the day. There were some benches at the side of the room, but apart from these the Pump Room was empty of furniture. This was just as well as there seemed to be hundreds of people there. There were men and women in almost equal numbers; the women were mostly walking about in twos and threes, glancing at each other's bonnets, and the men were exchanging newspapers. There were two fireplaces, one at the top and the other at the bottom of the room, but on this fine morning very few people were bothering about them.

'Let's have a drink of the water,' said our uncle, and he guided us over to where there was a giant urn with another more elegant urn on top of it. Water flowed continuously from the four taps on the top of the urn and he handed me a mugful. It tasted disgusting, I thought – warm and with a strange flavour and a smell of old eggs. I drank it down politely and listened to his lecture on how good it was, but Jane barely tasted hers and told him that anyway she was never ill.

She seemed more interested in the large clock at the side of the room which Uncle told her had been standing in that very place for over eighty years. It showed ten o'clock and the hour struck just as he finished speaking. Jane's eyes went to the door. For a moment I was puzzled. Surely she did not expect Eliza to be up as early as this, but then I saw a tall figure block the sunlight for a moment and realized who she was waiting for.

Harry Digweed seemed to be very ill at ease as he pushed his way through the crowd, trying not to tread on the various wildly yapping small dogs that fashionable ladies had attached to very long leads. I thought of him in the woods and fields of Steventon with his well-trained black pointer and felt sorry for him. He seemed like a fish out of water in this perfumed world of fine gentlefolk. He had seen us though, and he was coming towards us.

'Let's go and write your mother's name in the list of new arrivals,' proposed Uncle.

'You go, dear Uncle,' said Jane demurely. 'I would like just to rest here on the bench for a moment and gaze on this great clock.'

'I'll go with you, Uncle,' I volunteered. After all, there could be nothing wrong in Jane greeting an acquaintance in this crowded room. Even if there were private talk between them, no one could overhear with the music from the orchestra playing in the gallery above and the buzz of hundreds of voices.

By the time Uncle had finished putting our details in the huge visitors' book that lay, ready opened, on an ornate stand, Jane was making her way towards us, followed by Harry. I noticed a finely dressed young gentleman lift his quizzing glass and eye Harry's breeches with a sneering smile on his lips. I suddenly felt very sorry for Harry and experienced a great rush of loyalty towards him.

'Uncle,' I said excitedly, 'that young man is the son of one of Mr Austen's greatest friends, Mr Digweed of Steventon Manor.' I did not add that the Digweeds only rented the manor from the Austens' cousin in Kent, but perhaps even if I had it would have made no difference to one of

Mr Leigh-Perrot's generous, hospitable nature.

Jane did everything beautifully, introducing Harry and explaining that he was staying for a couple of nights in Bath and had come here to drink the waters and, to his surprise, saw us. It seemed a little unlikely that a young and extremely healthy-looking man like Harry would have bothered to come to drink the waters in Bath, but our uncle was not suspicious. He greeted Harry with great cordiality, inviting him to join us in a turn around Sydney Gardens and then to come back to the house and have some lunch with us.

Harry agreed to the walk in Sydney Gardens, but declined the lunch — rightly so, I thought, as Mrs Austen would have been a little suspicious about his turning up.

'I am going to the ball at the Assembly Rooms tomorrow night,' he said in stilted tones, which showed that Jane had carefully coached him. 'I hope to have the pleasure of seeing you all there.'

'Isn't that wonderful?' said nice Uncle James. 'Well, girls, at least you will know one young man there. You will have to share him between you though.'

And I smiled at him sweetly and hugged my secret to me. Wait until Uncle sees my Thomas, I thought exultantly, and when we went into Sydney Gardens I engaged him in conversation in order to give Jane and Harry some time together. My uncle was very unsuspecting and was only too pleased to tell me all about his fine property in Berkshire. And he told me the whole story of how a rich great-uncle, Thomas Perrot, had left him the estate when he was only fourteen years old and how lucky he had been to marry such a wonderful woman as his wife.

'I had just to add Perrot to the name of Leigh, and there I was in clover for the rest of my life,' he said.

I smiled back at him and took a quick peep over my shoulder. Jane and Harry were now quite a long way behind us. Wouldn't it be wonderful, I thought, if Harry had a rich great-uncle somewhere who would leave him an estate? I kept remembering what Eliza had said about the Digweeds – *good family, birth and breeding, but no money.*

'Oh, a brass band! Let's go and listen to it.' I dragged my uncle across the grass. Harry and Jane would find plenty of quiet benches and little nooks where they could sit and talk together while my uncle's attention was on the splendid noise that the huge instruments were making.

After lunch, Jane and I went to visit Eliza. My two aunts were planning a visit to the shops at Milsom Street, so we all walked together down George Street, then down Gay Street, Aunt Leigh-Perrot pointing out various Bath notables. Then we were in lovely Queen's Square, with its stately buildings shining in the afternoon sun and the pretty poplar trees casting long shadows.

'You fixed that up with Harry, didn't you, Jane?' I asked when we parted from my aunts at the corner of Wood Street and crossed over to the bottom quarter of Queen's Square. A couple of young men, racing their gigs, passed us and Jane, making no reply to my question, said that she was sure they were both young lords and that she could see by the eyes of the second one that he had fallen madly in love with her. This made us both giggle and we quickened our pace almost to a run.

Then we knocked on the door of number 13 and were immediately shown up to Eliza's lodging by a fat woman in mourning clothes, who had a little black kitten running behind her. On the way up I teased Jane about arranging to meet Harry at the Pump Room, but she just smiled mysteriously. I wondered whether that had been a secret meeting – and if so, did Jane carry out her plan of kissing him???????

Eliza was only just getting dressed, but she looked quite at home. Gowns peeped from closets and presses, frilly petticoats spilled from half-open drawers and the surface of her dressing table was almost completely covered with her possessions. While Jane was relating an account of our morning, including the appearance of Harry Digweed, I sat on the bed and made a list in my mind of everything that Eliza had there.

This is the list:

A small box of pomade

A glass bottle full of little holes for sprinkling
    powder

A powder puff on a delicate pale blue saucer

Four scent bottles
A small glass of wine
A hand mirror
Four candles in silver candlesticks.
A tray of breath-scenting lozenges
A miniature of her little son, Hastings (but none of
 her husband, Monsieur le Comte)
A glass dish with a pearl necklace coiled in it
Strips of lip-reddening crimson-coloured leather
A set of ivory manicure sticks
A lace handkerchief
A fan (of course)

That's all that I can remember — I think there could have been a dozen more items, but my attention was distracted by a soft knock on the door and a strange-looking woman sidled in.

'Ah, Phylly,' said Eliza. She jumped up and made a big fuss of her, introducing her and making sure that Phylly had a comfortable chair to sit on.

Philadelphia Walters is about the same age as Eliza (though no one would have guessed as she looks ten years older). She is only about thirty, I think. She is also Mr Austen's niece, but this time through his stepbrother, William-Hampson Walters. She is an unmarried lady who lives with her elderly parents in a small village in Kent, a strange little person, who was dressed in a very dowdy, old-fashioned gown. She has an odd habit of putting her head on one side and looking at you with  very bright beady eyes, which makes her look rather mouse-like — or perhaps more like a little sparrow.

'You know dearest Jane, don't you, Phylly?'

Head on one side, Cousin Philadelphia surveyed Jane, from the toes of her neat flat-heeled shoes, right up her spotted yellow muslin morning dress with its tightly buttoned yellow spencer to the tip of her straw bonnet, and then nodded vigorously.

'Yes, of course . . . I remember you when you were about twelve – dear, dear, dear, what a strange little girl you were then! I remember thinking that it was a shame that your elder sister had all the good looks.' This was Philadelphia's amiable reply, which she followed by saying, 'So this is Jenny? Not a bit like her mother, is she?' and peering at me in a disapproving fashion.

Jane made a face at me and turned to look out of the window.

'Are you going out, Eliza?' she enquired, ignoring Phylly. 'We were hoping to go for a walk with you up the hill through the park. We have lots to tell you.' She cast a quick frowning glance at Philadelphia, who had now wandered over to Eliza's dressing table and was sniffing distastefully at a jar of hair powder.

Eliza looked a little worried as she said, 'Phylly, darling, why don't you have a little siesta – after all, you were out at all sorts of early hours this morning when I was still *endormie*. I'll look after the two girls.'

'No, Cousin Eliza, I came to Bath to bear you company and I won't desert you now.' Phylly was grimly resolute. 'Not that I enjoy Bath,' she went on. 'I can't stand the shiny newness of the place and the glare and the chatter, and of course it is so noisy that it's no wonder that your poor nerves are shattered by it, Eliza. Don't you worry – you just take your ease and I will entertain the girls. Perhaps they would like to visit St Swithin's church?'

'No, we wouldn't,' said Jane abruptly. 'Let's go out then, Eliza, if you're ready.'

Eliza gave a last pat of the powder puff to her face, squirted on some scent, arranged her hat, with its elaborate bunches of cherries, to frame her small heart-shaped face and then picked up her parasol and announced herself ready.

'We might as well have gone with Mama and Aunt,' Jane hissed furiously at me as we followed the two ladies, Philadelphia talking continuously about her good works back home in Kent and how she insisted on some unfortunate village child learning to read and told his father to beat him because he had been slow and inattentive at her lesson. I decided that I didn't like this Phylly very much. I could see why Jane disliked her – everyone else said that I looked like my mother, so I think she meant to imply that I was plain.

'Let's visit some shops,' said Eliza over her shoulder. 'Come along, Phylly. I insist on buying you a new hat. Do allow me the pleasure.'

'And then the hat that she has on can be returned to the scarecrow.' Jane made the observation in a low tone, but definitely not a whisper. Philadelphia swung round sharply, but Jane just smiled sweetly at her.

'What I admire about you, Cousin Philadelphia,' she said amiably, 'is your great sense of humour. My father is always talking about it. No one has a greater sense of fun than my niece Philadelphia, that's what he says.'

Jane uttered this with the earnest countenance that she always assumes when telling an outrageous lie, and Phylly gave an uncertain smile and continued walking.

'Bother,' said Jane in my ear. 'Why didn't she take offence and go back to their lodgings? Is there any way of getting rid of her? Could I push her under that omnibus, do you think?'

I looked at the omnibus and its four horses. It looked rather fun to be in, with its passengers of excited girls and gallant young men.

And then I saw Harry, with a smart new hat which he was doffing as he came up to us.

'Good afternoon, Miss Jenny, Miss J-Jane.' Harry had a slight stutter from time to time. I thought it added to his attractiveness and I beamed encouragement at him as I curtsied.

Jane held out her hand to him in her impulsive way. 'Eliza, you know Harry Digweed, don't you? You met him at the play.'

'Oh, the play,' broke in Phylly before Eliza could open her mouth. 'I've heard all about that play. Your mother, Jane, wanted me to come and join in, but my principles wouldn't allow me. It's a nuisance to have been brought up with such strong Christian principles, but there you are, we can't change who we are, can we?' The last phrase was aimed at Harry, who – dear Harry! – immediately stammered that she was quite right.

Jane gave him an annoyed glance, which disconcerted him, and he turned bright red and tapped the brim of his shiny new hat against a lamp post in his confusion.

'Let's walk up towards the Crescent,' said Eliza soothingly. 'Will you come with us, Mr Digweed?'

He looked unsure for a moment, glancing from Philadelphia's unwelcoming face to Jane's annoyed one.

'Do come, Harry,' I said and earned myself a suspicious, head-to-one-side, bird-like look from Philadelphia.

'Tell me about your school, Cousin Philadelphia,' I said, moving up beside her and allowing Jane to fall behind and walk beside Harry. Eliza felt it her duty to keep Phylly and Jane at a distance from each other. So she walked beside me, gamely putting extra questions to Phylly about her teaching methods (involving mainly, we understood, the use of a small sharp ruler which stung the backs of the children's fingers when they made a mistake in their reading) and then, once she ran out of stories about the village school, hearing about Phylly's exciting ball at a nearby town where a gentleman actually asked her to dance for the second time!!!

Eliza, in her generous way, was very merry about Phylly's beau and her teasing remarks almost relaxed her unpleasant cousin into an odd, bird-like giggle. She even went so far as to tease Phylly about the impression that she had made on Harry, and Phylly graciously conceded that she thought he was a well-behaved young man.

*

I loved my first view of the Crescent when we eventually got there. It was as if someone had taken one huge mansion, gently bent it into a semicircle and set it on top of the hill to look down over the parkland. I couldn't count how many houses there are because we stayed just at the edge of it. (But my uncle told me at supper that there are thirty.)

Eliza was very interested in the quality of the luggage being taken into number I, the Crescent, where a huge travelling coach was unloading an enormous amount of goods and smartly dressed footmen were rushing in and out. Someone in the first rank of fashion must have hired the house, Eliza surmised.

I asked her if she was going to the Assembly Rooms tomorrow night and she nodded vigorously and was delighted to hear that Uncle James approved of the idea.

'And Jenny, you will wear your so beautiful white gown, *n'est-ce pas*? And Jane?' Eliza looked thoughtfully over at Jane, who was looking up at Harry, but then was forced to reassure Phylly, who was making a fuss about whether or not she should go to a ball.

Harry then decided that he should leave us. He is a sensitive young man and he felt that Phylly didn't like him. Nothing that Jane or I could say made him change his mind. Jane went with him to the top of the gravel walk, and I could see that she was giving him some directions. It was funny to watch them from a distance, he bending his fair head over Jane's dark one, she vehemently talking and gesturing and he nodding from time to time.

And then we all went off to buy the new hat for Phylly. We went from shop to shop to shop until eventually the troublesome woman chose something in pink and green in Gregory's shop, right down at the bottom of the town in Bath Street, near to the Pump Room. After all that, on the way back to Queen's Square she kept talking about remaking the bonnet.

Just now without a word Jane handed me the rough copy of something she had been writing. 'That's to put in your journal,' she said. 'It's in honour of Phylly. I'm thinking of dedicating one of my novels to her.'

Dedication

Madam: You are a Phoenix. Your taste is refined, your Sentiments are noble, and your Virtues innumerable. Your Person is lovely, your Figure elegant, and your Form magestic. Your Manners are polished, your Conversation is rational and your appearance singular. If therefore the following Tale will afford one moment's amusement to you, every wish will be gratified of

Your most obedient

humble servant

The Author.

Jane does make me laugh (I like the way she spells majestic). Poor Phylly!

Friday, 22 April 1791

The noise of the traffic woke me early this morning. Jane is still asleep so I will fill in the time by writing in my journal.

Yesterday evening Franklin and Rosalie escorted us to the supper party. Even now I keep giggling when I think about it, but I must explain it properly.

Mr and Mrs Forster are quite an elderly couple who own a fine house at Laura Place, down in the lower part of the town beyond the Pump Room. Their granddaughter Frances has just left school so they were having a little party for her and some of her friends before she left Bath to join her parents in London.

'It sounds very dull, doesn't it, Franklin – a party for schoolgirls,' said Jane as we walked down the hill followed by Rosalie carrying our slippers in a neat bag.

'Perhaps Mr and Mrs Forster thought it would be a treat for their granddaughter to meet two grown-up young ladies,' said Franklin soothingly.

'We'll instruct her, won't we, Jenny?' said Jane with a grin. She stuck her nose in the air and said in loud, lofty tones, 'My dear young thing, pray do not bother me with talk of globes and such things. Let us discuss our beaux. I've got four or five myself and I can never decide between them.'

'Miss Jane!' exclaimed Rosalie in a horrified voice, but Franklin just threw back his head and laughed so heartily that he set up an echo from the surrounding houses of Queen's Square.

But when we were delivered to the door of number 3, Laura Place, we were surprised to see four cocked hats lying on the table in the hall.

'Military men!' whispered Jane in my ear as the stately butler was escorting us towards the drawing room. Her delighted eyes were round and full of excitement. It looked as though the supper party wasn't going to be so dull, after all.

There were, indeed, four young men in the drawing room dressed in full regimentals. Jane's eyes sparkled with delight when she saw them. They were all young and all handsome. I heard a little gasp of surprise from behind me and whirled round to see Lavinia and Caroline Thorpe – again!

'So you are Mr Leigh-Perrot's little nieces. Which is which?' Mrs Forster, an elderly white-haired lady, swept forward, her silk gown trailing on the expensive carpet.

'I'm Jane Austen and this is Jenny Cooper.' Jane gave a haughty stare at the two Thorpe girls, who were smirking as we were being introduced.

'Both looking as shabby as servant girls,' whispered Lavinia. I could tell that she intended the whisper to reach us but not Mrs Forster.

I curtsied to Mrs Forster and kept my eyes fixed on her. I had stood up to Lavinia and Caroline at the Assembly Rooms at Basingstoke, and I would stand up to them again if they tried to bully me.

The girl at the piano turned out to be Frances Forster, and one of the military men, Colonel Forster, was her brother. Oh, and there was another girl, Charlotte Manners — very quiet, but sensible-looking.

'Now, my dears, let me introduce the gentlemen to you. This is Lieutenant Carter, Lieutenant Denny, Lieutenant Brandon and Colonel Forster, my grandson.'

'La,' said Jane, 'a colonel! And so young! You are truly blessed in your grandson, ma'am,' she said gravely to Mrs Forster.

Mrs Forster looked a little taken aback; Lavinia Thorpe sniggered and gave a sly look at her sister Caroline.

Colonel Forster, however, swept Jane a very deep

bow. 'You pay me too much honour, ma'am,' he said respectfully.

'Pray tell me, sir, how do you like Bath?' enquired Jane in rather a middle-aged fashion.

'Very well indeed, ma'am,' he returned.

'I mean to like it very much myself, but I have yet to make an appearance at the assemblies,' said Jane coquettishly.

'I feel quite assured that you will be a huge success, ma'am!' Colonel Forster was a good-looking young man. The scarlet uniform suited his dark good looks and he had a magnificent pair of grey eyes, fringed with jet-black lashes. He seemed amused by Jane, and I could see that Lavinia Thorpe had ceased to look scornful and now had an angry flush on her cheeks.

'Pray, ma'am, do you plan to dance the minuet at the Assembly Rooms?' Lieutenant Denny had left Caroline Thorpe's side and joined his friend Colonel Forster.

'I require some practice first, sir,' said Jane. She sighed. 'Alas, I live in the depths of the countryside and I haven't danced the minuet for many a long year!'

'Oh, we can't have that,' said Colonel Forster. His face was very serious, but his large grey eyes were full of laughter. 'Grandma, you will play a minuet for us, won't you? Denny, Carter, Brandon, move the furniture back like good fellows.' He swept Jane a low bow and said, 'Pray take my hand, ma'am.'

Jane curtsied. 'I'm vastly obliged to you, sir.' Her

eyes had a wicked glint in them as they flicked towards Lavinia Thorpe, but she wore a demure smile as she went forward.

Jane, of course, is an expert dancer, and Eliza had taught us both the minuet, but Jane artistically made a few errors and all in all she managed to keep both lieutenant Denny and Colonel Forster busy instructing her until supper was announced.

After supper – which was quite a fun meal with Colonel Forster and the three lieutenants exchanging witticisms with Jane – Mrs Forster suggested that Frances might like to bring the young ladies to her bedroom to freshen up and tidy their hair and the girl took us off. She was quite friendly to me but very cold to Jane. Lieutenant Denny had been sitting by the piano next to her when we arrived, but had deserted to instruct Jane in the minuet. Charlotte asked us a few polite questions about what it was like to live in the country, but she didn't seem interested.

The two Thorpe girls just scowled at us both.

'How are you enjoying Bath?' I asked Lavinia, in an effort to make conversation.

'What concern is that of yours?' she replied with a sneer.

'Tch,' said Jane reprovingly, clicking her tongue in a motherly way. 'Dear girls, you are shortly to enter the world where you will meet with many wonderful things; let me warn you against suffering yourselves to be meanly swayed by the follies and vices of others!'

'You are so ridiculous, Miss Jane Austen,' said Lavinia, turning away disdainfully. 'My dear creature,' she said to Frances, linking her arm affectionately, 'pray take no notice of those foolish girls. Let's go back to the drawing room.'

'Oh yes, let's,' said Jane enthusiastically. 'I can't wait to dance with Colonel Forster again.'

'Just you watch out, Jane.' Caroline's face was blotched with angry red patches. She plucked at Jane's sleeve to delay her and hissed, 'Colonel Forster is my sister's beau. Don't you go stealing him!'

'As if she could,' said Lavinia disdainfully, turning back. She shifted her glance from Jane to me and muttered. 'Jenny, you're just as plain as ever. Do you think that you will ever grow?'

I could feel Jane stiffen by my side, but I put a hand on her arm.

'Don't, Jane,' I said. 'Perhaps these girls can't help being ill-bred. They may never have learned proper manners. We have to remember how lucky we have been with our good upbringing. Pray let us go back with no more hard words spoken.'

Lavinia's shocked expression was so amusing that I entered the drawing room with a smile stretching from ear to ear. Lieutenant Carter was at my side instantly.

'I say, what a beautiful smile. You must favour me with this dance, Miss Cooper.'

Not just Colonel Forster but also Lieutenant Denny

came forward to claim Jane's hand.

'Pulling rank on me, old boy, aren't you?' said the lieutenant cheerfully as Jane went off triumphantly on the colonel's arm.

So Jane and I lined up for a country dance, and Lieutenant Denny asked Frances to dance. Lieutenant Brandon looked in a worried way at the remaining girls, but as Charlotte was the only agreeable-looking one of the three, he bowed before her. Both Lavinia and Caroline were left to gaze out of the window.

When the dance was finished Lavinia came up to us. She ignored me and just spoke directly to Jane.

'Come into the bedroom,' she said abruptly.

'Certainly,' said Jane. The light of battle sparkled in her eyes. She went eagerly forward with the two Thorpe girls. I followed unwillingly behind. I could not desert Jane, though I don't like quarrelling.

'Now look here, Miss Jane Austen,' said Lavinia aggressively when the door had closed behind us. 'I don't suppose you are going to the Assembly Rooms tomorrow, but if you are and you dance even one dance with Newton Wallop, then you'll be sorry.'

'Oh, will I?' enquired Jane in a surprised tone. 'Well, I suppose that I might. He's not a great dancer and he may stand on my foot. Is that what you mean?'

'You know perfectly well what I mean,' hissed Lavinia, turning an ugly shade of red. 'I'm warning you.'

'You keep warning me,' complained Jane. 'I wish you'd tell me what you are going to do. And then I could decide if it's worth dancing with Newton — that's if he is going to be at the Assembly Rooms.'

'I'm going to tell all Bath about you,' hissed Lavinia. 'I shall tell them that you come from a beggarly family and that you are just desperately trying to find a rich husband. I'll tell that you are determined to steal other girls' beaux and that no one can trust you.'

'Thank you,' said Jane gravely. 'I'm glad to know that you are more interested in Newton than you are in Colonel Forster. Now I know which one to concentrate on.' She smiled sweetly at Lavinia and swept past her, saying, 'Come on, Jenny, I must keep in practice.'

And she went straight over to Colonel Forster and asked him to tell her all about his regiment. Soon the small crowd of military men were gathered around Jane and myself, while the other girls pretended to be interested in some books of artworks.

And then Franklin and Rosalie arrived to escort us back.

And the four officers decided that they had to go also!

Jane has just woken up and asked me what I am writing. I told her that I had just written about the party last night and warned her that Lavinia Thorpe would probably tell the whole of Bath that she was a dreadful flirt.

'Don't care,' was Jane's answer to that. 'I mean to have hundreds of beaux before our holiday in Bath is over.'

Poor Harry, if he is interested in Jane — I don't think that he has much of a chance, I thought, but I didn't say anything.

Jane has just given me this, saying, 'You know you are my best friend. I promise to dedicate a whole volume of my writings to you.'

Cousin
Conscious of the Charming Character which in every Country and every Clime in Christendom is Cried, Concerning you, with Caution and Care I Commend to your Charitable Criticism this Clever Collection of Curious Comments, which have been Carefully Culled, Collected and Classed by your Comical Cousin.
The Author

The Assembly Rooms at Bath

Jane and I are dressing for the ball at the Upper Assembly Rooms. Mrs Leigh-Perrot sends up her own maid to help us, but we are almost ready by the time she arrives. We are in our chemises, waiting until the last moment to put on our beautiful ball dresses – both made from the same material: a gorgeous sprigged muslin, whiter than snow and with tiny sprays of silver dotted all over it.

Each of them is made in the latest fashion, fitting the figure softly, tied with a sash under the bosom and then flowing out into a train behind. My train has some exquisite blue glass beads sewn to it – they were part of my mother's wedding gown and she had saved them for my first ball gown – but otherwise the gowns are the same.

'Let me fix that curl for you, miss,' says Rosalie after admiring our dresses. She is obviously skilled at hairdressing because she reties my side curls into a beautiful bunch on top of my head and fastens the blue velvet rose to them with great dexterity. Afterwards she pulls one short curl out from the bunch and allows it to rest on my forehead and fastens the gold chain around my neck. I gaze into the looking glass and admire the beautiful cross studded with tiny seed pearls that Thomas gave me for my birthday.

Then Rosalie does Jane's hair, fastening her chignon with a red velvet rose, and helps us both to pull our gowns

very carefully over our heads.

'Don't worry about partners, girls,' says Aunt Leigh-Perrot kindly after we have been admired. 'The master of ceremonies at the Assembly Rooms, Mr King, is very good indeed about finding partners for visitors. He is a great friend of mine and we can rely on him finding a pair of suitable young men.'

I can see Uncle just about to open his mouth and tell about the young man we met at the Pump Room yesterday morning so I quickly ask whether we will walk to the Assembly Rooms.

This works well to distract him. Uncle suggests the landau. Aunt is against that. It won't be worthwhile for a couple of blocks. She suggests sedan chairs for herself and Mrs Austen. Mrs Austen thinks it is ridiculous to go two blocks in a sedan chair and says that she will walk, so Aunt Leigh-Perrot decides to walk also.

So we all set out, with Rosalie carrying our dancing slippers in a bag, and we go a little way down George Street, then up Bartlett Street, and then we walk triumphantly past hundreds of carriages lining up to drop off their ladies and gentlemen, past sweating sedan chairmen, each staggering uphill with a lady or gentleman peering out from behind curtains. Then we are going up the steps and in under the arches to the Assembly Rooms.

I feel sick as I follow the others into the cloakroom, where we leave our wraps and put on our dancing shoes. What if Thomas has not managed to come?

And then Jane and I follow the two ladies demurely across the octagonal hallway and through the door into the ballroom.

It is so, so beautiful.

Enormous.

High, high walls with windows set about twenty feet above the floor – all blue walls – the very palest of blues and the creamiest white surrounding the windows and the four pillared fireplaces and the carved doors . . .

And the light! Magnificent chandeliers. I have never seen anything more exquisite. Five of them . . . Sparkling, crystal-like tiny icicles – and the blaze of thousands of candles! I can't lower my gaze from them, they are so beautiful.

And then a voice, Thomas's voice, chocolate smooth:

'Good evening, Mrs Austen. Sir, madam, at your service.' Now he is bowing to the three adults. And then a bow to us. 'Miss Jenny, Miss Jane, I hope I see you well.' And then he looks at me, and although it is only a second, it seems like there is no one else in the room but he and I. The look that he gives me is so full of love, of longing, of promise and hope, that I wonder how I have been able to breathe without him.

Although his tone is very formal, something about the

warmth in his brown eyes makes me feel that we are back in the garden at Steventon, that I am wearing my night-gown and in his arms. I blush and look at the splendid polished wood floor.

Mrs Austen is wonderful. She is greeting Thomas with a nice mixture of surprise and pleasure, just as if he is an old friend of the family. He makes easy conver-sation, chatting about Bath and about the roads and the problems with his ship which prevented him from going to see his uncle, the admiral. I hardly follow it all. I try to control my breathing. There is a thundering noise in my ears and I feel the colour rise hotly to my cheeks. How handsome he looks in his blue-and-gold navy uniform. I can see a lot of girls stealing glances at his tall figure. They just see that. They don't see all the tiny things that I love about him – the way his eyes change so suddenly from being dark and piercing to the softest and gentlest of golden brown; the way he laughs; how he remembers everything that I say and, best of all, the way he makes me feel completely loved and protected. I stand there, drink-ing him in as if I have not seen him for a year.

'Perhaps Miss Jenny will favour me with the first dance?' asks Thomas. I curtsy silently. I dare not speak. My feelings are bubbling up inside me so that I fear that if I open my mouth I will probably laugh or cry – or both at the same time.

The crowd is swelling by the minute – everyone press-ing forward to see the minuet dancers – only they are allowed to dance the first dance. I move a little closer to

Thomas and now I can feel the warmth of him and I can barely wait until we are alone on the dance floor. The orchestra plays softly and the moves on the dance floor are made with no word spoken between the dancers.

And then it is all over – everyone claps. The elaborately dressed ladies and gentlemen retire. The floor is now empty for a moment. We all line up, facing our partners, for the country dance. First one couple, then another and then myself and Thomas, followed by Jane and Harry and then dozens more.

This is a dance I have danced a thousand times before, back in the parlour at Steventon or in the little Assembly Rooms in Basingstoke. But now it is different. Thomas and I touch hands, part, come together again, exchange a word, a glance . . . And every time that we part I almost feel as though I have lost a part of myself, something important to my life and happiness. And when we come together again it's as if two broken halves have been joined. My happiness seems to brim over and I suddenly feel scared that this might be the last time in my life when I will feel complete like this. Perhaps Augusta and Edward-John will manage to part us after all.

And then I look at Thomas and forget everything else. Wouldn't it be lovely to finish the evening in each other's arms and then to go out into the moonlit night and drive away, just the two of us? I think this, but I dare not say it.

Now the first dance is over. People are moving in every direction. Some crowd around the fireplaces, others meekly return to their chaperones, others like Jane stand talking and laughing with their escorts. Suddenly Thomas bends down, kisses my hand and whispers, 'Have you got the forget-me-nots safe?' I whisper, 'Yes,' but I dare not tell him that I have tucked the pressed flowers into my stays! Jane sees Newton and calls across to him. Phylly, who is talking with some gentleman by the fireplace, cannot restrain herself from saying, 'Jane!' sharply, and everyone looks at Jane, who laughs.

And in this moment of confusion, when no eyes are upon us, Thomas leans down and kisses my hand – his gaze never leaving mine. Even through the silk of my glove I can feel the warmth of his lips and it takes all my strength not to fall into his arms.

Jane is telling Newton all about her cousin Phylly.

'And then she put on this hat and stood on her toes and peered into the mirror in the shop and she gave this little chirping sound and said, "Oh, fancy me! How pretty!" She was just like a little parrot in a cage! I could have died laughing!'

Newton laughs heartily, though with a slightly guilty look around, to make sure that Phylly has moved away. But she is talking earnestly to Harry, so Jane and Newton start exchanging jokes about her and about parrots. I am just thinking of asking Thomas whether we should join them, when I notice an elderly gentleman in naval uniform staring at me. He sees that I have seen him, but he does not smile nor move towards us. He has a rather disagreeable face, I think.

'My uncle!' exclaims Thomas. 'He must have got my

letter and followed me to Bath. Wait for me,' he says abruptly. He takes me over to Jane and then crosses back across the room towards the gentleman in uniform. They talk while I watch anxiously. The man in uniform takes a folded letter from his pocket, holds it up rather threateningly towards Thomas and then speaks vigorously, tapping the letter against Thomas's chest as if to emphasize his point. Thomas faces him with a hard look, saying nothing, just bowing slightly from time to time. Jane speaks to me, but I don't reply. I am watching intently.

They have finished talking now and Thomas is leading him towards me, threading his way through the throngs of people laughing and talking happily.

'May I introduce my uncle to you, Jenny?' asks Thomas. His voice has the crisp, assured note that I am now beginning to recognize means battle. He takes me by the arm and I drop a curtsy to his uncle – very splendidly attired in the full uniform of an admiral of the fleet. 'I didn't know that he was in Bath, Jenny,' he says in my ear.

'Miss Cooper, this is my uncle, Admiral Williams. Sir, I have the honour of presenting Miss Cooper.'

The admiral bows stiffly and I curtsy again wordlessly, thanking my lucky stars that Jane and I had been practising our curtsy earlier in front of the splendid looking glass in our bedroom. He does not speak to me, but addresses Thomas in a brusque tone, 'Your sister, sir, was without a partner for that dance. She is standing over there with that fool of a governess that you engaged for her. She's too young for this sort of affair. She would be better off in school. Anyway, Bath is not what it was in my young day. Where is the master of ceremonies? It's his business to find partners for young ladies and gentlemen.'

Thomas is calmly saying something about Mr King, the master of ceremonies, but his uncle cuts him short and orders him to fetch his sister.

Now I am alone with the admiral and I stare at him wordlessly, wondering whether I should say something as he looks me up and down, as if mentally assessing the cost of my muslin gown and my white cotton gloves. I am on the point of asking him whether he is enjoying Bath when I hear a voice behind me, a familiar voice with the Hampshire burr in it.

'And she's a lovely little dog, that black pointer of mine. I could give you one of the puppies when she has them in June.'

There can be only one man in Bath who would be discussing black pointer dogs at a ball so I swing round quickly as Jane says thoughtfully:

'I quite fancy myself in a shooting jacket. Dearest Harry, could you get one of those for me, also?'

And then she dropped a neat curtsy right before the astonished admiral.

'Jane, this is Thomas's uncle, Admiral Williams. My cousin, Miss Jane Austen. And this is Mr Harry Digweed of Steventon Manor,' I say.

Admiral Williams bows to Jane and then nods at Harry. He stares intently at me. I get the feeling that he does not think much of me. A tall, thin, kind-looking woman comes up, followed by Thomas. A blonde girl is clinging to his arm, looking up at him with adoring eyes.

Thomas smiles down at her and then, taking no notice of the admiral, says, 'Jenny, I'd like you to meet my sister Elinor. Elinor, I've told you about Jenny.'

I smile at Elinor, but she does not smile back. She moves even closer to Thomas, squeezing herself up against him and looking up at him as if she is about ten years old. My heart sinks. I had hoped that we would be friends, but she is now eyeing me with an air of dislike. I wonder whether she is jealous of Thomas's interest in me. I suppose since their parents died when Elinor was very young, she has got used to thinking of Thomas as her property. Neither she nor the admiral seems anxious to welcome me as a new member of the family.

I try to keep a smile on my face. I so want her to like me, for us to be like sisters. Elinor is a pretty girl, a little younger than me, I think – very pale, very thin – even her blonde hair is pale. Thomas has his arm around her now and is smiling down at her, his little sister. I find myself feeling slightly irritated. After all, she is not that young!

And then I look at the admiral who is still glaring at me critically. He glances up at the balcony where the orchestra are beginning to tune their instruments.

'My dear,' he says to Elinor, 'I think if you look at your card you will see that the next dance has been given to Sir Walter.' He looks at the governess and abruptly tells her to escort her charge. Then he says, 'Perhaps, Miss Cooper, you will do me the honour of dancing this with an old man. Thomas, the Honourable Clotilde Wallop is here. You should ask her to dance. It was very kind of the Earl to put you up when you were in Hampshire. Come with me – I must greet her also. Excuse us for a moment, Miss Cooper.'

Thomas gives me an apologetic look and I try to smile cheerfully.

And now Thomas is bowing before Clotilde, the eldest sister of Newton Wallop. She is beautifully dressed in a flowing gown of gold silk embroidered with gold thread. As the daughter of the Earl of Portsmouth she will have a huge dowry. When the admiral makes his way back to me the look of satisfaction on his face is sickening.

'And your family comes from Bristol?' he says to me when we reach the bottom of the line and have the opportunity to talk to each other.

I nod silently.

'And your father, is he a . . . merchant?' He pauses before the word 'merchant'. I'm not sure whether he is pleased at the idea – after all, most merchants in Bristol are rich – or whether he thinks I am under-bred, but I tell him briefly that my father is dead, but that he used to be a clergyman. This makes him look as though some bad smell has reached his nose. I see Jane laughing with Newton and I envy them their easy companionship. They are sharpening their wits on each other and whispering in each other's ears.

'Good, good,' says the admiral, but the tone of his voice says, *Bad, bad*. 'And where did you meet my nephew?'

'At Basingstoke Assembly Rooms; my cousin Frank Austen introduced us,' I say. I feel my face flush guiltily. What would he say if he knew that we had met at midnight on the streets of Portsmouth?

Thomas and Newton's sister seem to be getting on very well. Of course he knows her – they were probably great friends when he stayed at their house not long ago. He is laughing at something Clotilde says, throwing his head back, the candlelight shining on his black hair. I gaze at it, wishing I was in his arms. Then I realize that the admiral has asked a question, so I apologize.

'I just asked whether you are enjoying Bath.' He sounds annoyed and I drag my eyes away from Thomas and tell him that I love Bath. I try to be enthusiastic about the Assembly Rooms, but he just nods in a bored way and then I fall silent. He asks me whether I have had a season in London and I am so taken aback that I blurt out the fact that my family could never afford something like that for me. He raises his eyebrows and greets an old acquaintance over my shoulder, but says no more to me, and I can't think of anything else to say.

When the dance finishes, I curtsy to him and he allows me to make my own way over to where my two aunts are sitting with Phylly perched on the bench below them. He doesn't think that I am worth paying any more attention to. I am acutely miserable and feel that I should have tried harder to impress him.

'Who is that?' Aunt Leigh-Perrot is staring at the admiral.

'Admiral Williams, Aunt,' I say. 'Where's Eliza?'

'Dancing with a Frenchman,' says Mrs Austen. 'Is that the uncle of Captain Thomas, then?'

I nod; she looks interested, but I think I have made rather a mess of it. Harry and Jane come up at that moment. Harry very nicely asks Phylly to dance and she bounces up from the seat and looks triumphantly at Jane.

And then Newton comes to claim Jane once again and I am still waiting, scanning the crowd, looking for Thomas. Now he is talking with another lady. He knows so many people here at Bath.

I can see Newton's sister deep in conversation with Elinor – they are laughing and talking as though the best of friends. And now the music begins.

Then Thomas comes to claim me and everything is wonderful again. I decide not to think about relations. My brother and sister-in-law don't like Thomas, and his uncle and sister don't seem to like me. I'll worry about it tomorrow, I tell myself.

Evening has come and the windows at the top of the walls have turned dark – they are like black mirrors, and the reflections of the five chandeliers sparkle in their panes. The fires burn with a red glow, but the crowd is so thick that I have a feeling that we are in our own little bubble of light.

'I have written to your brother,' says Thomas softly

in my ear. 'I am going to see him tomorrow. I shall set off first thing in the morning and be back in Bath by evening.'

And then he is gone, crossing hands with Phylly while Harry twirls me around and I skip neatly under our clasped hands.

'You're a good dancer, Harry,' I say, and he smiles.

'Thanks to Mrs Austen! She wouldn't let any boy get away with doing it clumsily. We boys, the four of us, had such fun at the parsonage in the winter evenings. My father and mother aren't too sociable, and the old manor house is a terrible tumbledown old ruin – old as the great King Henry VIII, they say – but there was always a welcome for us at the Austens'.'

And then Thomas was back and he and I went down the line. Jane, I notice, is chattering happily with Newton Wallop and both of them are laughing again. I look to see if Lavinia is dancing, but she isn't – just standing beside her mama, fanning herself so vigorously that no one can see her face. Phylly comes up to her and starts chatting. They both look across at Jane. I turn back to Thomas and blush when I see the look in his eyes.

'What are you going to say to Edward-John?' I ask when we reach the end of the room.

'I will make him see reason,' he says airily, and then he frowns. 'Why on earth does my uncle allow Elinor to dance with Sir Walter Montmorency?' He spits the words out through clenched teeth. His expression is dark and stormy. 'I don't care for that fellow; I've heard some stories about him, some scandal...' He looks down at me and seems to decide to say no more.

'He looks very charming,' I say. I must confess that I don't want to talk about Elinor. 'Anyway, your uncle seems to like him.'

Thomas shakes his head. 'I don't trust my uncle,' he says. 'He'd like to make a splendid match for Elinor – she's barely sixteen, too young to be thinking of getting married. She's young for her age,' he adds hastily as he sees me smile. 'She's scared of the admiral though, and she'll do anything to please him. The trouble is that he can't resist telling everyone that she will have a dowry of twenty thousand pounds from him when she marries with his approval.'

'What about you?' I ask anxiously. 'Do you have to get his approval before you marry?'

Thomas shrugs. 'He can keep his money, as far as I am concerned. I want to choose my own bride.'

He hasn't said no, I notice. I want to ask him whether he will forgo any fortune from his uncle if he marries me, but he is looking across at his sister again. His face softens as he watches her. 'It's different for poor little Elinor. She's a child that craves approval. She can't stand up for herself.' He looks down at me and says, 'Will you try to keep an eye on her for me, Jenny? Perhaps you and your cousin could befriend her. She is very shy and timid. It would do her good to have some girls of her own age to have fun with. She's a funny girl; I can't make her out. She's always trying to please, and it makes her seem scared stiff half the time. It's as if she has no mind of her own. She shouldn't be thinking of marriage for another few years.'

I smile to myself when I think how Thomas asked me to marry him although I am not much older than his sister. Privately I'm not sure that his view of Elinor as a sweet little child is quite accurate. There was something rather spiteful in the way that she looked at me and she definitely seemed to be gossiping about me to Newton's sister. However, I promise him that Jane and I will do our best to be friendly.

I look thoughtfully over at Elinor. She is still dancing with Sir Walter. He is a very elegantly dressed man in pale primrose-coloured breeches. His hair is rather long, but it suits him. He has a very handsome face, almost as though he is a carved statue. I wonder what the scandal was, but guess that Thomas won't tell me. Elinor is looking up at him timidly, her uncle watching her with a smirk on his face. Obviously he approves of her partner!

And then Thomas dances down the line and I wait, marking time. I see Elinor glance over at me. A look of dislike crosses her face. She stands on tiptoe, her mouth at Sir Walter's ear. He looks across at me and doesn't lower his voice.

'A country parson, no breeding, no family, no fortune? What can your brother be thinking?'

My heart sinks.

And then Thomas is back and together we dance to

the end of the line. Now we will wait here until our time comes to dance again. I decide that I won't tell him about Sir Walter's words. I don't want to cause any bad feeling, and I still hope that Elinor and I might be friends eventually.

While we mark time Thomas starts to tell me about his home on the Isle of Wight and how his house is near to his uncle's, and both of them overlook the sea but Thomas's house has a woodland to the back of it.

'If only I didn't have this trip to the East Indies,' he says, 'and if only you could come and visit in May. The beech woods are full of bluebells then. I'd love to see you standing there among them – just you and the carpet of blue and green. It would make such a beautiful picture. Your eyes are the exact shade of the bluebells.'

And now the bell goes for supper. Everyone is streaming through the door leading to the Octagon Room. The card players are coming in from the card room. Elinor and her governess are just ahead of us and the admiral pushes his way past us to join them. There is no sign of Sir Walter Montmorency now, and the admiral looks angry. Colonel Forster comes up to ask Jane for the after-supper dance, and she writes his name on her little dance card. I see Lavinia glare at Jane and whisper to a girl sitting next to her. I do hope Jane is not getting herself a reputation in Bath!

And then we have reached the opposite side of the Octagon Room and manage to enter the tea room. The room is almost as beautiful as the ballroom, the walls a delicate shade of salmon pink and the three fairy-tale chandeliers lighting up the dozens of circular tables spread with snowy-white linen cloths. At the top of the room there is a row of white marble arches and beyond a long table spread with the most delicious food: sweetmeats, jelly, biscuits, cold ham, turkey and many other wonderful things.

'Oh la,' says Jane from behind us. She is with Harry now and I am touched to see how happy he looks. I'm glad I thought of suggesting that he come to the Assembly Rooms.

Jane seizes me by the hand. 'Let's join Eliza,' she says rapidly. 'The tables are just for six so that will save us making conversation with my mother and my aunt and uncle – not to mention dear Phylly!'

Eliza and her escort are already sitting at a table just next to one of the four fireplaces. She is smiling and waving so I follow Jane while Thomas and Harry go to get a tray of food and cups of tea for us.

'Jenny,' says Eliza softly, 'your dear uncle, Mr Leigh-Perrot ... who is his heir?'

I look at her in astonishment and she laughs. 'You don't think of these things at your age, *ma chérie*, but they are important, nonetheless. There are no children and will never be, so the fortune – and it is a considerable one if you add Mrs Leigh-Perrot's to her husband's – well, it will doubtless be left to one of the family – perhaps one of his nephews.'

'To Jane's eldest brother?'

'Or to Edward-John,' says Eliza. 'Don't think your brother won't have thought of this. Let's make sure that Mrs Leigh-Perrot is in favour of your marriage to Captain Williams.'

Harry and Thomas have returned with two large trays of food, and Eliza turns her attention back to her French escort. She is speaking French to him but calling him 'Monsieur Baddy', which he seems to find very funny. They are discussing whether they like syllabub or not – they all do, except Harry, who thinks it is too sweet. Thomas and I are in our private little world, eating very little but just looking into each other's eyes. I find the courage to tell him how much I am going to miss him. I can hardly bear to think that he will be away for almost a year.

'How much do you love me?' His mouth is very close to my ear. Everyone is talking so loudly and music is playing in the background so that there seems to be a solid wall of sound all around us. I turn my head so that my mouth is near to him. 'I love you more than the sun and the moon and the stars,' I say, and I don't really care if someone hears.

The others at our table are playing a noisy game of 'likes' and 'dislikes' – everything that Jane likes Harry likes – even syllabub, which a few minutes earlier he had said he disliked!

'I don't think your uncle liked me,' I say to Thomas.

'Probably jealous of me,' says Thomas. He doesn't seem to care whether the admiral likes me or not and that cheers me. I did wonder though whether the admiral was regretting that Thomas was not having tea with an earl's daughter.

'What if he cuts you off without a penny for marrying a lowly person like myself?' I say it in a light-hearted way and he responds instantly with an equally light-hearted 'Who cares!' and I hope that he means it. Perhaps Thomas will also get twenty thousand pounds if he marries according to the admiral's wishes. When he is away from me, will he remember that? And will the thought of a marriage with someone like Newton's sister, Clotilde, be more attractive to him?

And then I realize that Mrs Leigh-Perrot and Mrs Austen have come over and are standing beside me.

The three men stand up and Eliza introduces Monsieur Baddy (who turns out to be Monsieur le Comte de something or other). Mrs Austen mentions Harry's name, and Mrs Leigh-Perrot nods at him and tells him that he has grown since she saw him last – and Harry goes bright red. Then she looks at me expectantly.

'Aunt, may I introduce Captain Thomas Williams,' I say.

'Delighted to make your acquaintance, Captain Williams!' Mrs Leigh-Perrot sounds quite enthusiastic. 'Harry,' she says, just as if he were still a small boy, 'perhaps I could borrow your chair? You could get me a cup of tea while I have a chat with Captain Williams.'

'Would you like to sit down also, Mrs Austen?' asks Thomas politely, but she shakes her head and says guiltily that she must get back to Phylly.

'Let's go and arrange our hair, girls,' says Eliza gaily. 'Monsieur Baddy –' she taps him on the arm with her fan – 'you behave yourself while I am gone. You may fetch yourself one more cake, but only one. There are many dances to come, so not too much cake.'

And then we are on our way, pushing through the crowded tables, leaving Thomas alone with Mrs Leigh-Perrot. I see that Elinor is still sitting with her governess and her uncle, none of them talking, and I feel sorry for Elinor. Perhaps we should have asked her to join our party. And then I get a shock. She is looking at me with a strange expression – almost as though she hates me.

And yet, she has only just met me!

'Look, Eliza,' says Jane as we pass through the Octagon Room. 'There's still one table of people there in the card room. Don't they want any supper?'

'Hush, they'll hear you,' I whisper, but I realize that the people at the table have eyes and ears for nothing but cards and the bets.

'*Oh la, ma chérie*,' says Eliza. 'There are some men, and women too, who cannot stop gambling. To give up a supper! Pouf! *C'est rien!* Nothing! I've known men to put a fine house and a great estate on the throw of a card.'

Eliza looks around to make sure that no one is within earshot and then hisses, 'Do you see that woman over there, the one with a very large hat with cherries and apricots on it? That's Georgiana, Duchess of Devonshire, and she cannot stop gambling; 'tis said she owes fifty thousand pounds!'

I have a quick look at the duchess, a plump fair-haired woman with a very large hat, but I'm more interested in the handsome Sir Walter Montmorency and the expression of despair on his face as he flings his cards on the table and pushes over the pile of money in front of him. He looks even more upset than the duchess, despite all of her debts. I begin to understand why Thomas doesn't want him as a husband for his sister despite his charm and good looks.

And then the dancing starts again. I forget about Elinor, forget about the admiral, forget about everyone, because I am in the arms of the man that I love . . .

Saturday, 23 April 1791

Such a wonderful evening at the Assembly Rooms! Dancing with Thomas, in the magnificent ballroom with its blue walls and five sparkling chandleliers. Having tea with Thomas in the pink-and-white tea room, peeping into the long, thin grass-green card room. And last of all, saying goodbye.

If only we could have slipped outside to the moonlit street. If only we could have gone anywhere. I shut my eyes and try to imagine what it would be like to be in that bluebell wood with Thomas.

But could I ever have said goodbye in a place like that?

So Thomas and I had to say goodbye in the Octagon Room under the watchful eyes of the Leigh-Perrots and Mrs Austen and half the population of Bath.

I don't think I will ever forget the Octagon Room. The eight slanting walls of primrose yellow, the four double doors, the four marble fireplaces and the sixteen paned windows above them.

And Thomas, very formally holding my hand in his, bowing to me.

But his hand, even through our gloves, burned through to mine, and his fingers pressed my fingers so tightly . . .

And his eyes when he raised his head . . .

Suddenly all the noise faded and it seemed as though we were alone . . .

Looking at each other . . .

'I'll be back,' he said softly.

'If only Thomas's uncle and sister liked me and Edward-John gave permission for the marriage, then I would be just so happy,' I remarked to Jane as we were getting ready for breakfast.

'Well, at least you have found the man of your dreams,' pointed out Jane. She sighed theatrically, saying, '*Hélas,*' in just the same way as Eliza does.

'Jane,' I said, diverted from my own troubles, 'don't be ridiculous. You have the whole of Bath paying court to you. You just have to choose. Who exactly do you like best, Newton Wallop, Captain Forster, Lieutenant Carter, Lieutenant Denny, Lieutenant Brandon or any of the other men who have been queuing up to dance with you?'

Jane sighed again. 'I need some advice, I think. My love life is getting too complicated for a simple country girl like myself.'

And then the bell rang for breakfast and we raced down, giggling as usual.

We have just finished our dinner, and Jane and I have come up to our bedroom for a little rest. We are all going to a concert in the Lower Rooms in the evening.

My uncle thinks that Thomas will be unlikely to be back from Bristol today, so I shall have to wait for tomorrow morning to see him. He has promised to take me to call on his sister Elinor after church so that will probably be the time.

Jane has just lifted her head from her paper to ask me whether I have written about our new gowns yet so I must do that now.

This morning at breakfast time our uncle asked us if we had enjoyed the evening. We were both so enthusiastic that he beamed at us, and even Mrs Leigh-Perrot gave a smile.

'They were both looking very pretty, I thought,' she said to Mrs Austen. 'Those white muslins are so fresh. Just right for girls of that age.'

'And what are you going to wear at the ball next Saturday?' asked Mr Leigh-Perrot.

Jane and I looked at each other. Another ball in seven days' time!

'The same,' I said after a minute.

'Oh no, you can't do that.' Mr Leigh-Perrot was as aghast as if he were a leader of fashion.

'We've only got one ball dress each,' said Jane, ignoring her mother's frown. 'Our old ones were falling apart.'

Mr Leigh-Perrot looked at his wife. 'What do you think, my dear? Shall we make the girls a present of a new gown each? Do you think that your dressmaker could make them in time?'

'I'm sure that she could.' Mrs Leigh-Perrot was also in a good humour. 'You can get up-to-date fashions here in Bath, as fine as London. No, no, Mrs Austen.

Your brother and I would love to do this. Now, girls, as soon as you finish your breakfast, go upstairs and put your bonnets on. We'll take Franklin with us to carry the parcels,' she added to her husband, and he nodded benignly.

Jane and I were first down. Franklin was already waiting for us, standing outside by the railing, wearing a top hat and a pair of white gloves.

'Franklin,' asked Jane as soon as we reached him, 'have you got a wife?'

'Not me, Miss Jane,' said Franklin. He had a very dignified air when he answered the question and I felt embarrassed that he had been asked.

I think Jane was a bit embarrassed too because she thought for a few moments before speaking again – and that is not like her.

'I just asked because I wondered if you could give me advice on choosing a husband.'

Franklin laughed at that for a long time. I liked the way that he did it. He just threw his head back and roared quite loudly. I saw a few passers-by look at him with surprise.

'Don't you worry your head about that, Miss Jane,' he said when he had recovered. 'Your father and mother will do the choosing, and they will choose someone just right for you.'

Jane made a face. When the two ladies came out Franklin walked in front of them, and Jane, taking my arm, fell back a little.

As we were walking along the west side of Queen's Square I heard a bright squeaky voice saying, 'Come along, Eliza, let's go for a brisk walk. That's what we need after being cooped up in those stuffy old Assembly Rooms yesterday evening. Walk quickly, dear. You'll be glad that I got you out of bed at a reasonable hour.'

'It's Eliza,' I said quickly.

'And Phylly,' groaned Jane.

Queen's Square had a garden in the centre of the four lines of houses. There were some tall bushes on the side we were walking, but in a moment Phylly emerged, strutting along quickly and followed by a very sleepy-looking Eliza.

Mrs Austen grinned at the sight. 'You're up early, Eliza,' she said.

'*Chère Madame*, I don't think I ever got up as early as this since I was a child,' said Eliza earnestly, doing her best to smother a yawn. 'That is unless I hadn't gone to bed the night before,' she added.

'Uncle and Aunt are going to buy Jenny and myself new gowns! Do come with us, Eliza, and help us to choose,' said Jane enthusiastically. She dropped back and allowed the Leigh-Perrots and Mrs Austen to get ahead of us. She turned eagerly to Eliza, but Phylly pushed her way between them.

'Dear, dear, Jane,' said Phylly, 'may I give you a word of advice?' She stood on her toes and whispered loudly into Jane's ear. 'I'm just a little worried about you. You should not get too interested in balls at your age. You are getting quite a name as a flirt. A little bird told me last night that you set out to steal young men from other girls, and that is not nice at all. There's another thing too, Jane dear, if you will forgive me mentioning it. I think you are trying to turn the head of that nice young man Harry Digweed. I'm sure that he is too sensible to take very much notice of you, but you have to be careful about your reputation, you know.'

Then she stood back from Jane and nodded sternly. Jane stared at her in wide-eyed innocence and Eliza looked from one to the other in an embarrassed fashion and then took matters into her own hands by decisively changing the subject.

'What style of gown will you have?' Eliza took my arm and Jane's and teetered along on her very high heels between us.

Jane told her that we weren't sure, and Eliza immediately began discussing the latest fashion, still walking fast and doing her best to catch up with the other three. She didn't look too upset when Phylly, from behind us, said disdainfully, 'Well, I am going to continue my morning constitutional. I've made a resolution to go ten times around the square's garden every morning. Otherwise my health will suffer in this stuffy city.'

'How strong you are, Phylly dear,' said Eliza admiringly over her shoulder, but to our relief she made no effort to persuade her cousin to accompany us.

'I'd like to have something in the latest fashion from Paris,' said Jane with determination. 'Something which would make a lord with ten thousand pounds a year immediately seek my hand in marriage.'

'Jane,' I said reproachfully. I felt sorry for Harry, who was so devoted. Even Phylly had noticed that. Harry wouldn't care what Jane wore.

'What about the latest idea of having an under-skirt, a train and an overskirt each of a different colour?' suggested Eliza. She released both our arms and stood in the middle of the pavement making wide gestures with her hands over her own body, outlining a loose style gathered in under the bosom, flowing out to a train behind and then outlining a sharply point-ed V-shape in the front. I could see immediately what she meant. Something like this:

We were now in the middle of Milsom Street and a small crowd of interested shoppers be-gan to gather around to listen to Eliza's mixture of French and English. She was so fashionably dressed herself that most people had a look of earnest attention that made me shoot a glance at Jane, and I could see that she, like me, was having a hard time stopping a giggle escaping. Mrs Leigh-Perrot had an air of annoyance, but Mrs

Austen just wore the usual look of amused tolerance that she reserved for her husband's eccentric niece.

'*Voyons*,' concluded Eliza. 'Let us go in. This is the shop, *n'est-ce pas*?'

The drapery shop was built like a small version of a church, with pillars dividing the space into lanes. Very cleverly each pillar was encircled with a band bearing five or six large hooks which were used to drape long swathes of muslin or silk in assorted colours. In between the pillars and set against the walls were numerous tall cheval looking glasses and the colours were reflected in them. While Mrs Leigh-Perrot had a friendly conversation with the owner, Jane and I wandered up and down the aisles, gazing at the beautiful fabrics.

'Muslin or silk?' Eliza joined us.

I quickly told her muslin. Silk would be very expensive, and I did not want to take advantage of the Leigh-Perrots' generosity. In any case, silk was difficult to clean, whereas muslin could be washed again and again. Jane had been admiring a glossy gold-colour silk, but she nodded reluctantly when I explained the advantages of muslin to Eliza. By the time Mrs Leigh-Perrot joined us we had both decided on muslin.

'Much more suitable for young girls,' said Mrs Austen decidedly, and I could see that she was pleased with our decision.

'I think I'd like this one, but what would I have for the underskirt?' Jane was examining a pale yellow.

'Too pale for you, *chérie*.' Eliza was always very definite about these things. She moved with quick, almost dancing steps between the draped pillars. Jane and I followed her obediently.

'. . . too much liberty given to children nowadays. They are asked what they want, rather than told what to do. When I was five years old I was put on a ship without a mother or father or any relation and I was sent all the way from Barbados to England and put in a boarding school. I didn't see my family for another ten years. Didn't do me any harm.'

Mrs Leigh-Perrot was carrying on this conversation with Mrs Austen now as the shop owner hovered around us. I wondered if she thought we were getting our own way too much in being allowed to choose the stuff for our gowns. Hurriedly I moved away, leaving Jane and Eliza staring at some yellow muslins, and walked down the long aisle trying to make my mind up. The trouble was that every one of the muslins was so beautiful. I thought about the Duchess of Devonshire, whom we had seen playing cards at the Assembly Rooms. If I were her I would spend fifty thousand pounds on muslins rather than waste it at the card table.

'What about this?' Jane was eying a rich yellow. I came back and joined them. It was easier to choose for Jane than for myself.

'*Parfait!*' enthused Eliza, picking up the end of the muslin and holding it against Jane, glancing quickly from Jane's deep brown hair and dark hazel eyes and then back at the material.

'I rather like it,' said Jane. 'It's the colour of daffodils. My favourite flower.' She lowered her voice and whispered wickedly to me, 'And Harry's favourite — don't forget that.'

Suddenly I made up my mind. Jane's remark about the daffodil had given me an idea.

'What about a bluebell colour for me?' I asked Eliza, and she nodded enthusiastically. While Jane dithered between two different shades of pale yellow for the train and the V-shaped panel in the front of the gown, I walked along scanning all the blues. But funnily enough it was Mrs Austen who, getting tired of Mrs Leigh-Perrot's reminiscences of her childhood and the shock of an English boarding school after the warmth and fun of Barbados (she had probably heard them all hundreds of times), called me over to a dark corner.

'Look, Jenny,' she said.

This pillar was draped in nothing but soft shades of blue. The shop owner was down in a minute. 'You'll need some light to see them properly, madam. Abigail, bring a lamp.'

Abigail brought the lamp. Mrs Austen said something about seeing them by daylight, but Eliza, who had now joined us, leaving Jane contemplating her daffodil yellow, shook her head firmly.

'My dearest aunt, not daylight – *Quelle horreur*! These gowns are meant to be seen by candlelight. Fetch two candles, *ma petite*,' she said to Abigail, who handed the lamp to her mistress, curtsied, flew down the shop and returned with two candles and a lighter.

'Don't set the place on fire, Madame de Feuillide,' said Mrs Leigh-Perrot frostily but Eliza took no notice.

'*Regarde-moi*, Jenny,' she said. 'Let me see those eyes. Ah, *ravissante*!'

I could feel myself getting rather pink in the face. Everyone was staring at my eyes.

'Another lamp, if you will be so kind,' murmured Eliza, and the shop owner sped off.

Before she was back, however, Eliza had taken down one of the muslins. The colour was soft, not pale – and yet not the blue of the sea, nor the blue of the sky, not a dark blue, nor a cornflower blue; this blue glowed warmly and richly with the faintest hint of green in the intensity of its colour.

Mrs Leigh-Perrot seized the lamp and held it in front of my face as Eliza draped the muslin over my shoulder, letting it flow down in front of me.

'Perfect match,' murmured Mrs Austen. 'Well done, Eliza.'

I said nothing. I was lost in the colour. I could almost smell the bluebells that Thomas had been talking about.

'Darker or lighter for the panel in front? What do you think, Jenny?' asked Eliza.

'Have it lighter,' advised Jane. 'I'll be a daffodil and you'll be a bluebell. Bluebells are lighter in the centre.' Then she whispered so that only I could hear, 'Thomas will think you quite ravishing in this!'

I smiled at her, but suddenly I felt like crying. Thomas would not be at the ball on Saturday. He would be away on his ship. He would not see me in my bluebell gown. After tomorrow, I would not see him for perhaps a whole year.

And now I am sitting in our bedroom in number I, the Paragon. The material for the two gowns has been delivered to the dressmaker, our measurements have been taken and we will go for our first fitting on Tuesday morning.

Tonight we are going to a concert. I'm not sure that I want to go.

Oh, I wish, I wish, I wish that Thomas were here. I

miss him terribly. I can't wait. I wish that I could know how his talk with Edward-John has gone. Surely, surely, surely it will go well and I can be happy again.

Jane has just given me this piece of paper to stick in my journal, and I must say that it has cheered me up! It's some more about Phylly.

From a Young lady crossed in Love to her freind –

WHY should this last disappointment hang so heavily on my Spirits? Why should I feel it more, why should it wound me deeper than those I have experienced before? Or is it that our feelings become more acute from being often wounded? I must suppose, my dear Belle, that this is the Case, since I am not conscious of being more sincerely attached to Digweed than I was to Neville, Fitzowen or either of the Crawfords, for all of whom I once felt the most lasting affection that ever warmed a Woman's heart. Tell me then, dear Belle, why I still sigh when I think of the faithless Harry, or why I weep when I behold his Beloved, for too surely this is the case. My Freinds are all alarmed for me; they fear my declining health; they lament my want of Spirits; they dread the effects of both.

Affectionately yours,
Philadelphia Walters

Monday, 25 April 1791

I hate my brother! I hate my brother! I hate my brother! I hate my brother! I hate my brother! I HATE my brother!

I wish that I had been there in Bristol yesterday and that I had been able to tell him how I felt. How could my mother have left him as my guardian? She must have known what he was like and how much he was under his wife's thumb. She should have asked the Austens to look after me. Or even the Leigh-Perrots.

Thomas told me that he was thinking of challenging Edward-John to a duel, but that he thought he shouldn't in case I was fond of my brother. His hand touched the sword by his side when he said that, and I felt a shiver run down my back.

'Not that,' I said hastily. Was I fond of Edward-John? At the moment I thought not, but he was my only brother and my nearest relation.

'But what are we going to do about Edward-John?' I asked him. I had not cried, not yet. My eyes were dry. I just had a terrible pain in my head and a feeling of despair.

Thomas just shrugged. He looked as though he did not think that Edward-John was of much importance. That somehow or other he would persuade him to agree, or force him to agree.

'You don't understand,' I said hopelessly. 'You

think it is just a matter of repeating arguments, that Edward-John will eventually come to his senses.'

'Of course I don't understand!' Suddenly he was angry and he glared as if at an unseen enemy before him. 'I can't understand how any brother could treat a sister the way that your brother does. He has no interest in you, no care for you.'

'It's not so much Edward-John,' I said despairingly. 'It's Augusta. You don't understand that, drop by drop, Augusta is feeding poison to him: I must not get married: they must not relinquish control over my little fortune; that's what she makes him think.'

'Nonsense,' he said impatiently. 'The man can't be as great a fool as that. What's fifty pounds a year? I told him that he's welcome to keep it. Wait till you see what I can bring back from a voyage, I said to him, but that sister-in-law of yours seemed to think that I was insulting them and used it as an excuse to finish the conversation. I thought it best to leave while I still had control of my temper.'

'She didn't even care that she could retain my dowry?' Now I really began to despair. That, at least, might have been understandable, but now I knew that Augusta hated me so much that she would do anything to make sure that I wasn't happy. 'She'll never give in,' I said. 'You don't understand . . .'

Thomas was suddenly angry. 'No, my darling,' he said hotly, 'you don't understand. There is nothing in the world that will stop me from making you my wife – especially not your hen-pecked brother and his harridan of a wife! I shall make my fortune, and you and I will not care for any disapproving relative.'

He took me in his arms and kissed me and I smiled as I kissed him back. . I could not spoil our last moments together. We were alone. Jane had made a big fuss of going into the best parlour with us, and then slipped out by the side door to the stairs when no one was around. It had been nice of her, and I should not waste the time. Soon he would go and I would not see him for another year at least.

'Let's not talk any more about my idiot brother,' I said. And when he stretched out his arms to me, I went into them instantly.

He took me upon his lap and cradled me in his arms. One arm was around me and the other was on my cheek, one broad thumb pushing my hair from my face. And then he kissed me.

Was it a minute?

Or was it an hour?

I don't know, but I remember that when Mrs Leigh-Perrot's voice sounded in the hall we broke apart.

Then the other door opened and Jane slipped in, only a minute before the Leigh-Perrots and Mrs Austen entered by the door from the hall.

And then all the formal goodbyes were said and Thomas kissed my hand and I smiled and wished him a good voyage and everyone else did the same.

And then he was gone. And I won't see him again for a whole year.

I waited until he had gone before running up to our room, throwing myself on my bed and breaking out into a fit of wild weeping which frightened me.

If I had not had Jane, I don't know what I should have done!

She kept everyone from the door, telling them that I wanted to be by myself. She sat by me, stroked my hair and brought me drinks and bathed my eyes with lavender water and then, when I began to yawn and turn my head towards the pillow, she drew the blinds and seated herself at her writing desk just by the window.

I have drawn a picture of her there, as I could see the outline of her face against the dim light, just before I fell asleep.

And now there is no more to be said.

This morning when I woke with the same pain in my heart I no longer sobbed, but my eyes were sore and my throat was dry.

I struggled through breakfast, but I could feel the tears welling up again, and Mrs Leigh-Perrot gave me a few drops of laudanum to calm me and I stumbled up the stairs back to bed. I had a terrible feeling that I might never see him again. One of my great-grandmothers was supposed to have the gift of second sight. I hope I haven't inherited it from her.

When I woke again I knew by the light that it was late afternoon. Jane was still there and she was still writing. I sat up in bed and looked across at her.

'What are you writing?' I asked. I was surprised to find that my voice sounded the same. I had seemed to have gone down into a dark pit, but somehow I had come up again. I was still Jenny. I was still in love with the most handsome, the bravest and the kindest man in the world.

'I'm making a list,' said Jane. 'While you were asleep Uncle Leigh-Perrot has been tiptoeing to the door every half-hour, wanting to know what he could do for you. He had a lot of strange suggestions. He keeps asking Franklin's advice.'

In spite of my misery, I had to laugh. I could just imagine our uncle pacing up and down and consulting with Franklin about what was to be done about his niece. Jane laughed too and looked encouraged to see me smile.

'Well, here's what he has been suggesting. You can stick that in your diary:

Olives
A blancmange shape
A new bonnet
Some sweetmeats
A piece of ginger
A slice of ham-and-veal pie
Some black butter and a pair of widgeon

'I told him that you would do better to sleep for the afternoon, but I suggested that we would have a good supper tonight and then visit the fireworks at the Gardens. That was Franklin's suggestion also. He tells me that they are mighty fine.'

'You go; I'll stay.' I struggled out of bed and looked at my face in the looking glass.

'I think you should go,' said Jane, watching me anxiously. 'If you don't go, I shan't enjoy it, neither will our uncle, neither will Franklin. We will all worry about you at home here lying on your bed. Come on, come down now to supper. I've heard the clock strike seven. Isn't it nice to be in a house full of timepieces of all sizes and shapes?'

And before I could argue Jane had brushed my hair, dabbed under my eyes with a little of the rosewater that had been left in a Wedgwood bowl for our use, and taken a fresh muslin gown from the hanging press and slipped it over my head as if I were her little sister.

'Come on,' she said, and blew out the candle.

*

Jane was in her element at supper. She had made a new plan.

'Of course, Jenny's brother, Edward-John, must think very highly of you, ma'am,' she assured our aunt as she smiled at Franklin to put some more chocolate pudding on her plate.

Mrs Leigh-Perrot preened herself. 'Well, I must say that he does always pay attention to what I say. Visits often also.'

'I thought that,' said Jane demurely. She caught Franklin's eye and glanced towards the cream jug. Obligingly he poured a generous allowance on top of her second helping of pudding. 'Jenny was saying that he is always quoting you — sometimes even in his sermons,' she continued with that bland expression she always wears when telling an outrageous lie.

I wondered what Jane was up to and saw Mrs Austen shoot her a suspicious glance.

'I was thinking about that today, when we heard he was being so unreasonable about Jenny's marriage to such an eligible young man as Captain Thomas Williams.' Jane sounded as prim as a middle-aged spinster. She even pursed her lips, though slightly spoiling the effect by then licking some chocolate from the corner of her mouth. 'I was thinking . . .' she went on, putting another large spoonful of chocolate pudding in her mouth, but still managing to talk through it, 'I was thinking that if anyone could influence him towards the right opinion on this, it would be someone whom he respects so highly – someone like you . . .'

Jane is just so clever, I thought as I tried to swallow some chocolate pudding – less to please myself than to please Franklin, who was watching me so anxiously with his kind eyes.

Now she had turned to our uncle and was questioning him about how chocolate was made. Jane, of course, had realized that our aunt, though sympathetic, was sharp and authoritative. She would not take kindly to anyone telling her what to do, let alone a young girl of Jane's age. During all the long explanations about cocoa beans, and about an Irish man called John Hannon who invented the first chocolate mills, Jane never once glanced towards Mrs Leigh-Perrot.

I did though, as I struggled to eat, and I could see her thoughtful expression. I noticed also how Mrs Austen shot a quick appraising glance at her sister-in-law and then lowered her eyes to her own plate.

Towards the end of the meal Mrs Leigh-Perrot, without a word of apology, rose abruptly and crossed the room towards her writing desk. There was a moment's silence as she drew out a sheet of paper and dipped her quill in the ink, but then Jane asked whether cocoa beans had shells and, if so, what happened to them. Franklin and Mr Leigh-Perrot started to argue about this and by the time they had solved the question Mrs Leigh-Perrot had sealed her letter, written the address and handed it to Franklin with instructions to take it to the post as soon as possible.

'It was to Edward-John,' said Jane when we went up to our room – with instructions from our uncle to put on warm wool spencers under our cloaks and to wear woollen stockings.

'Are you sure?' I asked, doing up the waist button of my spencer.

'Certain!' said Jane, getting her muff from her travelling bag. 'I had a look when I bent down to tie my lace.'

So I've quickly written all of this into my journal.

I wish I could stay in the house and write my thoughts about Thomas, but it wouldn't be fair to Jane.

In any case, I suddenly feel more cheerful. I've seen for myself how very rich the Leigh-Perrots are – number 1, the Paragon is just their residence in Bath; they also have an estate and fine manor house in Berkshire.

I told myself that Edward-John (and Augusta) would agree to anything if they thought they might inherit all this wealth.

Tuesday, 26 April 1791

It's raining this morning so I have time to write down everything about our experience at the gala night at Sydney Gardens.

This is how our evening began:

'James, you must have a sedan chair. If you walk down all the way to the gardens with that gouty leg of yours, you won't be fit for anything. It will spoil your enjoyment.' Mrs Leigh-Perrot sounded really worried about her husband when she said this.

'Nonsense, nonsense. As if I would allow four beautiful ladies to walk while I get carried! That would be a fine thing for a gentleman to do.' My uncle sounded resolute, but I had noticed how he limped rather heavily.

'Why don't you both go in sedan chairs and I'll walk down with Jane and Jenny? It'll only take us fifteen minutes at the most. That will be the best thing,' said Mrs Austen.

'Let's have sedan chairs for everyone. It will be fun for the girls.' Mr Leigh-Perrot sounded so cheered by the idea that Franklin smiled happily. Mrs Leigh-Perrot didn't look quite so pleased. Sedan chairs, I knew, cost sixpence to hire, and it did seem a terrible waste to have them for two healthy energetic girls who could easily walk or even run down the hill to the riverside gardens.

'Oh, Uncle,' said Jane. 'You are the kindest man in

the world. How did you know that of all things this is what I wished for? How can a novelist write about her heroine in a sedan chair if she has never experienced such a thing?'

'Well, that settles it,' he said, looking as pleased as if someone had given him a present. 'Franklin, run down to the chair house in Queen's Parade and order five chairs.'

I don't know about Jane, but I think I would have preferred to walk. The chair looked very beautiful on the outside, but it was stuffy and a bit smelly inside and I didn't like the way the chairmen raced along the pavements, knocking people out of the way and bouncing me from side to side. Still it was quite exciting, I suppose. Perhaps I'm just having what Jane calls 'a fit of the dismals'.

When we got out of our sedan chairs at the entrance, Eliza and Phylly were coming down the hill.

Eliza was tottering on her high heels, trying to keep up with Phylly, who was striding along briskly – I'm sure she had a stout pair of boots under her frilly gown which, I suspect, belonged to Eliza.

'Well, girls, did you enjoy that?' Our uncle had struggled out of his chair and was distributing six-pences to the chairmen.

'It was lovely, Uncle,' I said feebly, but Jane did better.

'It elevated my thoughts to a high level,' she assured him, and then gave him a quick kiss.

'Shall we go and see the illuminations?' she went on, tucking her arm through mine, while Phylly interrogated the Leigh-Perrots on their reasons for hiring sedan chairs for everyone and reminded them of how much it cost.

'Where's the waterfall?' Jane was spinning around in so many directions that she almost turned me giddy.

'This is what I call romantic!' Her voice was loud, and in spite of the band playing in the distance many people around heard her. I could see smiles on their faces, and I had to smile myself. The gardens did look so wonderfully romantic, with lights everywhere turning the colours of the trees, grass and flowers into strangely deeper and more mysterious versions of their everyday selves.

I suggested that we should go and see the grottoes, but Jane didn't answer. She had gone over towards the direction posts and was studying them.

'There it is, over there; the waterfall is down that pathway.'

'Jane,' I said sternly. 'You haven't made an assignation with a young gentleman, by any chance?'

'Quick,' hissed Jane, taking no notice. 'Let's go before we have to endure Phylly's company.'

The waterfall was spectacular. Lamps illuminated it — turning the water to shades of green and blue and a rosy red. Beside it was a tall, blond young man, looking more at home than the last time we met in his usual dress of riding boots, breeches and a well-worn olive-coloured riding coat.

'You go on, Jane, I must fix my shoelace.' I would give them a few minutes together — just as Jane gave me my private time with Thomas. I was so busy with my laces that although I heard the words, 'Good evening,' I didn't take much notice of them, and it was only after Admiral Williams repeated the phrase, 'Good evening, Miss Cooper,' that I realized that he was standing over me.

He was as upright and starchy as ever. Beside him was Elinor, looking very pale, and on her other side was Sir Walter Montmorency. The governess was slightly behind the other three.

'May I help? Have you a problem?' His voice was cold, as always. No one would ever think that his nephew had told him that he was betrothed to me. There was no acknowledgement of that in his aloof, rather distant manner. It was as if I was just some distant and not particularly interesting acquaintance. I was still bending down, fiddling with my lace, but I didn't stand up. If I did, I might have to join them and be escorted back to Mrs Austen and the Leigh-Perrots. And then I would betray Jane.

'Good evening, Admiral, Miss Elinor, Miss Taylor,' I said, trying to sound self-assured. 'No, there's no problem. It's just my bootlace. My cousin and my aunt will be back in a moment.' I prayed that he couldn't see Jane and Harry romantically silhouetted against the shining colourful waterfall.

He hesitated for a minute, glancing at the crowds milling around and at a group of young officers laughing loudly. 'Well, perhaps Miss Taylor will wait with you,' he said, beckoning to the governess without even glancing in her direction. I thought him very rude to the poor lady, I must say. I could see why Thomas disliked him.

'Sir Walter, could I ask a great favour of you? Would you be kind enough to escort my niece into that labyrinth? She has a fancy to go, and I can't abide these places. In any case, I have just seen an old acquaintance in the distance and he will be quite offended if I don't greet him. Go along, my dear,' he said to Elinor, who turned even paler. 'Sir Walter will take good care of you.'

I didn't think that Elinor looked happy about this arrangement. She did murmur, 'Uncle,' but he shooed her along as if she was a chicken in his way. She looked very young, very small and fragile beside the tall, god-like figure of her escort, who gave me a cool up-and-down look.

'I'll take good care of her, sir.' Sir Walter smiled down at Elinor as he tucked her arm under his and assured the admiral that he would make sure that no rough men would come near Miss Williams. I watched them go towards the labyrinth. Groups of girls with male escorts were giggling as they streamed into the maze of secret passages. I could imagine what fun it would have been if only Thomas were still here and perhaps Jane and Harry could join us. But Elinor didn't look as though she was having fun. She seemed to shrink away from Sir Walter. Her head was bent and her bonnet hid her features. I watched her go with concern and she looked up and caught my eye. Abruptly she rearranged her expression to one of haughty arrogance. Somehow or other, I thought that it was as though she were acting a part. There was no doubt that she was jealous of me and Thomas, but was he right? Was she just a child – a child who needed protecting? Or did she just dislike me intensely for no reason other than jealousy? However, it was the one thing that Thomas had asked of me and I couldn't fail him. I stood up and looked after them, feeling rather worried. There wasn't much that I could do, I told myself.

And yet I had promised Thomas. I remembered what he said about Sir Walter being involved in a scandal. He was no person to trust a young girl to.

'Miss Taylor,' I said rapidly. 'Would you mind waiting here for a moment? I must see my cousin. She is expecting me.'

I had a quick glance over my shoulder as I went towards the waterfall. Miss Taylor had retreated to one of the rustic benches set into little arbours. Couples occupied every one of the others, and for a moment I almost felt that she looked slightly comic, seated there, so stiffly, all by herself. But then, as one of the linksmen passed, bearing a flaming torch, I saw her face. It was drawn into tight lines of anxiety and I realized that she was deeply worried about Elinor.

Harry and Jane were laughing together about one of their childhood games when I approached – something about building a house in the woods when Jane was eight years old. They didn't look particularly romantic so I didn't mind interrupting them. I told Jane about Elinor and Sir Walter Montmorency going into the labyrinth alone and how I had promised Thomas to keep an eye on her. Jane was immediately intrigued.

'How did she seem?' she asked.

I hesitated and then said that I thought she looked pale and worried. And that the governess looked worried also. I told them what Thomas had said.

'Let's follow them,' said Harry. I could see that the words 'dastardly baronet' were trembling on Jane's lips, and I agreed immediately with Harry. The sooner we followed them the better. I wondered whether

I should tell Miss Taylor, but then I thought that the admiral, if he heard, would think that officious of me. After all, he was the one who suggested Sir Walter should accompany his niece to the labyrinth.

The labyrinth would have been such fun if I hadn't been worried about Elinor. Even though we could see the centre of it, with the famous Merlin swing, like a gorgeously decorated boat, up high above us, the passages, with their ten-foot hedges, continually ended with only a choice of going left or right, but never went straight ahead in the direction needed. Groups of couples wandered up and down, laughing and calling out to each other, most people seeming quite happy to be lost.

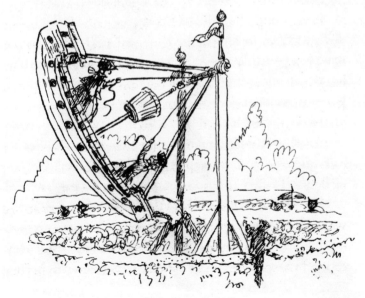

I began to despair of finding them – there were so many people and so many voices from unseen people – lots of shrieks from girls and laughs from men – but no trace of Elinor and Sir Walter.

After about ten minutes I said to Jane that I was perhaps making a fuss about nothing and that I didn't want to spoil their enjoyment. Perhaps we should just concentrate on searching for the Merlin swing in the centre of the labyrinth.

'No, we should go on looking for her, because once we get to Merlin's swing we'll have to go out,' said Jane, but the way her face lit up and then fell when I mentioned Merlin's swing was enough. I knew that she was dying to try it out. Harry looked from one to the other of us.

'No, let's go,' I insisted. 'Can you see it, Harry?'

'I can see it,' he said. 'This way.'

Even from inside the hedged paths, Merlin's swing was easily visible to everyone who was not as small as I was. To make it even easier to find, a man stood on it when it was not occupied and shouted encouragement to couples who looked as though they were getting desperate – though many, snuggled into benches in leafy alcoves, seemed happy to be lost forever!!!

It wasn't easy to find though as the paths threaded in and out and turned direction in a most confusing way. Harry, however, was a man who was used to finding his way through dense woodland. At every corner where men and girls were debating which way to turn, he made an instant and decisive choice, and within a few minutes we were at the centre of the labyrinth, being congratulated by the attendant.

'Don't look so worried, Miss Jenny,' whispered Harry as the attendant assisted Jane to climb into the boat-like swing. 'I've just thought that we might be able to see your friend from the swing. You're very high up in that. We should be able to see the whole of the maze from up there.'

I thanked him. Harry is becoming more and more impressive, I think.

'In you go, young lady,' said the attendant. 'Don't worry – it's as safe as houses.'

The Merlin swing was more like a boat than a swing. It hung from a bar between two twenty-foot-tall posts. By pulling the ropes alternately the boat goes higher and higher. It was so exciting that I screamed at one stage, but Jane only laughed and pulled her rope harder. Then she stood up, and Harry stood up and the boat really flew through the air. We could see everything – all over the gardens!

And then I remembered Elinor. I stood up too, pulling hard on the rope. I should have been scared, but I was concentrating too hard to be frightened.

There was a small grotto – very romantic-looking, filled with moss and tiny white flowers – at the end of one of those passages in the maze that led to nowhere. There were two figures in it – very closely entwined. The lights were bright though and I could see the purple gown and the pale blue coat. It was definitely Elinor and Sir Walter.

'Harry, there she is,' I said, and I pointed. He nodded grimly and at once began to slow the swing. Jane did not protest. This was a situation after her own heart: the dastardly baronet and the inno-cent young girl. It could have come straight out of *Clarissa*!

'Thank you, sir,' said the attendant. He was probably used to groups swinging for as long as they possibly could and was grateful we had stopped so quickly of our own accord. 'This is the way out, sir; you'll get straight back to the main pathway if you go through that gate just there.'

I wondered what Harry would do. Obviously the man wouldn't allow people to go back into the labyrinth from here. I could see him looking puzzled, running his hand over his blond hair, his blue eyes unsure and anxious. It was left to Jane, of course, to deal with the situation.

'Oh no!' She gave an artistic little scream as she felt at her neck. 'Oh, Jenny, I've lost the miniature of my great-uncle! Do you remember that I was showing it to you when we were sitting in that grotto? I wonder whether I left it there. Oh, what will I do?'

She gazed at the attendant with the distraught ex-pression of a devoted great-niece who has lost what she values the most.

'Don't you worry, miss,' he said reassuringly. 'I'll

just slip you out here. I'll show the gentleman where to go too. It's just next to the entrance. You'll go back out that way when you find it though, won't you? I'd get into trouble if you came to have a second chance of Merlin's swing.'

'We'll certainly do that; it's really very kind of you,' said Jane with one of her most charming smiles, and Harry and I murmured our thanks.

Once out, Harry was back in control again and he strode along the pathways looking determined.

'Shame I don't have my gun,' he said to Jane with his attractive lopsided grin.

'Duelling pistols would be more appropriate to a hero,' said Jane primly, and Harry laughed.

'In here,' he said after a few minutes and we turned down a short avenue between two hedges. At the top of it was the grotto that I had seen from high on Merlin's swing.

There were still two figures there. But they were entwined. The blue coat enclosed the purple gown; the baronet was kissing the lady!

And the lady was not struggling.

Not pulling back.

Not trying to scream.

Just there, in his arms.

Perhaps Elinor does love this Sir Walter????

After all, I suppose brothers aren't always aware what is in their sisters' heads – I should know!

I've just stopped writing to ask Jane how she felt at

the moment when we realized that Elinor was kissing Sir Walter.

Jane has been thinking about this question and this is her answer. She counted her feelings out on her fingers:

'Firstly, I felt embarrassed.

'Secondly, I felt that it wasn't a real love scene.

'And then,' she went on, 'I began to look at her carefully when they stopped kissing, and this is what I thought . . .

'I thought she looked frightened.

'I thought that, although she looked excited and sort of thrilled, she looked ashamed at the same time.

'I thought she didn't look happy.'

We went on discussing love for quite a while.

'You should know all about this, Jenny,' said Jane, in the severe tones of a schoolmistress. 'You are the one in love. Pray tell me, dear girl, what does being in love make you feel like?'

'I'm not sure . . .' I hesitated and Jane cut in immediately.

'Come, come, my dear, you can do better than that. Think hard!'

'It's a bit like sitting in front of a blazing fire, drinking hot spiced wine and knowing that something very exciting is going to happen,' I said eventually.

'Excellent!' said Jane in a mock-patronizing tone. 'You are doing well, Jenny dear. Now tell me – do you ever feel sad about loving Thomas?'

'Never!' I exclaimed.

'And how do you know that he is the right man for you?'

'Because I never have any doubts.'

'You answered that nice and quickly,' said Jane approvingly. Excited, happy and certain. I must remember that for my novels. And, of course, for that wonderful moment when I too meet my hero.'

I smiled. 'Do you know who I think acted like a hero in Sydney Gardens?'

'Dear Harry,' mused Jane. 'Yes, he was rather splendid, wasn't he?'

Here are some of our comments about Harry.

'I liked the way he said so calmly, "Miss Williams, your governess sent us to find you." This was mine.

'I liked the way that he casually slipped his hand into his pocket as if he had one of a pair of pistols there.' This was Jane's.

'And the way that he looked at Sir Walter and didn't look at Elinor.' I had thought that very sensitive of him because once Elinor had seen us she burst into tears.

'The best bit was where he said, "Please take my arm, Miss Williams," and he just waited even though she was in tears. I couldn't believe it, with Sir Walter blustering and shouting, "I'm having a private conversation with this lady, young man. You are an ill-mannered puppy, sir!" but Harry just took no notice, held out his arm to Elinor with a lovely smile and acted as though Sir Walter wasn't even there. And Elinor clung to his arm as though he were her brother.' Jane keeps laughing so much that she is jogging my elbow. That's why this handwriting is so bad!

'And then when Sir Walter shouted after us, "You'll hear from my friends, sir!" and Harry just said, "That'll be good. I miss my daily session of shooting rats and such-like vermin in Hampshire." And he said it without even turning his head. That was the best bit, I think.' I laughed when I said this, but Jane just looked thoughtful.

'Dear, dear Harry! I never saw him stand up to someone before now. He was always such a gentle boy. All his brothers bullied him, and so did my brothers — all except Frank.' Jane looked so serious when she said these words that I decided not to discuss Elinor any more. Jane needs time to think about the men in her life to sort out what she really feels for Harry. Elinor is my responsibility, not hers.

I feel worried about Elinor. Jane is right. She didn't look like a girl in love.

So why was she allowing Sir Walter to kiss her?

Did she feel that she had to obey her uncle? Obviously he wants Sir Walter to marry her and perhaps Elinor thought that was the right way to engage his affections.

Or was it that no one gives her much love and affection? That governess looks dreary and worn out.

And Thomas is away so much that she can see very little of him. Perhaps she found it comforting to be shown affection by Sir Walter because she receives very little from anyone else.

And the admiral is rather terrifying.

This morning, Jane and I shall call on her.

We called in at the lodgings in York Street, down near the Pump Room, just after lunch but we couldn't persuade Elinor to be friends. We couldn't even get her to speak to us.

It's difficult to talk to someone who makes it plain that they dislike you – I realize that Thomas is her hero and she can't forgive me for taking him away from her but, to be honest, I don't think that she likes Jane either. It was like talking to a ghost or someone who was scared stiff. Unfortunately the admiral was there. Every time that either Jane or I asked Elinor a question, she hesitated and then the admiral jumped in and answered it for her – just putting in, 'Is that not so, Elinor?' at the end of each reply.

And Elinor would say, 'Yes, Uncle,' in a very small, quiet voice.

Sometimes the governess spoke for her and then she would say, 'Yes, Miss Taylor,' in the same tone.

An invitation to walk up Milsom Street and look into the shop windows was firmly refused by the admiral on the grounds that it might rain.

Elinor didn't look disappointed. Or even interested.

Just went on staring at the floor.

She was dressed in yet another purple gown – it was silk, but a harsh colour, more like something that an elderly lady would wear than a proper gown for a girl of our age.

'What does Sir Walter Montmorency see in her?' asked Jane in a puzzled voice when we were walking away from the house. 'I would have thought he would look for something more sophisticated. She's not really even pretty. She's too washed-out looking.'

I told Jane that I thought it was the purple gown that made Elinor look so pale.

'Why does she wear that awful colour? It looks dreadful on her.'

'It's a pity she wouldn't come out with us,' I said. 'We could have taken her to that lovely shop and shown her some muslins; the admiral is very, very rich, you know, and Thomas told me that he is giving Elinor a large dowry. He wants her to make an excellent match.'

And then Jane stopped, dead in the middle of the pavement, earning herself an annoyed glance from an elderly gentleman with a stick who had almost bumped into her.

'I know what it is,' she said in a loud, clear voice. 'I know what the dastardly baronet is up to.'

'Shh,' I whispered. 'Everyone will hear you. Quick, come in here, into the abbey. We can talk quietly there.'

Giggling together we ran along York Street and rushed into the abbey.

Many of the people examining the wonderful carvings and admiring the stained-glass windows turned round when we came rushing in. We crept to the back of the church, to a dark corner where there didn't seem to be anything of interest, and we fell on our knees with our bonnets touching.

'What?' I hissed.

'He's after her fortune, that's it,' said Jane. Her dark hazel eyes were sparkling with excitement. 'Do you remember we saw him gambling – in the card room? He may have lost all his own money – just like that Duchess of Devonshire. What sort of fortune will the admiral give Elinor?'

I told her I wasn't sure but thought it would be quite large eventually, and even now he had settled fifty thousand pounds on her.

'Well, that would be two thousand, five hundred pounds a year for a start,' whispered Jane, who was good at arithmetic. 'Imagine! My father only has five hundred pounds a year.'

'And my fortune is fifty pounds a year!' I felt a bit sorry that I was not worth more to Thomas, but then I didn't think he was the sort of man to want to marry a girl for her fortune. He was too independent. He was certain that he would make his own fortune in the navy.

'But, Jane,' I said after a minute, 'I suppose even if

that is true, if Elinor likes him, then there is no reason why we should interfere. Let him ask for her hand from the admiral, like an honourable man.' And then I giggled a little because that did sound like something out of one of Mrs Radcliffe's novels.

Jane shook her head wisely. 'Jenny, you and I know that is not the way things are. Do you know what Harry was muttering when you were talking to Miss Taylor? Well, he was saying no honourable man would take advantage of a young girl like that. Wasn't that splendid?'

I agreed that it was splendid, but it troubled me. There was something very wrong about the situation between Elinor and Sir Walter Montmorency.

Oh, Thomas, I will do my best for your sister. Jane's probably right; there is something wrong.

Tuesday evening, 26 April

This afternoon we had some luck, because as we went down towards Sydney Gardens we met Elinor and her governess.

We asked permission to accompany them and Jane suggested going into the gardens. Miss Taylor agreed enthusiastically, but just as she was in the middle of her sentence Elinor interrupted her and said that she didn't want to go – that she hated the place. She sounded quite rude and I was surprised.

Miss Taylor said nothing for a moment and then just said, 'Very well, dear, as you please. Where would you like to walk?'

'I don't mind, Miss Taylor,' said Elinor. Now she spoke in her usual dull tones and we didn't get much out of her. Even when Miss Taylor stopped to talk to an acquaintance, telling us to walk on, Elinor said nothing. Jane and I grew tired of trying to get her to talk and started to chat to each other. Jane was making jokes about a man in such black clothes that she reckoned that he must be going to his own funeral. I was trying hard not to giggle when I caught sight of Elinor's face under her bonnet. She didn't look shy, she didn't look bored, she didn't have that same dull expression that she wore customarily; she looked jealous!

I had guessed already that she was jealous of me because of Thomas. But perhaps she was jealous that

I was Jane's friend, or even that Jane was my friend. Or that we were having fun and she wasn't; perhaps that was it. Certainly she was a strange girl, perhaps a bit spoiled and at the same time neglected.

'Jane!' I said suddenly on an impulse. I stopped and rubbed my ankle and then continued, 'You've forgotten that you promised to call on Cousin Eliza this morning to give her a message. Miss Taylor, would you accompany her? I know that my aunt and uncle do not wish her to be alone in Bath, and unfortunately I seem to have twisted my ankle. Perhaps Elinor won't mind keeping me company and we will sit on this bench and wait for your return.'

I calculated that it would be at least twenty minutes before Jane and Miss Taylor arrived back from Queen's Square so perhaps I should be able to get Elinor to talk in that time. As soon as they disappeared I seized the opportunity and asked her whether she loved Sir Walter Montmorency.

'It's none of your business,' said Elinor in furious tones. 'And none of your friend's business either, coming along like that and interrupting a private conversation.'

'We were only trying to help,' I said. 'If anyone saw you, it would have been bad for your reputation.'

'I told you . . .' Her voice rose so high that a man passing looked at her in a startled way. 'I told you that it is my business, not yours,' she repeated in a lower voice. 'I don't interfere in your affairs; why should you interfere in mine?'

'I think of you like a sister,' I said quietly. 'When—'

'Well, don't!' she burst out. 'And as for your getting married to Thomas, you can think again. The admiral has plans for him and what the admiral wants, he gets. Thomas won't dare stand up to him. You'll see; Thomas will marry the daughter of the Earl of Portsmouth.'

Perhaps she was right, I thought. I sat on the bench miserably looking across at the square.

'That's my uncle's plan anyway,' she muttered. She seemed a little uncomfortable now. After a minute she said in quite a gentle way, 'Does your ankle hurt?'

'It's not too bad,' I said, giving it a rub. I felt rather deceitful, but she was looking at me in a much friendlier way now. I didn't think it was true that Thomas was frightened of the admiral or that he would be willing to be dictated to by him. He was just not that kind of man.

'Was your uncle very strict with you both?' I asked that question with interest. Thomas and Elinor seemed so different that it was hard to believe that they had been brought up by the same man. I felt that I wanted to know more about the admiral.

'Very,' said Elinor. Suddenly she seemed more willing to talk. Perhaps that outburst had got rid of her feelings of resentment and that had done her good. 'He used to beat Thomas – but not me,' she added hastily as she saw the horror in my eyes. 'But I was always terrified that he might. I think I annoyed him. He liked Thomas much better than he liked me. I never remember him being kind to me or praising me for anything.'

'But you had Thomas, didn't you?' I felt very sorry for her. She had spoken so bleakly.

Elinor shrugged. 'Not often. He went off to naval college when he was twelve and then into the navy as a midshipman. Sometimes I didn't even see him in the holidays because he would go to stay with a friend. He was always very kind to me though, and he took me away from that awful boarding school. He had a big fight with the admiral, my uncle, about it, and my uncle was furious. Thomas engaged Miss Taylor, but my uncle then insisted on paying her wage, so she just thinks about pleasing him.'

She stopped for a moment and then added, 'And now Thomas wants to get married, so my uncle would like me to be married also.'

I told her that she didn't have to get married and that if Thomas and I ever managed to get married then she could live with us, but I don't think she believed me. And then Miss Taylor, followed by Jane, came trotting down the hill and rushed Elinor away.

I've just asked Jane what she thinks about Elinor and she looked interested but didn't reply — instead she started scribbling on a piece of paper. When she had finished she handed it to me.

'Stick that in your journal,' she said. 'I think I'll write a story about someone like her some day. I'll call her Fanny. I always think that is a silly sort of name and she will be a silly sort of girl – creeping around like a little mouse and saying yes to her uncle no matter what he says. This is what someone says about her.'

I do not quite know what to make of her. I do not understand her. What is her character? Is she solemn? Is she odd? Is she prudish? Why did she draw back and look so grave at me? I could hardly get her to speak. I never was so long in company with a girl in my life, trying to entertain her, and succeed so ill! Never met with a girl who looked so grave on me! I must try to get the better of this. Her looks say, "I will not like you, I am determined not to like you".

'Who's the "I" in that?' I asked as I glued it into my journal.

'The baronet, perhaps,' said Jane doubtfully. 'Or perhaps it's a man who really loves her. Or perhaps it is another girl. A sort of fun-loving girl . . . I haven't made up my mind yet how the story is going to go. I know what Fanny/Elinor is going to be like though – very annoying to someone like me! I can't stand people who are too good. Pictures of perfection make me feel sick and wicked.'

I told Jane that I didn't know why she found Elinor annoying – 'After all, you never stop talking, so I would have thought you would like someone silent.'

Jane made a face and said that Elinor didn't even laugh at a joke. I knew what she meant, though I teased. It's very hard to make conversation with someone who just says yes or no – and even the best jokes fall flat if someone doesn't laugh at them.

'Do you think that she is in love with Sir Walter?' I really wanted to have Jane's opinion on this as I found it very hard to make up my mind.

Jane shook her head firmly. 'She doesn't look like you when you are with Thomas, all dreamy and adoring; she just looks scared.'

I suggested that we could, perhaps, get her to fall in love with someone else. And then I got a sudden inspiration. Perhaps, I thought, Elinor's jealous look at Jane was inspired by a love of Harry.

'What about Harry Digweed?'

'Certainly not!' said Jane sharply. 'What a union! Harry Digweed and Elinor!'

'It would be a good match for him. Think of it. She has a dowry of fifty thousand pounds. He seemed fond of her and concerned about her that night at Sydney Gardens. He was even prepared to fight a duel on her behalf.'

'A girl like Elinor is unworthy of being peculiarly, exclusively, passionately loved by Harry Digweed!' said Jane dramatically. After a minute she said pensively, 'I wish Harry would go back to Steventon. What is he doing hanging around Bath for so long?'

Before I could answer she said abruptly that she was going downstairs and she slammed the door quickly after her so that I could say no more.

I wonder . . .

Wednesday, 27 April 1791

This morning we went for our second fitting. The gowns were looking beautiful but I won't write about that now because something very strange happened afterwards.

Jane and I had noticed that Mrs Leigh-Perrot was not as generous and open-handed as her husband; in fact, she was quite careful about money. Instead of buying herself a new gown for the ball on Saturday – she had worn all of hers at least twice to the Assembly Rooms during the season – she had decided to get an old gown remade in a more modern style.

It had been a rich gown in its day. It was made from brocaded silk – coloured green with red flowers. Originally it probably was a wide, full-skirted gown, such as Mrs Austen wore, the sort of gown that, ten years ago, would have had panniers under it to hold it out at the sides, but now the dressmaker had cut away most of the fullness, just leaving a loose back falling in straight folds. It had an under-gown made from muslin, which showed at the bosom and wrists. Jane and I signalled with our eyebrows that we did not think much of it, but Mrs Leigh-Perrot seemed very satisfied and asked the dressmaker to wrap it up.

So then we set off, Mrs Leigh-Perrot, an upright stately figure in her well-fitting green pelisse, carrying her gown in her basket, and Jane and I trying hard not to dance down the pavement. It was so exciting to be in Bath. I was feeling cheerful and full of energy. This morning Mrs Austen had whispered to me that Edward-John and Augusta (of course) were coming on Friday and going to stay for the weekend. She patted me on the shoulder with a smile on her face, and I knew she thought that my troubles might be over. It was one thing a poor clergyman like Mr Austen, with his nine children to provide for, asking Edward-John to consent to my marriage with Thomas, but another thing completely for the wealthy and childless Leigh-Perrots to ask the same favour.

And then Mrs Leigh-Perrot stopped in front of a shop in Bath Street. It wasn't as nice a shop as most of the ones on Milsom Street. It had a faded, run-down look. The windows were dirty and the paint peeling. I remembered the place – it was Miss Gregory's shop, where Phylly eventually consented to choose a bonnet, after we had tried every other shop from top to bottom of the city of Bath.

'Let's go in here, girls,' said our aunt. 'I want to get some black lace to trim the gown. My maid will be able to do it for me.'

'Why is she going into that horrid shop?' whispered Jane as we followed the stately figure in.

I frowned at Jane and shook my head. I wasn't going to risk offending Mrs Leigh-Perrot now, just two days before Edward-John arrived. In any case, it was her own business where she chose to buy lace. Probably it was a few pence cheaper there than elsewhere!

She spent a long time choosing her black lace, doled out the one pound, nineteen shillings that it cost and then insisted that it should be wrapped up in the same parcel as her gown.

So the man assistant took away the brown paper package to his own counter, undid the string and wrapped up the card of black lace and did up the parcel again while Aunt Leigh-Perrot inspected all the other cards of lace − black, white, pink, green and blue − to be certain that she had got the best bargain that the shop could offer.

Jane got bored with all of this and told Mrs Leigh-Perrot that we would wait for her outside on the pavement.

When we got out we saw Eliza chatting to Monsieur Baddy just outside the lending library. He had taken a small flat package from his pocket, which he presented to her. Eliza did a quick little dance of joy on the pavement and he kissed her hand with a very grand air and went on down the street smiling happily to himself.

Then Eliza waved to us and we crossed the street.

'*Madame*.' Eliza curtsied respectfully to my aunt, who had just joined us, and then hugged and kissed the two of us.

'How pretty you look,' she said. 'Oh, to be young again!' She sighed and looked melancholy for a moment, but then her eyes sparkled again.

'I have news,' she said. 'The Princesse de Lambelle

is in town!' She said it with such a dramatic air that passers-by turned their heads to look at her.

'Who's the Princesse de Lambelle?' asked Jane.

'*Ma chérie!*' exclaimed Eliza. 'Do you not know?! The Princesse de Lambelle is one of Queen Marie Antoinette's very best and most intimate friends. She is come straight from my beloved Paris.'

My aunt was interested in this news and wanted to know immediately where this Princesse de Lambelle was staying. Upon hearing that the Princesse de Lambelle and her household had rented number I, the Crescent, she nodded her head sagely. I remembered how we had watched a huge travelling coach unloading enormous quantities of goods, and how the smartly dressed footmen were rushing in and out on the day when we had walked up there.

'And that is not all,' said Eliza, her eyes going from my face to Jane's. 'There will be a ball there and *mon petit ami* Monsieur Baddy, has procured four tickets of invitation. What do you say to that, *mes petites*?'

'Oh, Eliza!' gasped Jane. 'Do you mean us? Go to a ball given by a princess! Oh, Jenny!'

We hugged each other right in the middle of the street, taking no notice of Mrs Leigh-Perrot.

But then Phylly appeared from the library doorway, declaring loudly that there was nothing there that it was possible for someone like herself to read.

'Idle scribblings lead to an idle, dissipated life,' she declared.

Suddenly my heart sank. Four tickets. Phylly was Eliza's guest. She would have to be one of the four. The same thought obviously occurred to Jane, and she stared at Phylly in dismay.

And then Eliza's happy face became worried. All three of us looked from Phylly's disapproving face to one another.

The terrible thing was that Phylly would probably hate the ball, make Eliza uncomfortable and conscience-stricken during the evening, then spend the following day criticizing everything and everyone.

However, she was Eliza's cousin and guest so she had to go. And Jane was Eliza's cousin. I was no relation. I was the one that had to be left out.

I was just opening my lips to say this, but Jane was quicker.

'Eliza was just telling us about the Princesse de Lambelle, the best friend of Marie Antoinette,' she said in solemn, hesitant tones. 'What do you think of Marie Antoinette, Phylly?'

Phylly pursed up the lips of her tight little mouth. 'It's not for me to criticize a queen,' she said to my disappointment, but then couldn't resist adding sharply, 'however, she is not a good example to young girls like yourself.'

'Oh, why?' breathed Jane, opening her eyes in wide innocence.

Phylly hesitated but could not resist it. 'Debauched,'

she said bluntly. 'That is the only word that can describe her.'

'Oh!' Jane looked shocked. 'And what about her friend, Madame de Lambelle?'

Phylly shuddered. 'I should prefer not to talk about her!' she said. 'I cannot bear to relate the scandalous stories that I have heard.'

Eliza now decided to lend her own considerable acting ability to Jane's performance.

'But, Phylly,' she said with a gay little laugh. 'No one cares about these things nowadays. That is very *démodé*. I'm sure you will want to accompany me to the ball that the Princesse de Lambelle is giving next week.'

'Certainly not,' said Phylly piously. 'You could not ask that of me, Eliza. I will be happy with my Bible and a dish of tea. You go to the ball and I will wait up for you.'

'If you're sure, Phylly dear,' said Eliza meekly and allowed herself to be dragged away by Phylly who wished to pray at the abbey. As they went along, Eliza glanced over her shoulder and gave us both a tiny wink.

And then I spotted Miss Gregory coming out of her shop. She crossed the road and stopped squarely in front of us.

'Excuse me, ma'am, but did you by mistake take a card of white lace as well as the black?' she said to Mrs Leigh-Perrot. Her tone was superficially polite but there was an edge of insolence under it.

'Certainly not,' said Mrs Leigh-Perrot sternly. 'I bought, and paid for, a card of black lace and no other.'

'There must have been some mistake. My assistant says that a card of white lace is missing from the pile that you looked at.' The woman was still polite, but quite insistent. I saw the man who had wrapped the parcel come out of the door of Miss Gregory's shop.

'Look for yourself,' snapped Mrs Leigh-Perrot. She handed the basket impatiently to Miss Gregory and stood back, staring at the woman with a frown on her face.

It only took one minute for the parcel to be unwrapped. The card of black lace bought and paid for by my aunt was on top of the remodelled gown, but underneath it, hidden in the folds, was a card of white lace.

'Well,' said Mrs Leigh-Perrot eyeing it stonily, 'your young man must have put it in there by mistake. It was he who wrapped the parcel.'

'No such thing, no such thing!' Miss Gregory screamed the words out in a loud and agitated voice, adding, 'You stole it. You're guilty of theft.'

'Take it away and mind your tongue,' snapped Mrs Leigh-Perrot. She snatched the basket from Miss Gregory, thrust the white lace into her hands and set off at a great pace. We hurried after her, exchanging glances, but she did not speak to us until we reached the end of George Street.

'Not a word to your uncle about this,' she said. 'I won't have him worried.'

'Do you think that she did it?' Jane whispered to me, but I told her not to be silly.

And then we had a nice discussion about our new gowns. I thought that we should save them for the ball at the Crescent as I thought this would probably be a more grand affair, but Jane wanted to wear her 'daffodil' dress at the Assembly Rooms on Saturday.

Then I realized that I was being obtuse. Of course, Harry would be at the Assembly Rooms on Saturday night, but there was no chance that he would have an invitation to a ball given by a French princess. So I proposed that I would wear my white gown on Saturday and Jane would wear her new yellow gown. Then the following week, Jane would wear white and I would wear my bluebell gown.

I would have to have a little talk with my uncle and assure him that ladies never wore the same gown twice in a row and explain to him that I really, really wanted to keep my beautiful bluebell gown for the ball given by a real 'princesse'.

Thursday, 28 April 1791

Something terrible happened today.

Two terrible things, really.

But one will probably turn out to be just a ridiculous mistake.

When Jane and I came downstairs Franklin was already putting letters by the plates.

'Cassandra,' said Jane, examining the folded piece of paper beside her mother's place at table. It seems awful now, but we were both giggling over a teary splash on the ink of the capital P of Paragon on the address.

'Perhaps she's eloped with Tom Fowle,' said Jane dramatically. 'This is her letter of penitence. *Dearest Mama . . . love conquers all . . . I could no longer resist his manly arms . . . I have lost my virtue . . . pray consent . . . my tears flow as I write . . .*'

And then Mrs Leigh-Perrot arrived, closely followed by her husband. A minute later Mrs Austen came in and plumped down in her place.

For a moment she hardly noticed the letter – she was busy sipping her tea and crunching the toast that Franklin handed to her on a silver dish, straight from the toasting fork. She liked her toast hot and crisp, with no butter or honey on it.

Then she looked at the letter and gave an amused smile, recognizing Cassandra's handwriting.

'Some trouble with the laundry, or the hens, no doubt,' she remarked tolerantly, breaking open the seal.

There was a moment's silence. Mrs Leigh-Perrot was reading her own letters, Mr Leigh-Perrot was busy with his newspaper, which Franklin had just warmed at the fire to make sure that the ink was dry on all the pages, and Jane and I were immersed in drinking the frothy hot chocolate Franklin prepared for us every morning.

When I looked up I saw Mrs Austen on her feet, her weathered complexion drained of colour.

'I must go home,' she said, gathering up her reticule, first having stuffed the letter from Cassandra into it.

'Goodness gracious, sister, what is the matter?' Her brother looked very alarmed. My heart stopped for a moment. Could Jane have been right? Perhaps Cassandra had eloped.

But no, Mrs Austen was looking anxious, almost frightened, but certainly not annoyed. It seemed to take her a minute to speak, almost as though her throat had swelled for a moment.

'My little boy, my little Charles,' she said. 'Cassandra writes that he is in a high fever . . .'

I saw Mrs Leigh-Perrot open her mouth as if to say that children get fevers all the time, but then she shut it at the expression on Mrs Austen's face.

'I must leave. Jane and Jenny, go and pack your

things!' And then she stopped. Her face contorted. 'What am I thinking of? No, I can't bring you girls back into the house.' She looked at her brother. 'Cassandra says that he has pustules on his face and body. The apothecary fears smallpox.'

A moment ago that breakfast parlour had seemed the snuggest place on earth with the warm velvet curtains, the flames from the fire reflected by the highly polished Sheraton furniture, but now that terrible word, smallpox, seemed to turn everything cold and grey – and to go on echoing for a long time afterwards. We all knew that people died in huge numbers from smallpox. Those who did manage to survive were usually scarred for life. I thought of Charles's smooth young skin and the tears rose to my eyes. I bit my lips, swallowed hard, and saw that Jane was doing the same thing.

Mr and Mrs Leigh-Perrot were very practical and sensible. Jane and I were to stay in Bath – that would be no trouble. Franklin was sent running down the hill to the White Hart Inn to ask the stagecoach to stop outside the house and pick up Mrs Austen. It was not normal to pick up passengers in that way, but it would be on their way to the London road and my uncle was confident that the stagecoach would do this in the case of a mother being summoned home to a sick child.

'Don't mention the word *smallpox*, Franklin,' advised my uncle, putting some coins into Franklin's hand – no doubt for the coachman. 'Just say the child is very ill.'

In the meantime, Mrs Austen had gone upstairs to pack, sternly refusing any assistance. Jane and I looked at each other uncertainly when she was gone. I suspected that Mrs Austen wanted to shed a few tears in private, but it did seem bad not to help her to gather her things together. Neither of us spoke, and although we managed to hold back the tears I think we probably both envied Franklin running at full speed down the hill towards the White Hart Inn. It would have been good to have had something to do.

'Would you like me to escort you to Steventon, sister?' asked our uncle when Mrs Austen reappeared with her bags. She shook her head resolutely and told him cheerfully that he should stay and look after his gouty leg, so he had to be content with lending her his own special travelling rug and telling one of the maids to pack a small basket of things to eat.

Franklin arrived back in style, sitting up beside the coachman. Mrs Austen kissed us all in an absent-minded way and was in the coach before her brother could even lend her his hand.

No one quite knew what to do after she left. Jane and I wandered around aimlessly and then Jane decided to practise her music. Mr Leigh-Perrot went off, accompanied by Franklin, to drink the waters at the Pump Room and his wife settled herself down with a little-used embroidery frame.

And then there was a loud peremptory knock on the door.

And this is how things went then.

The maid came in to say that a constable was at the door; Mrs Leigh-Perrot said to send him in. She sounded quite cheerful — she probably welcomed a break in her thoughts about smallpox. The constable was probably just coming about some wild young soldiers who had been doing various tricks, like stealing carriage lamps in the neighbourhood.

And then the constable came in looking embarrassed. He asked her to confirm her name and address, which she did in a slightly annoyed way.

Then he told her that she had to come down to the Roundhouse in Stall Street, where the police constables had an office and a small jail. My aunt frowned at him and asked him why.

Then Jane came in. She had been crying, I could see, and I had noticed long pauses in her playing. However, she looked from her aunt to the constable with eyes that held just a little of their usual sparkle.

The constable consulted his notebook and enquired whether my aunt had bought some white lace at Miss Gregory's shop on the day before.

'I did not.' My aunt's voice was harsh and her face had darkened. The constable looked at her in surprise and then consulted his notebook again.

'I beg your pardon; I meant to say black lace.' He sounded a bit nervous, and I didn't blame him as Mrs

Leigh-Perrot looked very fierce. He dived back into his notebook.

'Miss Gregory says that you also took a card of white lace for which you had not paid. We would like you to come down to the Roundhouse and make a statement about this matter.'

'Certainly not!' exclaimed Mrs Leigh-Perrot. Her eyes were flashing and she stood very tall and straight.

'W-what?' stammered the constable.

'Go to the Roundhouse alone and unprotected! Certainly not.'

'Your husband can accompany you, of course.' The constable seemed to breathe a little easier at the thought of Mr Leigh-Perrot. 'Perhaps I could speak to him.'

'My husband is not at home,' said Mrs Leigh-Perrot firmly. 'In any case, this silly business has nothing whatsoever to do with him. Now take yourself off, my man.'

As Jane said later, that was where things began to go wrong. Mrs Leigh-Perrot might have done better to stick with the lone-unprotected-female line of conversation, said Jane.

'I'm afraid there is a very serious complaint made against you, Madam. You are accused of theft. You know the law of the land. Any stolen article over the value of five shillings – and this lace was worth twenty shillings – is classified as grand larceny.'

Jane and I were quite frightened by this. We looked

at each other. Mrs Leigh-Perrot showed no signs of anxiety though.

'May I ask who makes this complaint?' Her voice was haughty and quite loud.

'The complaint was sworn by Miss Gregory, the shop owner.'

'A woman,' said my aunt with emphasis, 'without moral or financial probity.'

Jane's eyes glinted. She liked these sorts of phrases. The constable snapped his notebook shut.

'You will kindly attend the Roundhouse in Stall Street as soon as your husband comes home, madam.' He then picked up his hat and strode out, banging the front door behind him.

An hour later my uncle came home, but nothing was said. We talked of Charles. We heard of Franklin's opinion that it probably wasn't smallpox, just some fever. We heard of the opinions of most of the people who drank the waters in the Pump Room, many of whom thought smallpox was nothing, some of whom had various recipes for herbal drinks and others who believed in bloodletting immediately. My uncle sat down to write to his poor sister with all this advice, but my aunt said not a word of the constable's visit.

It rained heavily for the whole afternoon and none of us ventured out. No one visited the Roundhouse to see the constable.

I've just asked Jane what she thought my aunt

meant by calling Miss Gregory 'a woman without moral or financial probity'.

This is what Jane said: 'She cheats her customers and lives with a man outside marriage.'

I said to Jane that in that case surely no one will believe her but Jane just replied, 'Grand larceny is very serious.'

Friday, 29 April 1791

Another terrible day. When Jane and I were talking it over tonight we both said that we guessed at breakfast that Mrs Leigh-Perrot had told her husband about the constable's visit and about the accusation.

Our uncle ate very little and he shot from the table when Franklin came in and whispered to him that the lawyer had arrived. Before he left the room I saw him touch his wife affectionately on the shoulder. She made no reply or gesture in return, but both Jane and I had a suspicion that her eyes were wet.

When the breakfast table was cleared she suddenly spoke for the first time to ask whether Eliza had two or three bedrooms in her lodgings at Queen's Square. Jane told her that there were three bedrooms, and Mrs Leigh-Perrot nodded calmly and said that was good because if there were some temporary problem then perhaps Eliza would have us to stay with her at Queen's Square.

'Why? What could happen?' asked Jane bluntly.

Mrs Leigh-Perrot gave a superior smile, 'Well, you know men and how they worry,' she said. 'Your poor uncle has got it into his head that this Miss Gregory might make trouble. Apparently . . .' and when she came to this our aunt turned her gaze away from us, stared at the window and finished by saying, 'apparently, she has some sort of . . . of friendship with the chief constable.'

Jane's eyes met mine and her eyebrows shot up. We neither of us had the spirit to make any jokes though, and when my aunt told us to go and write letters or something we did not even discuss the matter. We were both too worried about Charles and the possibility that the poor little fellow has smallpox. Jane is writing a letter to her mother and I am writing my journal.

At about eleven o'clock, Jane and I went out to have the last fitting for our new gowns. It was sort of sad, because our aunt declined to come. Since breakfast time she had worn a worried expression, and her husband, who seems devoted to her, kept casting anxious looks in her direction.

We set off alone, and were soon joined by Harry. I must say that I began to suspect that he kept a watch on the house because whenever we come out in our bonnets and cloaks — and alone — he is soon by our side.

Jane told him about Charles, and oddly for Jane, who seldom cries, tears overflowed from her eyes. Harry was very upset. I think that if I were not there he might have taken her in his arms instantly.

'He'll be all right; he's a tough little lad. I know about six or seven fellows who had smallpox when they were young. Got a few marks left, but he won't mind that. He'll be off to the navy school at the end of the summer, won't he? He'll be proud of a few scars then — make him look tough.' While he was talking, I could see how he was racking his brains to think of the right thing to say.

Jane gulped a little, and then laughed and then gulped again. She stopped by the railings of the Queen's Square garden and faced into the bushes. Once again I bent down to fiddle with my lace. When I took a peep upwards, Harry had his arm around Jane.

A moment later two ladies with parasols came along the pavement chattering noisily and Jane moved away.

'Dear Harry,' she said affectionately. 'I'll stop making a fool of myself and embarrassing everyone.'

When we returned from the dressmaker's shop, the stagecoach from Bristol was just coming up Gay Street. There seemed to be only two people in it, but a large number of bandboxes in the luggage carrier at the back.

'Two women,' I guessed.

'Or one man and one woman with many heads,' said Jane. She kept trying to make jokes all the morning. I think she was embarrassed that she had cried in front of Harry. He had offered to wait outside the dressmaker's while we were having our fitting, but Jane told him not to be silly and not to waste a nice fine morning and to go and have a ride around Sydney Gardens, or something. He looked very miserable when he went off, poor fellow.

I was so busy thinking about Jane and Harry and trying to work out whether she was in love with him or not that I didn't notice for a moment that the stage-coach had stopped outside the Leigh-Perrot house. It was only when Jane gasped that I realized that the tall, rather plump man who had stepped down on to the pavement was my brother.

'Oh no,' I moaned under my breath. I didn't think that I could stand having Edward-John and Augusta around as well as the worries about poor little Charles – and the worry about Aunt Leigh-Perrot being accused of stealing.

I felt embarrassed about seeing them again. The last time I was in such a temper with them that I just ignored them and didn't bother saying goodbye. Now I felt that I couldn't go up and hug them or even shake them by the hand.

Luckily the door opened just then. Franklin came running down, beaming with delight. He glanced at the stagecoach, but came quickly over to Jane. 'Good news, Miss Jane,' he whispered, and then went over to assist with the baggage. By this stage our uncle and aunt had come out, Uncle waving a letter and calling out, 'Nothing but chickenpox! The little lad is fine.'

Jane went so white for a moment that I thought she might faint. I put my arm around her as she held on to the black metal railings. After a minute, her colour came back and she laughed a little hysterically.

'Honestly, Cassandra! Couldn't she tell the difference between chickenpox and smallpox?!'

I tried to excuse Cassandra's mistake, saying that it was sometimes hard to distinguish between the two in the beginning stages, but Jane wasn't listening. She was shaking hands very politely with Edward-John and Augusta (I just dropped a quick curtsy and kept my eyes on the pavement) and saying in her most grown-up tones, 'What a shame that we have to run away the moment that you arrive, but we really must bring the good news to Cousin Eliza. She was so very upset when we told her about Charles.'

Instead of going to Eliza — she hadn't even been told about Charles's sickness — Jane and I went for a walk. Harry joined us and we went up to the Crescent and looked at the view from there. Then we had a good look at number 1, also. Even though it was still quite bright, we could see hundreds of candles already burning within the house.

'To think that we will be dancing there next week,' I said longingly. I felt a little guilty because Thomas would not be there, but then I imagined what a lovely long letter I could write to him describing the event (and give to Harry to post). Thomas had given me the name of a ships' post at Southampton. Apparently ships take letters for each other.

'I will be dancing with a *comte*,' said Jane, gazing up at the stately windows.

'Not Monsieur Baddy, I hope; you'll make Eliza envious,' I said.

'Every Frenchman is a count,' said Jane very positively, and Harry laughed. He knows her so well, and is always amused at her conversation, especially when she is living in one of her stories.

After supper we went up to our room, saying we were going to write letters. Mr and Mrs Leigh-Perrot looked as if they would be glad to join us but Augusta was talking about two brothers, friends of theirs, very rich merchants, who had shared the stagecoach with them and who were now staying at the Greyhound, which, according to her, is the best inn in Bath.

'There's Harry outside,' said Jane, going to the window to close the curtains. She gave a sigh. 'Oh dear, how romantic it would be if he were to pace the pavement until dawn! Do you think that is what he is going to do?'

'Poor Harry!' I went and joined her, pulling the curtain back a little so that I could see him. The movement was enough to attract his attention. He gave one quick look upwards and then took a folded letter from his pocket and pretended to be busy scrutinizing the address.

'Jane,' I said quickly, 'I think Harry has a letter for me. Or perhaps it is for you . . .'

'Let's go down.' Jane was already at the door. We both crept down the stairs and opened the front door as softly and carefully as we could.

Harry had a letter in his hand. The bold, upright handwriting in that very black ink almost jumped out at me; I hardly noticed the small, well-drawn anchor in one corner of the folded sheet. I knew instantly that it was from Thomas.

'For you, Miss Jenny,' he said. 'It was at the inn when I rode home.'

Harry melted away quickly as soon as I had the precious letter safely tucked under my cloak. In a moment Jane and I were back indoors and crept up the stairs to our bedroom. It was the first really long letter that I had received from Thomas. I will stick it in here now, and every day when I open my journal I will reread it.

My dearest Jenny,

It is almost dawn here at Southampton. When I look towards the east I can see a faint brightness in the sky. All the men are watching the sky also. They know that once daybreak comes I will give the order and then we will set sail. The tide is turning. There is always something magical about an ebb tide at dawn. The wind is blowing strongly from the east. And now, my darling, here is my wonderful news. My orders have been changed. Only I know this so far, but when I tell the men a great cheer will go up. We are not going to the East Indies, but to the West Indies. We will be home before Christmas.

I wish you could have seen my ship. A few minutes ago the rigging of the three masts was black against the pale grey skies, but I gave the order and now three enormous white sails have been unfurled and a faint line of gold has crept across the horizon. In a few minutes, I shall finish writing this and give it to the boat that is going ashore with everyone's letters. And then I will give the order to cast off. We shall sail from Southampton past the coast of Spain and then cross the Atlantic towards Barbados.

My darling, ever since you and I were together in the early morning on the day I was leaving Steventon, I always think this hour before dawn is the most solemn moment of the day, and now I am thinking of you and of the life we will spend together. It seems to me that I am like a man who has been walking a long and lonely road for many years and now I have come home to warmth and companionship. I find myself smiling at odd moments of the day when your face comes before me.

Perhaps one day you will come on a voyage with me and I can show you all the wonders of the world. In the meantime keep yourself well and happy, my darling, until the day when I come back and when we can be married.
With all my love,
Thomas.

P.S. Keep an eye on Elinor for me, won't you? I sense she is not happy.
PP,S Thank you for your lovely letter.

Saturday, 30 April 1791

Breakfast was a silent meal. Augusta kept eyeing me with dislike, and I wonder what was said last evening. Edward-John did not look at me at all and fawned on our uncle and aunt in a sickening sort of way.

Just after breakfast there was a thunderous knock on the door. Jane and I were on the staircase, but we stopped and waited until the housemaid went to open the door. When we saw the constable on the doorstep and heard him demand Mrs Leigh-Perrot we crept down the stairs again and waited in the back of the hallway.

I think that if it had been Franklin he would have left the constable standing in the hall and fetched Mr Leigh-Perrot, but the housemaid was flustered and immediately showed the man into the breakfast parlour. Jane and I could hear every word that was said. Jane has written it out like a play. I think it is mostly correct — written in Jane's unique style, of course.

Constable: Hi must hask you to haccompany me to the Roundhouse, madam.

Mrs Leigh-Perrot: What nonsense! Say what you have to say and be quick about it!

Constable: Hit is my dooty to hinform you, madam . . .

Mrs Leigh-Perrot: Don't you speak like that to

me, my man. Be off with you or I'll have the law on you.

Constable (very loudly): Hi ham the law, madam.

Mrs Leigh-Perrot: Pooh! Nonsense!

Constable: You must hanswer questions about a card of stolen lace, madam.

Mrs Leigh-Perrot: What do you mean – 'stolen'? I have no knowledge of stolen lace.

Enter Mr Leigh-Perrot

Mr Leigh-Perrot: My good man, are you aware of who I am? The mayor of this town is a personal friend of mine.

Constable (in loud, bullying tones): Be that as it may, sir, if the good lady does not report to the Roundhouse, then she will be harrested.

And then the constable marched out of the house, not waiting for anyone to show him the door. By this time Edward-John and Augusta were on the scene. I could see from the uncertainty in Augusta's eyes that she wasn't quite sure how to act. On the one hand, the Leigh-Perrot couple are very rich – Mrs Leigh-Perrot is an heiress in her own right. On the other hand it was thoroughly disreputable to be arrested and dragged off to jail by a police constable. Eventually Augusta solved the problem of how to behave by fainting noisily on to the sofa.

'It's good that you are here, Edward-John; you can

take care of your sister and cousin as your Uncle James has taken the notion into his head that he wishes to accompany me.' Our courageous aunt ignored the unconscious figure on the sofa and told the maid to bring her bonnet and pelisse.

'May we go with you? Please, Aunt, allow us to go.' Jane was also ignoring Augusta, who, realizing that no one but her husband was paying attention to her, now sat up with a faint squeak of horror.

'No young lady of true elegance could possibly visit such a place,' she said, frowning at Jane.

'We'll all walk down together,' said Jane firmly. 'Dearest Aunt, please do allow us. We are your family. My mother would want us to do this.'

Edward-John seemed to making some noises as if he too was going to offer, but Augusta put a stop to this by stretching out her arms to him and then fainting again.

'Certainly not.' Mrs Leigh-Perrot sounded her usual authoritative self, but she patted Jane on the shoulder and I think that she was quite touched by the offer.

'Bother,' said Jane as she eyed the couple going down the steep hill of the Paragon. 'It would have made such an exciting scene in a novel.'

I was quite shocked, but couldn't help a slight giggle as we went back upstairs to our bedroom in order to escape from Augusta and Edward-John. We sat on the window seat so that we could see the Leigh-Perrots when they returned and tried to guess if they would come in a cab or a sedan chair, or whether they would walk.

Lots of gigs, chaises and other vehicles passed, their horses labouring on the steep hill, but there was no sign of any familiar figures. Then a large omnibus lumbered past, taking a long time despite the four horses straining every limb.

When it had gone by a blond-haired young man emerged from behind it and crossed the road. The next minute we heard the doorbell.

'It's Harry,' said Jane. She gave a quick glance at the looking glass and then opened the door very quietly, shutting it carefully once I was through. Together we tiptoed down the stairs and reached the hallway before the maid.

'Go back to the kitchen, Rosalie, it's just someone bringing news,' said Jane in an imitation of Mrs Leigh-Perrot's stately manner and Rosalie vanished before Jane had edged the heavy hall door open and pulled Harry inside.

I had a quick look into the second-best parlour. It was empty, so I nodded at Jane who caught Harry by the hand and led him in there.

'Not another letter for Jenny!' exclaimed Jane.

Harry shook his head and explained that he had met Mr and Mrs Leigh-Perrot on their way into the town hall. He walked with them and they told him all that had happened. On their way there they had been handed a letter stating that if they were willing to recompense Miss Gregory, no more action would be taken. Harry described how the two had argued about it.

'It's a plot,' said Jane dramatically. 'A dastardly plot to extract money from an innocent woman.'

'Mr Leigh-Perrot wanted to send a ten-pound note and finish with the whole business, but Mrs Leigh-Perrot would not agree,' said Harry. 'She said she was innocent, and that she would prove it in the eye of the law.' She had told Harry that they had no need of assistance and that they would be perfectly all right and that no harm ever came to the innocent. But Harry, who could see that Mr Leigh-Perrot looked anxious, said that he was going that way in any case.

He told us he was glad that he had accompanied them when he saw the constable standing outside the town hall. According to Harry, the man addressed the elderly pair in a rather rude manner.

'So I stepped forward and asked Mr Leigh-Perrot whether I could be of any assistance to him if I accompanied him inside. I had a word with the constable about being civil to people. He said something rude back and unfortunately –' Harry gave an impish grin before finishing – 'my boot managed to trip him up when I was on my way in.'

'Harry, you will be the hero of my next story,' said Jane enthusiastically. I must say that I almost felt like kissing him myself. He was such a shy, quiet young man and yet he had plenty of courage when it came to a need for it.

'I just thought that that I should go in with them, as they might want someone to run errands for them,' explained Harry modestly.

'And what happened?' I almost expected Jane to run upstairs for her writing desk and start writing it all down as a story.

'Well, the mayor was a bit embarrassed,' said Harry. 'I think that he probably knows them very well. Once he almost called Mr Leigh-Perrot "James" and then just stopped himself. The magistrate wasn't so friendly, and that constable kept putting in bits like: "Well, we have two sworn testimonies that Mrs Leigh-Perrot is guilty, and only her word that she is innocent." They had Miss Gregory and that Filby man who works for her – supposedly – the two of them were there.' He hesitated a little and then said, 'I'm afraid that they are going to keep her in jail for the moment until Mr Leigh-Perrot can arrange bail. And he's going to stay with her. Mrs Leigh-Perrot wanted him to go back because she didn't want you two to be left alone, but her husband was saying that Edward-John and his wife could surely look after his sister and cousin.'

It was very selfish of me, but I must write my thought here in my journal. And it was this: *Now I am back under Augusta's rule again.* I tried to stop thinking of that and asked Harry whether Mrs Leigh-Perrot was very upset.

'Oh, she stood up to them,' said Harry with a grin.

'She put her nose in the air and said, "I certainly did have the white lace in my possession," and then she pointed at the two wretches – that's what she called them – and said, "But only they know how it came to be wrapped up with the black lace which had been bought and paid for."'

'Harry, what do you mean by saying that Filby was "supposedly" working for Miss Gregory?' asked Jane, eyeing him keenly.

Harry's cheeks flushed and he ran a hand through his hair.

'I have my suspicions about that fellow,' was all that he would say, and Jane did not question him further, though I could see her eyes sparkling with excitement.

Harry then produced a list Mrs Leigh-Perrot had given him for overnight necessities for herself and her husband. I offered to take the list to the chambermaid and I went off, leaving them alone. It had been nice of Harry to help the elderly couple, I thought, and then I felt ashamed of my brother that he had not done as much for his uncle and aunt.

After he had gone back with a well-packed bag, Jane told me that she guessed Harry suspected this man Filby was having some sort of irregular relation-ship with Miss Gregory – 'Living in sin,' she hissed when I looked puzzled.

6 o'clock Saturday, 30 April

Augusta has just declared that we should attend the ball at the Assembly Rooms, to keep the flag flying and to show the world that we don't believe what is being said about poor, dear Aunt Leigh-Perrot. I can't believe that even Augusta could be so insensitive. Jane and I had been hoping that Mr Leigh-Perrot might have obtained bail for his wife by now, but there has been no word, so the poor things will definitely have to spend the night in custody. Harry has just come back with a note for Edward-John. In the hall on the way out Jane whispered to him to make sure to be at the Assembly Rooms tonight and she would give him all of her dances so that they could discuss the affair and find out if there is a plot between Miss Gregory and Mr Filby to get money from the Leigh-Perrots. She is sure that the note that was handed to them on their way to the town hall means that they are being blackmailed. I felt a bit sick at the idea of going to the Assembly Rooms when the Leigh-Perrots are in such trouble, but I have to admit that Jane is full of practical ideas for their release.

It's selfish of me, but I must say that my heart sinks at the thought of what the admiral will say when he hears about this. It will be a great scandal and he will definitely not want his nephew allied to a family in such disgrace.

Back at the Assembly Rooms

The Assembly Rooms – so different and yet so much the same.

The same lovely chandeliers, the same elegant company, the same magnificent ballroom with the same five magnificent chandeliers, the same crowds of beautifully dressed ladies and gentlemen, the same primrose-yellow Octagon Room and narrow green card room, the same lovely pink supper room . . .

Jane in her daffodil-yellow gown flirting with Newton Wallop . . .

'My dear boy, where did you pick up such unmeaning rubbish? I suspect that you have been reading novels . . .'

But no Thomas . . .

Augusta comes up. She wants to introduce her dear friends . . . two very fat, rather greasy-looking youngish men – probably in their mid-thirties – bowing very politely. They pay all sorts of compliments to Edward-John, including congratulating him on his sermon last week. My brother looks a little surprised at that and I wonder whether these two – Augusta introduces them as merchants from Bristol – had really attended his church.

I am dancing with the younger of the two, Mr Stanley, quite a small man in comparison with my Thomas, with a rounded stomach sticking out under his embroidered waistcoat and over the top of his pale yellow breeches and

203

a large, round face with trickles of perspiration running down it.

He tries to make conversation, to impress me, talks and talks about how speedy his horses are and how clever he was to choose them. I don't take much notice, but then he says something that makes me gasp.

He is trying to make me guess how much his horse cost . . . 'Well, I'll give you an 'int.' He smiles down at me, his big greasy mouth splitting open to show his yellow teeth. He pauses for a moment and then says slowly and pompously, 'What would you say if I told you this horse cost as much as I got for ten darkies?'

'Darkies!' For a moment I am puzzled, and then I realize what he means. I stare at him with disgust and he grins back at me, baring his horrible teeth.

'Slaves from Africa, you know; I trade in them. Make lots of money, I can assure you. You must come and see my house some time, you and your sister, Mrs Cooper. You'd get lost in it! A great big place at Clifton, up on the hill over Bristol.'

I look away, look around the room, anything rather than look at this disgusting man.

Jane is dancing with Colonel Forster now. Phylly and Lavinia have their heads together, watching her with critical and hostile eyes. Phylly is some sort of second cousin to Lavinia, apparently. They seem very fond of each other. Eliza is dancing with Monsieur Baddy. Augusta is being whirled around by the brother of that oaf who is dancing with me. Both brothers look equally revolting. No doubt

Mr Jerome Wilkins is also a slave dealer. The fact that the brothers are rich would be enough for Augusta. I know her well enough to know that she worships money.

The dance finishes. I make an excuse that I have to find my cousin.

Now Jane is with Harry Digweed. They have their heads together in one corner of the ballroom. I don't want to interrupt and I go to the cloakroom. It's early in the evening, just one person is there – a girl sitting on the window seat, staring through the panes – staring at nothing. It's Elinor – her head is turned away from me, but I hear a muffled sob.

'Go away!' She shouts the words violently. 'It's all your fault! Why did you interfere? It was none of your business.' She raises her face towards me. I see a red mark on her cheek as if someone has slapped her.

'Elinor! Did the admiral do this?'

I touch her cheek. She flinches and pulls away, staring at me. 'Not the admiral,' she says.

'Who then?'

She seems about to answer but shakes her head. 'It's all your fault anyway!' she repeats.

She breaks away from me and goes back towards the ballroom. I follow her. I see Sir Walter come up to her and slip his arm around her waist. She looks up at him with tears swimming in her eyes and he pats her hand with an amused smile. He sees me looking, stares coldly at me and then walks away with Elinor on his arm.

Did he hit her?

And then Augusta is shrieking in my ear that Mr Stanley Wilkins is waiting to dance with me. Ghastly man, he takes me by the hand and leads me on to the dance floor.

I shut my ears to his voice and stare distantly over his shoulder so that I don't have to look at him. When the dance finishes I drop him a quick curtsy and go over and stand beside Jane. She is having a wonderful time, like a butterfly flitting from one partner to another. She has just allowed Newton Wallop to write his name on her card for the next country dance.

Lavinia Thorpe makes a sharp hissing sound behind us, and Jane says to her wisely, 'La, Miss Thorpe, I fear you are somewhat heated by the wine. Pray do seek relief for your disordered head and lovesick heart in the conversation of an intelligent woman like myself.'

Lavinia turns white and says, 'I warn you, Jane Austen!' but Jane takes no notice, gives Newton Wallop his dance and then one to Colonel Forster, another of Lavinia's beaux.

It's just before supper now. I am waiting at the door for Jane. Just as she comes along I hear Lavinia, surrounded by a crowd of girls, say to Caroline in a very loud voice, 'I always knew that Jane Austen and her relations were beggars, but I never knew until today that they were actually thieves as well. Let's hope that aunt of theirs will be hanged and then they will never be able to show their faces in society again. I can just imagine that woman dangling from the gallows, can't you?'

For a moment Jane's face freezes. Her eyes are very

large and her expression is a mask of horror.

And then Harry, who has been standing to one side, comes forward and says to Lavinia with great politeness, 'Excuse me, ma'am, but I think you mentioned the name of the aunt of a friend of mine. Or am I mistaken?'

He holds Lavinia's eyes for a few moments – and I hold my breath! – and then Lavinia looks down and mutters, 'I think you are mistaken, sir.'

And Jane's face relaxes into a smile and she says, 'Dearest Harry, come and join us for supper!'

Monday, 2 May 1791

Mr Stanley Wilkins and his equally revolting brother Mr Jerome Wilkins called on us this morning.

'Dear lady!' Mr Jerome spent a long time bending over Augusta's hand. They are so obsequious that it is nauseating. She smiled sweetly and looked coy. They fell over each other to give explanations as to why they did not pay the conventional calls yesterday after the ball.

'Problems with the cargo,' said Jerome with a sneer.

I was staring at them. I felt sick. Did that mean some poor unfortunate slaves had died?

'Young ladies don't like business talk,' said Stanley in a loud, hearty voice with a frown at his brother.

'Sit here beside me, Jenny dear,' cooed Augusta, trying to sound like a fond mother.

After they had gone Augusta lectured me on being so silent, but I just ignored her and told her that I had to go to keep an appointment with Eliza. Jane and I are finding that visiting Eliza is very useful. It allows us to get out of the house and also to meet Harry and talk about the Leigh-Perrots.

Harry had some more news for us.

'There's a woman in the town,' he said in a low voice as he accompanied us to Queen's Square. 'Her name is Mrs Blagrave and when she bought a veil in Miss Gregory's shop a couple of months ago she noticed that this fellow, Filby, put two veils in the parcel instead of one.

However, she spotted him and warned him not to "*try any of your tricks with me, young man.*"'

I asked Harry how he had found that out, and he said that the chambermaid at the Greyhound Inn had heard it from Mrs Blagrave's maid.

'What does this chambermaid look like?' Jane rather surprised me as she asked the question quite abruptly.

'Very tiny, with little blonde curls on her forehead,' said Harry. He blushed slightly as he said that and Jane scowled.

'I think that is very important about Mrs Blagrave,' I said. I couldn't see what the chambermaid's appearance had to do with the matter.

'So do I,' said Harry. 'I think that it sounds as though this Filby has a reputation for doing things like that. What do you think I should do?'

'Tell my uncle, of course,' said Jane. She sounded a little snappish, but Harry didn't appear to notice.

'I was thinking that I might have a word with the lawyer instead.' Harry didn't appear to notice Jane's mood. 'It's just that your uncle . . .' he was addressing both of us, 'just that he is such a nice, kind man, and I don't think that he would like to think too badly of anyone, or to do anything underhand like making enquiries of a maid.'

'Could you make enquiries of the maid yourself, Harry?' I said. He was a good-looking fellow with charming ways, and I thought he would be more likely to get something out of a girl than a lawyer with a threatening manner and legal language.

Before we parted we had it all worked out. Harry was to chat to the chambermaid, see if she could get her friend to go for a walk with her – perhaps in the gardens by the river – and Harry would meet them by accident, treat her to an ice and get all the information possible from her . . .

Jane and I have just got ready for the French ball, as Jane keeps calling it. We're both so pleased that Augusta has not been invited. And she is furious! She tried to get Edward-John to agree with her that we should not go with just Eliza to chaperone us, but Edward-John, who, like most men, finds Eliza madly attractive, refused to agree with her. For once he stood up to Augusta!!! He said that he thought it would be a great opportunity and that, in any case, he had no authority over Jane and it would be a sad thing if she had to go without her cousin's company. He had visited the Leigh-Perrots this afternoon and they had talked about the ball and had sent a message to say that they were looking forward to hearing all about it. When he mentioned the word 'Leigh-Perrot' Augusta became silent. Obviously she had in mind the desirability of Edward-John pleasing his rich and childless uncle and aunt. She even suggested that Rosalie should help us to dress and to do our hair! Thanks to Rosalie, we were ready in very good time. She is a very competent, well-trained lady's maid, but very starchy, as Jane puts it. We were very quiet as she dressed us both, as if we were a pair of dolls. Jane was thoughtful, and there were none of the jokes and wild fits of giggling that happened when we were getting ready with Eliza for a ball at Steventon. When we were both ready she stood us in front of the large cheval looking glass and said with satisfaction, 'You will be the two most beautiful young ladies at the Crescent tonight.'

We both looked very solemn, I thought, as I gazed at our reflection. One dark-haired, dark-eyed girl in a rich daffodil yellow gown and the other blonde with a bluebell gown that matched her eyes. (Jane had received so many compliments about her new dress that she decided to wear it after all.)

I've just asked Jane how long it will be before Eliza calls for us, and she said that it will be at least fifteen minutes – and that Eliza is always late for everything!

So there may be time for me to write about Harry.

Harry, I think, knows everything about the Leigh-Perrot household by now. He knows what time dinner is, when it finishes, and that Jane and I always go to our bedroom after dinner. In this household there are so many servants that we have no chores like helping to clear the plates from the table as we do at Steventon, so we just go straight upstairs – while aunt and uncle have a little sleep – and we chat. Now that it's just a matter of Augusta and Edward-John, we rush away as soon as the meal is over.

And Harry chose that moment to stroll up and down the Paragon on the opposite side of the road. We saw him from our bedroom window.

We slipped downstairs and beckoned him into the second-best parlour, closing the door quietly behind us.

'I've been to see your uncle and aunt,' said Harry. His eyes widened at the sight of Jane's new gown, but he was too shy to comment and just continued with his account of our poor aunt. 'The jailer has housed them in his own house instead of the ordinary prison,' he told us. 'I'd say that Mr Leigh-Perrot has had to give him a pretty good bribe for that!'

'How are they?' I asked.

'They're in good spirits — Mrs Leigh-Perrot especially. She was telling me a funny story about the jailer's wife stirring the fried onions with a knife, then licking the knife to clean it before giving it to Mrs Leigh-Perrot. Apparently your aunt was so appalled that she gave her dinner to the dog!'

Jane remarked that Franklin would be upset if he heard that, and I agreed. Poor Franklin was going around looking as if his world had fallen apart. He was devoted to his master and mistress. It was almost as if they had taken the place of the family that he had left behind in Barbados.

'But that's not all that I wanted to tell you,' went on Harry. 'I was having a chat to the stableman at the Greyhound Inn about the Leigh-Perrots — just mentioning the subject in passing like, and he told me that the chambermaid had an interesting story to tell about it. I asked him to finish grooming my horse for me and gave him sixpence – I pretended that I had hurt my shoulder and I stayed there, rubbing it – I'd guessed that he would like to tell the story, but I didn't want to scare him off by being too interested.'

'Harry, you are a man of genius!' exclaimed Jane and Harry blushed scarlet. 'Tell me that you got the story out of him!'

'Well, he didn't know too much – just that it was something about Gye the printer owning the shop premises – Miss Gregory's shop, that is. Apparently . . .' and Harry blushed again, 'apparently the printer's apprentice has some sort of relationship with the chambermaid.'

'What a dissipated place this city of Bath is!' Jane said these words with an air of such deep satisfaction that I couldn't stop myself giggling – though I was very, very sorry for my uncle and aunt.

'So I went to ask the chambermaid for some hot water. And when she brought it, I persuaded her to talk. She made me swear not to betray her name.' And now even Harry's forehead reddened. And yet there was a glint of amusement in his cornflower-blue eyes.

'Ah,' said Jane with great satisfaction, 'I do love secrets, especially those that require solemn oaths of inviolable secrecy.' She said the words almost breathlessly.

'Well, the chambermaid didn't exactly tell me anything, but she said that she had heard that the printer Gye, the man who owns the shop, had given presents to the apprentice, Sarah Raines, who works for Miss Gregory. The apprentice saw him put a shilling into a little packet and write the girl's name on the outside.'

'Bribery!' Jane and I said the word together.

'We'll have to get more evidence than that,' warned Harry. 'The chambermaid will never swear in court that the printer's apprentice told her that. And the printer's apprentice will never give evidence against his master.'

I asked Harry whether he really thought that it would go to court and he nodded with a quick, anxious look at Jane as if to make sure that she was not too upset. He should have known better.

'A court case!' exclaimed Jane. 'Oh, Jenny, I think it will be our duty to be there to support our dear aunt.'

Jane, I know, was very sincere about her feelings for her aunt, but I must say that I have a feeling that a court case may well appear in her writings!

'I'd better be getting back,' said Harry. 'I thought I might drop in on the printer, see about getting some cards engraved – I'm sure my mother would like that as a present from Bath.'

'And get the dastardly fellow to admit his crime!' said Jane excitedly, and Harry gave her his lovely smile and made ready to leave.

When we showed him out, Franklin was there at

the doorstep. His eyes looked red. I felt very sorry for him.

'What's the news, Miss Jane?' he asked eagerly.

'They are quite comfortable, staying in the jailer's house. My aunt is making jokes, Franklin, so you don't need to worry about them.' Jane said the words reassuringly, but Franklin didn't look relieved.

'I have to worry, Miss Jane,' he said almost roughly. I looked at him in surprise. He was always so very polite. He stared back at the two of us. 'The cook's been talking to me about it,' he continued. 'The punishment for stealing anything worth more than five shillings is death – she might be hanged!'

'What?!' I got a fright, but Jane patted Franklin on the arm and told him that would never happen to someone of Mrs Leigh-Perrot's stature in society.

However, as we went back up the stairs together she whispered to me that Aunt Leigh-Perrot might be transported to Botany Bay in Australia. Apparently they ship criminals out there and leave them there for the rest of their life.

'Don't worry,' said Jane when I exclaimed. 'Harry and I will find the solution to this. Dirty work is afoot!'

Jane has just gone to the window and said that she sees Eliza's hired carriage turning into the Paragon.

Now she is shrieking at the top of her voice about something.

Oh! Henry is here!

Tuesday, 3 May 1791

Dearest, dearest, dearest Thomas,

I love you. I wonder how often one can say that without being boring. I love you from the top of your head right down to your feet. When I see the sun it reminds me of how warm your love feels. When I am sitting by my candle, your face is there in front of me. When I hear something funny or something strange I immediately think of telling you.

Jane's brother Henry came to Bath yesterday with a message from Frank to say that there will be a small fast ship going out and it will meet your ship at Madeira, and to write immediately. Henry will bring my letter to Southampton as he is going to visit Frank - so my letter can be as long and as thick as I like and won't cost you a penny. So you will have two letters from me! I feared that my first letter would not reach you for months.

And I will have a letter from you, if you have time to write. Henry says that I should have it in a couple of weeks' time.

It's after breakfast. Jane has gone to practise the piano - in order to annoy Augusta, she plays very loudly and then says that she has promised her aunt and uncle to

practise faithfully every day. Augusta and
Edward-John were not speaking to each other
in the breakfast parlour when I slipped away
with the excuse that I had to write some
letters. I certainly didn't tell them that I
was going to write to you!

I was thinking about our wedding. When
we get married, could it be at Steventon?
It's so much more of a home to me than my
brother's place at Bristol. The little church
there is so lovely.

You notice that I don't say 'if' - now I
am as strong as a sailor's wife should be and
I say 'when' all the times Jane and I are
discussing it.

So, what shall I tell you about? Firstly, the
ball at number 1, the Crescent, and about the
Princesse de Lambelle. Eliza managed to get
an invitation for Jane and myself to go and
we were quite excited.

Jane's brother Henry had been sent by
his mother to visit the Leigh-Perrots (because
of this ridiculous accusation of shoplifting)
and, knowing that Edward-John and Augusta
were occupying the house in the Paragon,
he decided that it would be more enjoyable
to go and stay with Eliza. They called for
Jane and myself and, as usual, Eliza and
Henry were getting on so very, very well!

Henry was joking about Phylly and telling us about how Phylly claimed that Jane and I were leading dissipated lives in Bath. Henry, apparently, teased Phylly that she was the one with a string of lovers!

'And he was very naughty - very, very naughty - teasing poor Phylly all the afternoon,' said Eliza, leaning across the carriage and tapping Henry with her fan.

She and Monsieur Baddy, as she calls the French count who is her great friend, were sitting on one side of the carriage, and Henry was squashed in between Jane and me on the other side, but we were all very jolly.

And now I must write about the Crescent. Somehow Eliza, speaking rapid French, managed to get Henry admitted - as she said herself, an unattached good-looking young man is always welcome at any party!! Then we were through the front door, in the stately entrance hall with its marbled walls and beautifully moulded plasterwork, and up the stairs.

The Princesse de Lambelle - according to Eliza, she was half-Italian and half-German - that's where the princess part comes from - seemed to speak only French. She kissed Eliza on both cheeks, gave her hand to Monsieur Baddy to kiss and smiled kindly at the rest of us.

Would you like to know what a real princess looks like? Well, she looked about forty, with a very sad-looking, rather lined face, and she was dressed in an elaborate pale lilac silk gown, embroidered with patterns in deeper purple and trimmed with elaborate ruffles of gold lace.

The drawing room was magnificent. The walls were covered in green silk and a huge chandelier with thirty candles hung over the centre of the room. Fastened to various places on the walls were more candlesticks, each of them bearing two or four candles. Under each candlestick were small Pembroke tables with four gilt chairs placed around each so that some could sit and talk while others danced.

I danced with Henry, who was very interested to hear all about you and your interview with Edward-John and about your voyage, and he was so pleased to hear that you are going to the West Indies, not the East Indies, and that you will be home for Christmas. He's like you; he thinks that Edward-John will give in when you come back. I hope that you are both right!

Jane had a great time. Newton Wallop was there and they danced together for most of the evening. She kept saying things like:

'...Dearest Newton, at my time of life, I count myself safe from the perseverance of disagreeable lovers and the persecution of obstinate fathers...'

(that's a quote from one of her novels) and all the French ladies and gentlemen - those who can speak English - were looking at her in such an amazed way that I could hardly stop laughing.

Henry was my partner for supper. It was very formal, not at all like at the Assembly Rooms, where everyone just pushes their way into the supper room and chooses a table or queues up at the long table and chooses what they like to eat. This was more like a dinner party.

First a footman, all dressed up in silk knee breeches and powdered hair, came to the door, touched a gong, then bowed and announced:

'Le dîner est servi.'

And then slowly and in a very genteel manner, with lots of bowing and curtsying, the guests formed a long line after the Princesse de Lambelle and followed her down the staircase and into the dining room, which was on the left-hand side of the front door. While we were waiting in the queue, I peeped into the next room. It looked like a study because it had a desk and a jar full of quills and one of those flintlocks for melting wax and a magnificent bookcase (Chippendale, all of it, whispered Henry in my ear, adding that Chippendale and Hepplewhite furniture is 'très à la mode'). The little card tables were also probably made by either Chippendale or Hepplewhite, but what fascinated me was that at one of the tables, laying out the counters with an anxious face, was the Duchess of Devonshire - still playing cards! Do you remember me telling you about her? I wonder what her debts amount to now!

Then we moved into the dining room, where another footman found us two places towards the end of the long, long table. Eliza and Monsieur Baddy caused some confusion by moving along to sit beside us, and Jane ignored her partner, who was being directed further up the table, and came to sit by us also. He followed her, of course, but I don't think that he was very pleased as he said very little during the whole meal. But the Austens and myself were very merry in English and a mixture of French and Monsieur Baddy joined in to the best of his ability. He laughed when Eliza, having informed us that the long table was probably three tables put together, sent questions up and down the solemn rows to see who could spot where the join was under the immense starched linen cloth. So all along the table, stately powdered heads were ducking down and peering under the starched table cover, while the Princesse de Lambelle gazed at her guests in a bewildered fashion.

'On dit que she pay forty pound for just the dessert service,' whispered Monsieur Baddy. 'And the silver - oh là là!'

I giggled, thinking about my fifty pounds a year, and Henry pretended to try to put a teaspoon into his pocket. Jane of course was quite at home. When the footman tried to help her to some lobster salad, she said, 'Non, merci,' firmly. She shook her head also at the oysters, the veal escalopes and the mutton pie, and then pointed to the trifle and said in English, 'Some of that, please.' I decided to have trifle also, and just looked at the footman, and he obligingly ladled another large helping on to a beautiful Wedgwood plate. To my embarrassment everyone was looking at us and laughing, and even the sad face of the Princesse creased in an indulgent smile. I suppose we were the youngest guests *there, and everyone seemed to treat us a little like children, coming and talking to Eliza about us and admiring our gowns.*

I wish that you could have been there and could have seen my bluebell gown. The Leigh-Perrots gave us both a present of a new ball gown, and they are so beautiful - mine in two shades of blue and Jane's in a rich daffodil yellow.

I am imagining my love as one of those huge brightly coloured balloons that waft men through the sky, and I send it across the sea to you.

From your own Jenny

I have just sealed my letter to Thomas and asked Jane whether she enjoyed the party at the Crescent. She yawned and said, 'It will give me some material for my novels.' I didn't say anything and after a minute she yawned again and said, 'They don't seem real, these French counts, do they? You couldn't imagine going for a walk through the woods with them . . .' and then she went off to bed.

Wednesday, 4 May 1791

Just after breakfast Jane and I escaped for our morning walk. This time we were ready with the excuse that we wanted to say goodbye to Henry, who was returning to Steventon on the midday stagecoach.

There was no sign of Harry Digweed, so we walked down to Queen's Square and rang the bell at Eliza's door. For a wonder she was up and dressed, her face delicately powdered and the faintest trace of rouge on her cheeks.

'*Mes chéries!* Come in, come in, *mes petites!*' Eliza was in a cheerful mood. But then, with a guilty look over her shoulder, she changed to dramatic, tragic tones.

'How good you are, *mes chères petites filles*. You have come to cheer up your lonely *cousine*.'

'Lonely?' Jane and I looked at each other with raised eyebrows. By this time we were both in the drawing room. The mantelpiece above the fire was crowded with innumerable invitation cards; bunches of hothouse flowers, each dangling the name of the presenter, made the room seem like a garden. No one in the whole city of Bath looked less likely to be lonely than Eliza.

'It's Phylly,' exclaimed Eliza loudly in heartbroken tones. 'She is thinking of leaving me, going to Steventon. *Hélas!*' Eliza gave a gulp, which had the effect of making Jane giggle, but then Phylly strode out from the inner room, and Eliza stopped abruptly. Phylly was not wearing her cloak or her bonnet.

'I've changed my mind, Cousin Eliza,' she announced solemnly. 'I've decided that it would be improper of me to travel alone with a young man.'

'But he's your cousin, Phylly,' wailed Eliza, and Henry gave her a sharp frown, kissed all three of us, bowed to Phylly and declared that he had to be off straightaway. We heard him running fast down the stairs.

'He's going to be very, very, very early,' Jane muttered to me as we looked down from the window at her brother's fleeing figure.

'*Les jeunes* — life is fun and movement for them,' said Eliza sadly. But then she cheered up. 'Let's discuss the ball,' she said. 'Jane, *chérie*, you've made quite a conquest, haven't you. We might see our little Jane as the wife of an earl some time, Phylly!'

'An earl!' Jane stared at her. 'What are you talking about, Eliza?'

Eliza laughed. 'Listen to her, Phylly. She spent most of the night dancing with Newton Wallop, the son of the Earl of Portland, no less! And there she is with a face like a baby. He is so taken by her! He hangs on every word that she says. And Jenny, too, you naughty girl! I saw you with the *comte*. You two were laughing together.'

Jane and I giggled, but Phylly was not amused. 'I must say that all this flirting upsets me. What are you young girls thinking of! This sort of behaviour will get you talked about. I wish we could all leave this dissipated city and go back to our quiet country ways.'

'*Hélas*,' sighed Eliza, leaving it to our imagination to guess whether she was referring to the loss of the quiet country days or to the continued presence of Phylly.

'We have to leave you,' said Jane with a solemn face. 'We have an appointment with a young gentleman in this dissipated city of Bath and we cannot disappoint him. Who knows, but he may fall into despair and end his days in a stream. I wrote a poem about that last night.' She stood very still in the centre of the room, her toes, in her neat slip-on shoes, turned outwards, her hands clasped in front of her, clutching her reticule, and recited:

> *Here lies my friend who having promiséd*
> *That unto me he would be marriéd,*
> *Threw his sweet body and his lovely face*
> *Into the stream that runs thru' Laura Place.*

Then she bowed slightly towards Phylly. We both raced down the stairs and flew out into Queen's Square before exploding into a laugh.

On the way back we met Harry. What a surprise!!
'You're out early,' he said.
'Tell us the news,' commanded Jane. 'I can see that

you have some. I know that look on your face.'

These two have known each other since they were babies, I thought, looking from one face to the other. They've played together, gone for walks together, and spent evenings dancing together in the shabby parlour at Steventon parsonage. They probably recognize each other's every expression, understand every move.

'Well, I do have something interesting,' said Harry, his soft Hampshire accent standing out amidst the clipped speech of the inhabitants of Bath, who were hastening downhill for their morning bath in the spa waters or drink at the Pump Room.

'From your friend the chambermaid?' It was difficult for me to tell from Jane's voice whether she cared about Harry's friendship with this chambermaid. Harry, however, gave a small smile and a quick glance at Jane's high-coloured face.

'Yes,' he said, nodding. 'And she got it from her friend, the lady's maid to Mrs Kent.'

'Who on earth are Mrs Kent and her lady's maid?' said Jane impatiently.

'Ah, don't be rushing me now,' said Harry with a grin. 'I'm not a novelist like you, you know. You must give me time.'

'Let Harry tell the story, Jane,' I said, and he proceeded to tell it very well. It appears that Mrs Kent, a respectable widow living in Bath, had bought four pairs of gloves from Miss Gregory. When she got home and unwrapped the parcel at home she found five pairs of gloves. According to the maid, she was puzzling over how such a thing could have happened when there was a loud ring at her front door. It was Miss Gregory, who straightaway accused Mrs Kent of stealing the gloves. When the widow angrily denied this, Miss Gregory said that she was going to summon a constable. At this stage Mrs Kent got frightened and gave the gloves back to Miss Gregory with a ten-pound note tucked in between them. Jane and I both gasped at this. Ten pounds would feed a farm labourer's family for a year! However, Miss Gregory took the ten-pound note and then marched away, muttering to herself, according to the lady's maid. After that no more was heard!!!

'Harry, you must tell the lawyer this,' said Jane. 'It's obvious that this is a plot. They hoped to frighten my aunt and uncle into paying them money. They are in debt to the printer who owns the shop and this plan was concocted to get them out of trouble.'

Harry hesitated a little.

'I don't think that will work,' he said eventually.

'No, you must,' said Jane. 'Don't be shy.'

'What about your brother H-Henry? I thought I would get him to do it; he could pretend that he had found it out for himself.'

'Henry's gone back to Steventon,' said Jane impatiently. 'No, Harry, you must be the one to talk to them.'

'It's just that . . . it's j-just that I think your uncle and aunt won't take much notice of me . . . They might even think that I was meddling in their a-affairs,' stammered Harry, obviously uncomfortable.

I told Jane that I saw what Harry meant. I felt sorry for him, but someone like Jane, who wasn't shy, could not understand how Harry was feeling.

Harry went on: 'Anyway, I don't think that the lawyer would believe me. He'd probably tell me to mind my own business.'

'I wonder, could we go and talk to our uncle and aunt — pretend that we had overheard something?' I suggested.

'No, that wouldn't do either. Mr and Mrs Leigh-Perrot told Henry yesterday that on no account are either of you to be allowed to go into the prison. She said it would never do for girls of your age. She said the same thing to your brother, Miss Jenny.'

'I know what we'll do!' Jane was suddenly all lit up with excitement. 'I'll write a letter, an anonymous letter, and you can drop it in through the lawyer's door at darkest midnight, Harry. Then the lawyer can claim all the credit it for it — which is a shame really, when it was your cleverness, dear Harry — you should be rewarded.'

'I don't want any reward.' There was a smile on Harry's face, and I had a feeling that Jane's words, especially the 'dear Harry' part, were all the reward that he had ever wanted.

Jane rushed me back home, dying to get to work on

the letter and assuring Harry that it would be ready for him after our three o'clock dinner.

But when we came in through the hall door Augusta was there, all dressed up in a brand-new gown, trimmed with all sorts of lace billowing around her hips and falling into folds below her fur jacket and enormous fur muff.

'There you are,' she exclaimed when she saw me. 'I've been sending here and there, looking for you. I do declare you are running quite wild! Now go upstairs and get changed into something decent. What have you to wear for a visit?'

'Visit?' I asked, wondering where we were going. As far as I knew, Augusta had no acquaintance in the city of Bath.

'We're going to see Mr Wilkins and Mr Stanley Wilkins. They've invited you and me to their house in Bristol. You will be all right here, Jane, my dear? Edward-John will keep you company once he gets back from visiting your aunt and uncle.' She didn't wait for Jane's answer but was chivvying me up the stairs, peering into the clothes press to see what I might wear.

'I'll be perfectly all right on my own, ma'am. Thank you for enquiring, ma'am. I very much appreciate your kind concern for me.' Jane dropped a few curtsies, so ridiculous that I found it hard to repress a giggle as Augusta went through my scanty wardrobe with exclamations of despair.

'I suppose you had better wear that blue muslin,' she muttered eventually. 'I don't suppose that he will notice what you are wearing.'

'He??' Jane signalled me with her eyebrows and I shook my head silently at her, wishing that I had the courage to say no to Augusta.

The Wilkins brothers live side by side in two enormous houses in George Street in Bristol. I wondered why they have two houses, since neither man has wife nor family, but I suppose they have to display their wealth. According to Augusta both are 'wealthy beyond dreams' – her expression.

We went into Mr Stanley Wilkins's house first. We had to see all over the house, from the bedrooms with their beautifully carved beds, hung with finest muslin drapery, dressing tables in shining mahogany and delicate china on the washstands, and the kitchen, with its modern closed stove, to the drawing room, where I sat, uncomfortably squashed between Augusta and the hugely fat Mr Stanley Wilkins, right in the centre of one of Mr Chippendale's three-seater settees and gazed at the glowing carpet.

'If you look at the design on the carpet, Miss Jenny,' wheezed Mr Stanley, 'you will see that it exactly echoes the plasterwork on the ceiling. I had it woven for me specially.'

Augusta exclaimed happily about all the beauties while I craned my neck to look at the elaborate scrolls and tendrils above my head 'Now, I must just pop in and see your brother,' said Augusta brightly. 'It would never do to make him jealous, would it? You will look after my little sister, won't you, Mr Stanley?'

I hardly know how to write the next bit. After Augusta went, neither of us knew what to say. Eventually he rang the bell for some sweetmeats for me. I took one, but I hated it. It had a strange sickly taste – coconut, according to him. I chewed and chewed and wished that I could spit it out.

And then, when my mouth was full of this horrible flaky stuff, he suddenly got off the settee and knelt on the floor. At first I thought that he was going to point out another pattern on the carpet and obediently I looked down. I remember my attention being caught by the twisted, rather spindly legs of the settee and thinking that it was amazing that they held his weight as well as Augusta's and mine.

And then I realized that he was asking me to marry him!!!

And I was so embarrassed!!!

He was an old man – well, he might be less than forty, but he looks older because he is so fat.

He took hold of my hand and I thought it might be impolite to snatch it away.

And there I was with my mouth full of sickly coconut and my hand imprisoned by a fat old man.

Suddenly I felt angry. Augusta had planned all of this – left me alone with him while she went next door. She would marry me off to this rich old man – my little legacy of fifty pounds a year would be nothing to him – he would never demand that! In fact, he would probably bring lots of nice little items back for her from over the seas– I could just imagine what Augusta would get out of this marriage . . .

I swallowed the rest of the coconut sweet. I hardly tasted it now and I didn't care if I was sick all over his specially woven carpet. I stood up and dragged my hand away from his and thanked him politely for his offer of marriage but said that I had to decline it.

I was quite pleased with this little speech, but it didn't work. He tried to take me in his arms. I screamed! And then I managed to get one of Mr Chippendale's elegant Chinese lacquered chairs between him and me. I held it out in front of me, and when he grabbed the seat I suddenly let go and escaped by the long windows out to the front of the house and shrieked for Augusta.

Jane, who has been writing at her desk, has just interrupted me and asked me to read out my journal to her. This is how our conversation went:

Me: 'I don't want to.'

Jane: 'Well, at least tell me what he said.'

Me: 'I don't remember exactly.'

Jane (quite shocked): 'My dear Jenny, I don't think that you take your duties as a cousin to a novelist seriously. I don't seem to get any offers of marriage myself so I'm relying on you, who seem to get them every few days. How can I write about love scenes when no one will describe them properly?'

Me: 'That was not a love scene.'

Jane: 'Doesn't matter. I could turn it into an abduction scene. That might be more fun. I think I'll write it up about you being dragged screaming into his chaise. Wait a minute, though, and I'll write a letter that you can put under Augusta's door before you flee through the darkness to find your own true love and beg his protection.'

When I read Jane's letter I giggled a bit. I was beginning to feel better about the whole day. After all, I had stood up to that man and I had stood up to Augusta, and when we came home and she complained about me to Edward-John, I had stood up to him as well. I shouted at the two of them and told them that they could not sell me off to a slave dealer. I don't think I will give this letter to Augusta though. She is too stupid to understand that it is satirical, so I will stick it into my journal.

My dear Augusta,

I am the happiest creature in the World, for I have just received an offer of marriage from Mr Wilkins . . . I hardly know how to value it enough . . . and now, my dear Augusta, I want your advice whether I should accept his offer or not . . . He is quite an old man, about two and forty, very plain, so plain that I cannot bear to look at him. He is extremely disagreeable and I hate him more than anyone else in the world. If I accept him I know that I shall be miserable all the rest of my Life for he is very ill-tempered and peevish . . .

And now my dear Augusta, I want your advice as to whether I should really accept this offer or not, bearing in mind my utter hatred and detestation of the man.

I am, my dear Augusta,

Your obliged and humble servant,

Thursday, 5 May 1791

Augusta has not been speaking to me since our talk last night. She called me downstairs just after I had written my journal and told me how stupid I was being and what a fantastic (that was her word) match this would be.

'After all,' she commented, 'the family is rather in disgrace over this business of your aunt being imprisoned.'

Once I become Mrs Stanley Wilkins, apparently, I will have everything that I could possibly desire (and HIM, of course). I kept telling her that I consider myself engaged to Captain Thomas Williams and she kept shouting me down. And then she got Edward-John in to talk to me, but that didn't work either. I was very proud of myself. When Edward-John said that Mama had left me in his charge I replied very quietly and very reasonably, 'That was because she thought you, as my brother, would do everything for my happiness.'

And he went red and said no more.

Augusta then tried to be friendly and sisterly, shaking her head and saying: 'Jenny, Jenny, you really are a very sad girl and do not know how to take care of yourself. You must let others do that for you.' And she assured me that my 'timidity' had done me no harm with dear Mr Stanley Wilkins. She even told me — these are her exact words — that: '*In those who are at all inferior, it is extremely prepossessing.'*

But I held firm, and after a few minutes' silence from both of them said that I was going up to my bedroom.

Jane has just said that she can see Harry walking down the hill past the house. He will be waiting for us at Queen's Square Gardens. We are both going to take letters. Mine is to Charles, who is recovering slowly from the chickenpox, and Jane's is to her mother, telling all about the Leigh-Perrots. She has just been down to tell Augusta that we are going out to put our letters in the post. She tells me that Edward-John is entertaining Mr Stanley Wilkins in the breakfast parlour and that Augusta and Mr Jerome Wilkins are nowhere to be seen!

'Perhaps he has abducted her in his barouche,' said Jane.

Later on Thursday, 5 May

Now it is after dinner and I have two things to write down – three things really. One is that Augusta is still not speaking to me. It's quite funny actually, because at dinner she asked Jane to tell me that I should eat cabbage. Dear, kind Franklin looked rather troubled as he glanced from one to the other of us, but Jane enjoyed it all very much, putting Augusta's questions and orders into a very formal, old-fashioned style.

'Jenny, dear, I do assure you that it is a truth universally acknowleged, that cabbage brightens the complexion.'

Or,

'My dear Jenny, your sister wishes to request you to be good enough to remove your wrist from the table and hold your fork daintily, as becomes a young lady.'

The second thing is that we met Sir Walter, the baronet who is paying attentions to Thomas's sister, Elinor. He was walking along with his eyes fixed on the pavement and muttering to himself. He did not even appear to see us, which was quite strange after his quarrel with Harry at Sydney Gardens. I wonder whether he is thinking about his card games.

The third thing is more important because it is what Harry has found out. He has now established – no doubt through the friendly chambermaid – that Sarah Raines, Miss Gregory's apprentice, who had testified that she watched Mr Filby wrap Aunt Leigh-Perrot's parcel (and that he had definitely not put any white lace in with the gown), could not have done so. Apparently a girl in the shop opposite saw Sarah Raines come out of the pastry-cook shop with a large pie on a plate – and this was well before Mrs Leigh-Perrot had emerged.

'I shall have to write another anonymous letter to the lawyer,' said Jane with satisfaction.

I asked her what she had written in the first letter, and she promised to let me have a copy to stick in my journal.

We had a peaceful evening. Jane and I played cards and Edward-John stared at a book. Augusta had gone off to have supper with a friend who was staying at the Greyhound Inn. We know that's where she went because Franklin told us that he ordered a sedan chair to take her there and to pick her up again at ten o'clock.

Now I am going to put away my journal, but before I do so I will stick in the letters that Jane wrote to the lawyer. I must say that I would have liked to see his face when he broke the wax seal and unfolded the sheet.

Honoured Sir,

You will forgive me I am sure if I conceal my identity, though 'tis a highly respected one, under the pseudonym below. I am of the gentle sex who was brought up to be shy and retiring and the thought of my name being mentioned in public is enough to cause premature death in one of my sensitivity.

Now, sir, these facts that I will enumerate bear heavily upon a case in your charge. I refer to the false accusation made by Miss Gregory against your client Mrs Leigh-Perrot.

1. A Mrs Kent bought four pairs of gloves from Miss Gregory.

2. Upon unwrapping the parcel she found five pairs of gloves.

3. Almost immediately Miss Gregory arrived and accused Mrs Kent of theft.

4. After Mrs Kent's denial, Miss Gregory threatened to summon a constable.

5. Mrs Kent then returned the gloves with a ten-pound note tucked between them.

She heard no more of the matter.
I ask you, sir, to decide whether or not this is the act of an honest woman.

Yours truly,
A Respectable Spinster and Freind to Justice

Honoured Sir,

You may remember receiving a letter from me before now.

Once again I write to you as one who worships the truth and feels that scandal and malice should always be revealed.

False evidence has been given!

Sarah Raines has been guilty of an untruth. She was in a pie shop when she purported to witness the packing-up of Mrs Leigh-Perrot's parcel.

You may also wish to know that the printer Gye is owed rent on the Gregory shop.

And also that Miss Gregory is having an affair with that man Filby.

And that Filby and Miss Gregory have tried this trick on other citizens of Bath.

Yours truly,

A Respectable Spinster and Freind to Justice

Friday, 6 May 1791

This morning a letter came for Jane to say that her parents, along with James, would be arriving on the stagecoach on Sunday. Charles was very much better, and Mrs Austen felt that she should come to support her brother and his wife.

Augusta actually spoke to me this morning. It was only to enquire whether Rosalie had washed and pressed my blue muslin gown. I nodded silently and she gave me an annoyed glance and said, 'Come now, these sullens don't become a young girl. Look up and speak up; that's what I was told when I was your age.'

'And see how generally esteemed you are now, ma'am,' said Jane in her politest manner. I choked over a piece of toast and Franklin fussed over me, bringing a glass of water and bending over me. I thought I glimpsed the shadow of a grin on his face.

Augusta just smiled sweetly and cast a glance at Edward-John to see whether he was going to say something complimentary. My brother, however, seemed in a troubled mood. He was eating very little and drinking cup after cup of coffee.

'Come now, not you too,' his wife said to him impatiently. 'Pray, let us have some news, Mr Cooper! How are things going for the unfortunate Mrs Leigh-Perrot?'

'Well,' said Edward-John, making a visible effort

to rouse himself from his depressing thoughts, 'when I was there yesterday afternoon the lawyer came with some good news. Apparently this is not the first time that the clerk, Mr Filby, has wrapped up something not paid for in a lady's parcel. The lawyer thinks that is very significant.'

'Good gracious me, Mr C., how can you be so tiresome!' Augusta's voice was so shrill that it made the glasses on the sideboard ring. She stared at Edward-John in an exasperated manner. 'Why ever didn't you tell me that last night?'

'Because you went straight out to dinner with your friends, my dear.' His voice was quiet, but it seemed to hold a meaning in it. Jane and I exchanged glances across the table.

Augusta's face seemed to colour a little. I had never seen her blush before. But then she turned on me in a most vindictive manner.

'If I've told you once, I've told you a thousand times, Jenny. Pray sit up straight. Perhaps you can't help being dwarfed, but you can at least hold yourself properly.'

'You're quite right, ma'am,' said Jane, spooning some honey on to her toast with a calm expression.

'What?' Augusta looked at her suspiciously.

'Yes, indeed, I've heard you say so again and again. I have very good hearing,' she added with a bland expression as she licked the honey spoon. 'I'm always overhearing things that are not meant for me. My mama used to say, "Little pitchers have big ears," when I was small. She made sure not to talk about private business when I was around.'

As Jane and I were going back up the stairs to our bedroom I could hear Augusta from the parlour saying loudly to Edward-John, 'I'm not sure that I am too impressed with the manners of that Austen girl. She seems to me to have all the vulgarity of her mother combined with the slyness of her father.'

When we got into the bedroom I looked anxiously at Jane to see if this had hurt her, but to my surprise there was a broad smile on her face and her eyes were sparkling.

'There's some mystery here,' she hissed. 'Who was she having dinner with yesterday?'

I looked blank and she said impatiently, 'Go on, Jenny; think! Who's staying at the Greyhound Inn – and don't say Harry . . .'

And then suddenly something about her expression made me think. My mouth opened, began to form a name and then shut again.

Jane nodded.

'The Wilkins brothers!' I gasped.

Jane shook her head vigorously. 'Not the Wilkins *brothers* – remember, Mr Stanley is reserved for you, you lucky, lucky girl. No, I would guess that she dined with Mr Jerome Wilkins.'

I must say that first of all I was flooded with horror. What a terrible thing for Edward-John to have a wife who would dine alone with another man. But Jane's expression made me conceal my feelings. After all, why should I care about Augusta?

Jane was looking more than pleased though. She looked positively elated — with that expression that she wears when her brain is working fast. She went over to the window and began to mutter, 'Harry, Harry, where are you? Come on, Harry!' drumming her fingers on the glass all the while.

'Here he is,' she said after a minute.

I was glad to see him and to distract Jane from Augusta. I felt a bit uncomfortable talking about my brother the clergyman and his wife. However much I loathed Augusta, somehow I just could not imagine her doing something like that.

But then, as I was putting on my bonnet and cloak, I remembered the scene in Mr Jerome Wilkins's house. After I ran from the parlour it had taken a long time for Augusta to appear. Several maids and the butler had come through the front door and stared in alarm before she had arrived to see her disgraceful sister-in-law weeping hysterically on the front lawn. I had been so upset and so frightened at the time that I had not really considered Augusta's strange behaviour.

Why did she take so long to appear?

And what had she been doing in Mr Jerome Wilkins's house?

Harry greeted us with an air of quiet satisfaction

when we met him beside the garden in Queen's Square. He had already been to see the Leigh-Perrots — 'They keep early hours,' he said briefly, though I guessed that he wanted to have the most up-to-date information for Jane. The couple had been in very good humour. Mr Leigh-Perrot had engaged four lawyers from London, and letters testifying to the good character of Mrs Leigh-Perrot had come in from all quarters. The trial had been set for the following Monday, 9 May, and they were hoping that their ordeal would soon be over and they would be back in their own comfortable house on that very night.

I asked Harry whether he thought that it would really end happily or if they were pretending in order to keep their spirits up. I thought this was the sort of thing that a devoted husband and wife might say to each other, without really believing it. Harry tried to say that he thought it would, but he has a very open, honest face and after a few words he fell silent.

'Why shouldn't it?' asked Jane in an annoyed tone, interpreting his silence as I had done.

'Well, there's talk at the Greyhound that your aunt turned red and then white when Miss Gregory found the white lace in her parcel,' said Harry. He watched Jane's face anxiously before adding, 'They say that Sir Vicary Gibbs, the prosecuting lawyer, will make full use of that.'

'Nonsense,' said Jane. 'Anyone would look uncomfortable if they were accused of stealing. I wish I were a lawyer. I'd answer him.'

'The important thing is the jury,' said Harry. 'If they like Mrs Leigh-Perrot, and believe her, then they will acquit; if they don't . . . well, they won't.'

Harry had certainly changed, I thought, watching him gaze at Jane's worried face. He adored her, that was obvious, but these days he did not hesitate to disagree with her. However, he was very protective of her and did not like to see her troubled. Now he was anxious to put her mind at ease.

'Perhaps you could write to her,' he suggested. 'She definitely doesn't want you to come to see her, but you could write and offer to help her with her submission. The lawyer arrived this morning when I was there. On my way out I heard him tell her that she will have an opportunity in court to make a submission and that he always advises his clients to write it out beforehand.'

I could see a struggle going on in Jane's face. On the one hand, she would love to do this, I know, and I could just imagine how funny it would be when she had written it. But on the other hand this was a serious matter. She briefly told Harry that she would think about it, and then changed the subject.

'Harry, we need your help about something else,' she said. 'It's something about Jenny – something to ensure her everlasting happiness with the man whom she loves.' She delivered these words so dramatically that a passing lady escorted by a middle-aged maid passing by, gave her an icy glance.

Harry flushed a little and I went bright red.

'Jane!' I said.

'You know that terrible sister-in-law of Jenny's who is forcing her brother to refuse permission for the marriage – well, I was thinking that if we knew something about dear Augusta, something that might, shall we say, bring her round to understanding Jenny's point of view, well . . .'

'You're not thinking of doing a spot of blackmail yourself, are you?' enquired Harry with his attractive grin. 'Bath is having a bad effect on you. What would your father say?'

'I just thought you might have noticed her arriving by sedan chair at the Greyhound Inn last evening,' said Jane with her most demure air.

Harry was deeply embarrassed, I could see. He kicked at the railing around the gardens with a well-worn riding boot. Eventually he said in a reserved tone, 'Yes, she did come to have dinner with a gentleman.'

'Private parlour?' queried Jane with a lift of her eyebrow.

Again Harry gave the railings a few gentle kicks, but eventually he nodded.

Jane understood his feelings. Afterwards she said to me that all boys are like that – they hate telling tales. Jane is an authority on boys – as well as having her own brothers, she has been brought up with Mr Austen's pupils filling the house for most of the year. Quickly she changed the conversation back to discussing whether or not she should draft something for Mrs Leigh-Perrot's submission to the jury of twelve men at her trial. Harry was very enthusiastic about how well she would do that. He remembered, rather tenderly, I thought, a story that she had written when she was only eleven and how clever he had thought it. By the time he left us to exercise his horse, he looked quite happy again.

'Let's go and talk to Eliza about it,' said Jane as soon as he left us.

Eliza was still in bed, her hair under her nightcap still in its curling papers. She looked blissfully happy as she sipped her hot chocolate and nibbled her toast.

'Dear Phylly is out,' she said. 'She's gone to the early-morning service at St Swithin's and when that is over she will go to the post office. She spent yesterday writing letters.'

'Shame about that,' said Jane, sitting on the foot of the bed. 'Think what fun you would be having going ten times around Queen's Square Gardens in the fresh morning air, instead of lying there in your bed drinking chocolate.'

Eliza shuddered dramatically, but made no reply. One nice thing about Eliza is that she is very loyal to Phylly. Apparently Phylly used to write to her once a week during all the years that she was in France. Though Jane said to me privately, once, that was Phylly's way of tormenting Eliza. She knew that her cousin was too busy with her social life to write back more than once a month, and so Eliza had to apologize a million times to Phylly for the delay in writing. Phylly probably deeply enjoyed making her feel guilty, according to Jane.

'We wanted to ask your advice,' said Jane, taking a bonbon from a silver box on the dressing table and offering one to me also.

Between the two of us, we told her about Harry's latest news and his suggestion that Jane help her aunt with the submission to be read out to the jury. I had started to get quite enthusiastic about that idea. There was no doubt that Jane could put things into words very well, and Eliza would be able to tactfully tone down the exaggerations a little.

But Eliza disappointed us. She seemed unlike her usual flamboyant self – very, very cautious and cir-cumspect – very wary about interfering in the Leigh-Perrot affair.

'I think, Jane *chérie*, we should leave your aunt and uncle to work these things out themselves. They are both people of the world; they will know the right things to do. They have legal advice. They will be well looked after.'

We were both a bit taken aback by this, and to cover the awkward moment Jane began to tell Eliza about Augusta and her dinner at the Greyhound Inn. Immediately Eliza's eyes began to sparkle. '*Oh là là*,' she breathed. '*Quel scandale!*' In her excitement she spilt her hot chocolate on the silver tray.

'And listen to what happened to Jenny,' went on Jane, competently taking the tray and depositing the spilt chocolate into the slop pail.

I told Eliza all about how Augusta left me alone at Mr Stanley Wilkins's house and how she went into Mr Jerome Wilkins's house. Jane joined in with the account of how Mr Stanley had proposed to me and then tried to ravish me – 'ravish' was Jane's word and it made me feel like a heroine in one of Mr Richardson's books.

'*Alors!*' was Eliza's comment. She slipped her dressing gown over her nightdress and threw back the covers.

'We were thinking, Jenny and me, that we might hint that we know something – make her worried. What do you think about that, Eliza?'

Eliza powdered her face and then carefully outlined her eyes with something called kohl, one of the many gifts brought from India by her godfather, Warren Hastings. Then she took from a jewelled box a tiny black patch, which she placed to conceal a minute pimple on her left cheek. Only when that was done to her satisfaction did she reply.

'*Mais non.* Leave this to me.'

Quickly she pulled out a sheet of superfine writing paper, dipped her quill into the ink pot and began to write. The letter was short and soon folded and sealed with a drop of scarlet sealing wax. Then Eliza wrote the address on the outside.

'An invitation for your dear sister-in-law to a little tea-drinking tomorrow afternoon,' she said as she gave me the letter.

'Oh, but we want to be there,' complained Jane.

'I don't,' I said. 'Anyway, Augusta will say nothing if we are around.'

'Quite true,' observed Eliza tranquilly. 'I have asked her to bring you both, but I will send you out of the room to fetch some *petits gâteaux* from the pastry-cook. You will no doubt be able to listen well from the little kitchen and will arrive with the sweetmeats after I have finished talking about my daily visit to the baths and inviting Augusta to join with me in this health-giving process.'

'I'm sure that you never visited the baths in your life,' said Jane with conviction.

'But, *chérie*,' cried Eliza, 'of course I did. How else could I turn faint on the way home last Thursday and have to drop into the Greyhound Inn for a small glass of brandy to restore me?'

Jane has just asked me whether I have put in the cleverness of Eliza in finding an excuse for knowing about Augusta's visit to the Greyhound Inn, and when I told her that I had she said that she is pleased that Harry is not involved.

'In fact, I think I'll tell him the story about Eliza feeling faint after her bath and then he won't worry about being dishonourable. Harry is so very honour-able himself that he would never suspect Eliza of making the whole thing up.'

Saturday, 7 May 1791

At about four o'clock today we went out to visit Eliza. Augusta led the way, wearing her new and very magnificent purple pelisse and carrying her immense fur muff. Ever since I have come to Bath and stared in the windows of the shops with Jane I have begun to realize how much Augusta's clothes must cost. Today she was also wearing a brand-new pair of yellow nankin boots and carrying a matching reticule. Her walking gown was of silk and her immensely large hat, crowned with its luxuriant bunch of floating ostrich feathers, was of the finest velvet.

Eliza greeted us warmly, ushering us rapidly through her small narrow hallway and into the drawing room, with its views over the square. There was something different about the room and for a moment I could not think what it was. Then Jane's eyes met mine and I realized the plan.

At one end of the drawing room there was a large hatch with wooden doors that could be opened to hand food in from the tiny kitchen beyond. Today this hatch was screened off. Eliza had hung across it a hideous piece of embroidery, stitched by Phylly, with strange-looking flowers around the outside and a large text scrolled across the middle:

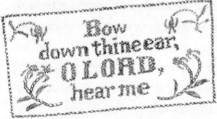

'Don't take off your cloaks and bonnets, girls,' Eliza was saying with well-acted haste. 'Something terrible has happened. The pastry-cook has not delivered the *petits gâteaux* for our tea. You must run down to Bath Street and fetch them. Here is the key for you to let yourselves back in again. Go quickly – *Madame* and I will entertain ourselves with gossip until you return.'

In a moment she had pushed us out of the room with a quick wink and a nod towards the kitchen. We waited until she had gone back in, then walked noisily, tramping on the floor, towards the hall door, opened it, shut it with a bang and then crept back into the kitchen, where we were not surprised to see a great array of little cakes spread out on pretty plates. Jane tiptoed towards the hatch, whose wooden doors were clipped open, and I followed her. We both perched on the table there and prepared to listen. With just the screen between the drawing room and us, we could hear every word spoken.

Eliza, I realized, was playing the part of a lifetime. Sophisticated lady-about-town, deeply admiring of Augusta's fashion sense, full of deprecating little jokes about 'admirers', sure that Augusta had many of these . . .

'We don't take any notice of men, do we?' she said to the rather impressed Augusta, who judging by her giggled response to '*agréables*', was flattered to be counted as a woman of the world by the sophisticated Comtesse de Feuillide, who was important enough to be invited to private balls at the Crescent by a *princesse*.

And then Eliza mentioned the baths. Perhaps she and Augusta could go there together one day, she suggested. Augusta was not keen, pretended that she could not go without Mr Cooper's approval. Eliza laughed at the idea of a mere man having anything to say on the matter. However, she told her how right she was.

'La,' she said. 'I do declare that the last time I went there — what with all this affair of wearing a canvas shift and the smell of the water, *oh là là* . . . and the crowds that were there . . . I felt quite unwell. In fact, on the way home — this was last Thursday — I felt so faint that I had the sedan chairmen stop at the Greyhound Inn to get me a glass of brandy. I fancy you may have seen me there . . .'

There was a long silence. I wished that I could pluck aside Phylly's embroidery to see Augusta's face. I almost thought that I had heard a quick gasp, and then Eliza spoke again, her tone light and teasing.

'Don't worry, *chère madame*,' she said. '*Les dames*,

they must have fun, *hein*? He is rich, this Mr Wilkins, *n'est-ce pas*?'

Augusta gave a shaky laugh. 'I've heard that you are a great flirt,' she said, trying to match Eliza's lightness of tone, but only succeeding in sounding vulgar and stupid, as usual.

Eliza sighed. 'Ah, flirtation!' she said, sounding deeply sincere. '*Hélas, mon amie*, I am too old for all that sort of thing now. But you, that is another affair. You are young, you must amuse yourself.'

Then there was a short silence. I imagined Eliza tapping Augusta on the arm with her fan and exchanging smiles with her. Eliza is only a few years older than Augusta, but my sister-in-law was probably quite happy to be taken for a young woman.

And then Eliza spoke again.

'However, permit me to give you a little advice. Have your fun, but be careful. Above all, be careful of sharp young eyes and sharp little ears. Keep them sweet, my dear. Don't set them against you.'

Still Augusta said nothing. Jane was mouthing the words 'little pitchers'. I shook my head at her. How was Eliza going to manage this? I wondered.

Eliza herself had no doubts though. Her voice was strong and confident.

'It was a mistake, *mon amie*, to make an enemy of your husband's sister and her cousin, *bien sûr*. They come to me, you understand, with stories . . . You must marry Jenny off. You don't want her back with you in your house, do you? Accompanying you on every visit? Talking to her clever little cousin about you? No, no, you don't want that. Give her what she wants – let her marry the captain.'

'She is so without ambition. I could have made a wonderful match for her with a very wealthy man,' sighed Augusta, but there was something about her voice, a sort of respectful sweetness, that made me think that she had understood the point. Her own flirtation – or whatever it was with that abominable man, the slave dealer – was more important to her than thwarting me and my hopes for the future. She had no doubt given up the thought of marrying me off to Mr Stanley Wilkins. He probably didn't ever want to see me again after the way I disgraced him in front of his servants and neighbours at Bristol.

'Talk to your husband tonight,' advised Eliza. 'He will be pleased to think that you have Jenny's interests at heart and that you just want the girl's happiness.'

I imagined a quick wink from Eliza at this point. I held my breath. Was it going to work?

Another deep sigh from Augusta. 'I suppose you are right,' she said. 'It's not as if she were a beauty or anything like that. I hoped to make a match for her – a very advantageous match, but her manners . . . her clumsiness . . . her stupidity – well, the gentleman will probably no longer be interested if she behaves again as she did a few days ago.'

'You have done your best,' said Eliza sedately. 'Now get her off your hands, before the captain too changes his mind. No one would blame him as you have refused his offer. Let her write to him as quickly as possible. *Alors*, tell me, are you going to Lady Russell's party next week? And have you heard the latest *on-dit* about her young admirer?'

Jane put her finger to her lips and slid carefully off the table. I followed her and we tiptoed down the hall. There was little fear of discovery – gales of laughter were coming from Eliza's drawing room. We edged the hall door open quietly and went down the stairs towards the front door. After waiting for a while we returned noisily, went straight into the kitchen and appeared in the drawing room with plates of small cakes in our hands and demure expressions on our faces.

But now it is ten o'clock at night and Augusta has not spoken to Edward-John. Or else she has spoken and he was unwilling to grant his permission . . .

What is happening????

Sunday, 8 May 1791

Dear Thomas,

I hope this letter will be in time for the small fast ship, but I fear that it won't. I told you about my aunt Mrs Leigh-Perrot and the accusation of shoplifting from Miss Gregory's shop in Bath. Well, she is in great danger. She will be tried tomorrow at Taunton Assizes. A boy - a fourteen-year-old boy - was found guilty there last week and has been hanged.

Until I heard of that today, I wasn't so worried. Jane and I hoped that rumours of Miss Gregory stuffing spare gloves - or lace in my aunt's case - into baskets and then blackmailing clients would serve to acquit our aunt, but now I am frightened.

Most people believe that my aunt will not be hanged, but many think that she will be transported to Australia. She'll die if that happens. Only the young and strong can survive that year-long voyage. And then to live in that strange, uninhabited place - wear chains and be treated as a common criminal!

Today Mr and Mrs Austen, with James, Jane's eldest brother, arrived off the stagecoach at midday. They want to be present at the trial of Mrs Leigh-Perrot and to assure her that her relatives believe in her innocence.

Mr Austen was his usual polite self to Edward-John and Augusta, but Mrs Austen was quite offhand with them. She barely nodded in reply to their greetings and made sure that she was the one who gave orders to Franklin and to the chambermaid about their luggage. James and Edward-John were not friendly. In fact, in Jane's expression, they eyed each other like two rival dogs. When we went up to our bedroom, Jane told me that her brothers Henry and Frank had been taking bets as to which of the two eldest nephews of Mr Leigh-Perrot would succeed to his fortune.

It was a horrible day today. The three Austens were tired, and Augusta had a headache and retired to her room. No one felt cheerful, with the terrible prospect of Mrs Leigh-Perrot being found guilty looming over us.

Tomorrow morning early we will all go to Taunton by coach.

I'm going to post this letter now and then I will write again and tell you the news about the trial.

I wish I could hear from you. I wish I knew that all the love that I sent you has arrived.

Much love, my darling, from your Jenny

The Day of Mrs Leigh-Perrot's Trial

I'm so sleepy that it feels like the middle of the night. I stumble out of bed while Rosalie wakes Jane. Neither of us speaks while we wash and dress.

Downstairs James is yawning over a cup of strong coffee. Mr and Mrs Austen have finished their breakfast and are waiting in the hall; she is dressed in a stout cloak and he in an old-fashioned greatcoat with many capes over his shoulders. Edward-John appears and says guiltily that Augusta is too ill to come. Jane looks sidelong at me but is too sleepy to make a comment.

Then we are walking down the hill to the White Hart Inn where we will get the stagecoach. The trial is not to be at Bath, but in another town called Taunton. In the coach I keep sleeping and waking with a start and sleeping again. James and his parents are playing cards, and Jane is sound asleep with her head on her father's shoulder.

'Taunton!' shouts the coachman, and we are here at last.

We get out, stretch our legs, eat a second breakfast with some wonderful tea and scorched toast, and then we are on our way up through the town until we reach the courthouse.

'It's in the castle,' says Jane, looking up excitedly. 'It's where Judge Jeffreys condemned all those two hundred men to be hanged in the time of King Charles II. He did that at the Bloody Assizes, you know.'

'Jane, be quiet,' says Mrs Austen fiercely, and I think it rather tactless of Jane to talk in this way. By the end of this day we will know the fate of our own aunt. I just can't believe that anyone could hang an old lady – even if she did take that piece of lace! And would transportation be any better? Could she stand the journey of a year out to Australia and then have to live as a convict? I start to shiver and pull my cloak closely around me.

The court is held in the great hall of the castle. There is a sort of raised platform at the end with a large chair for the judge. Then there is one boxed-off enclosure for the accused and another larger one where the twelve members of the jury are already seated. At the end of the platform, but at floor level, is a long table where the lawyers in wigs and long black gowns are sitting. Beside this is the witness box.

The hall is almost full – James says that he thinks there must be about two thousand people there. Mrs Austen takes a piece of paper and a pencil from her reticule, scribbles a note and tells James to take it to Mrs Leigh-Perrot's lawyer, Mr Jekyll.

In a couple of minutes he comes over and shakes hands with us all and finds us chairs at the side of the hall, quite near to the dock. He tells us that there are four of them, four lawyers, all to defend Mrs Leigh-Perrot. He speaks confidently, but when he goes back to the table and whispers to his three colleagues I think that they all look worried.

Then Mr Leigh-Perrot comes in by himself. He looks very old, and his gout is troubling him. He walks with a stick. Mr Jekyll jumps up to greet him and takes him over to a seat beside us, whispering loudly that this is going to be a famous case and that most of the big London papers have sent journalists to cover it. He points out the journalist from the *London Times*, standing leaning against the wall nearby, but Mr Leigh-Perrot ignores him. He hardly even notices us as he stumbles along. He has cut himself shaving this morning and his hair doesn't look brushed. His eyes have huge pouches under them as if he hasn't slept properly for a long time. Mrs Austen jumps up, hugs him, and gets him to sit down beside her. I notice that she holds his hand. This brother and sister are very fond of each other, I think, and I look at Edward-John sitting at the end of the row. He hasn't spoken one word to me today.

And then Mrs Leigh-Perrot is brought in from a door at the back of the platform. She is dressed very stylishly in her dark green pelisse, a fine muslin white scarf swathed around her neck, and a brand-new elaborate headdress in green velvet – not exactly a bonnet – is gathered in a sort of band around the front and covers her head, flowing down to her shoulders at the back in a very elegant style. She must have sent for this especially to wear at the trial. I had never seen it before, but Rosalie had been up and down to the prison with clothes for her mistress.

'Isn't she brave?' whispers Jane admiringly, and I nod.

Suddenly I feel tears streaming down my cheeks.

I hadn't realized quite how fond I have become of the elderly couple. They have been so good and kind to Jane and myself, buying us the new ball gowns and trying to arrange my marriage for me. I don't know whom I pity the most: Mrs Leigh-Perrot, erect and stately, bowing her head slightly to the jury and then taking her place, still standing, in the prisoner's box, or her poor husband, convulsed with sorrow at the sight of her.

And then the judge comes in. '*Mr Justice Lawrence,*' whispers James to his mother, and everyone rises until he takes his seat. Mrs Leigh-Perrot gives him a stately bow, rather as if he has come to one of her stylish receptions at the Paragon in Bath, and he bows back quite courteously. He takes his seat and then whispers to a court official, who comes over to Mrs Leigh-Perrot and obviously tells her to sit down.

'That's a good sign,' whispers Jane in my ear. 'He can't have fallen in love with her so quickly, so perhaps he thinks that she is innocent.'

Then the trial begins. Sir Vicary Gibbs opens the case for the prosecution. He is a small man, very small, perhaps only an inch or so bigger than I am – and I am only five foot two inches! Jane whispers in my ear that James told her Sir Vicary is called Sir Vinegar because he is so sour. He does seem sour, being very sarcastic and witty about rich ladies who think it is fun to steal from poor shopkeepers. Everyone turns to look at Mrs Leigh-Perrot when he says that, but not a muscle in her face moves as she sits there, quietly attentive. I admire her courage.

I think I would prefer to die rather than to sit there and have that horrible man say such terrible things about me.

'I will bring witnesses to prove that this woman stole lace worth over nineteen shillings,' he says loudly, and he reminds the jury to make sure that they are not in any way influenced by the wealth and rank of the woman in the dock.

I see Mr Leigh-Perrot shudder when he hears his wife, the heiress of vast estates in Barbados, called a woman. I don't suppose that she has ever been called that in her life before. She was probably called a lady from the time she was two years old.

However, I also notice that the foreman of the jury looks a bit offended at that piece of advice. Perhaps that was not such a clever idea from the chief prosecutor.

But then Miss Gregory, the first witness, is so precise and seems to remember everything so well that I begin to feel quite worried again. I hadn't even noticed her going downstairs for her dinner, leaving Mr Filby to wrap the parcel and the apprentice Sarah Raines to tidy away the cards of lace – though perhaps that happened after Jane and I had left the shop.

Then there is Mr Filby – again with the air of having learned everything by heart. He even admits that he lives with Miss Gregory, though they are not married. I look at the jury when he says that, but they don't look as though they care. And then Mr Bond, one of Aunt Leigh-Perrot's lawyers, rises to cross-examine Mr Filby. He makes a very good job of it, I think, and I feel quite excited. Mrs Kent and Mrs Blagrave are there in court and he bows towards them when he refers to them.

'It seems as if you are in the habit of wrapping up extra goods in your customers' parcels,' he says to Filby, and the man doesn't quite know what to reply. In the end he says that he perhaps has made the occasional mistake.

'But these ladies told you of your error,' says Mr Bond. 'What about others? What happens when the customer does not bring back the goods? It's not surprising, is it, that the shop does not make a profit. Or do you perhaps do it on purpose so that the shop *will* make a profit . . . ?'

I see Jane give a quick nod of her head when he says that. Her letter has been carefully read and the bit about Miss Gregory being behind with the rent for the printer, Mr Gye, has been noticed.

And then Sarah Raines the apprentice gives her statement, which is that she is sure that Mr Filby did not wrap up any white lace in Mrs Leigh-Perrot's parcel. Mr Jekyll cross-examines her and she gets into a great muddle. The judge tries to help her, and unfortunately she improves then and goes back to the statement that she has prepared.

But then Mr Jekyll calls the shop girl who is prepared to swear that she saw Sarah Raines come out of the pastry-cook shop with a large pie on a plate and that Mrs Leigh-Perrot was coming out of Miss Gregory's shop at the same time.

'So it looks as though you were not present while the parcel was being wrapped, doesn't it?' says Mr Jekyll with a sweet smile, and Sarah Raines just nods.

'Oh, well done, Harry,' whispers Jane in my ear. The jurymen are all sitting up and exchanging glances with each other.

And then Miss Gregory is recalled and now it is the turn of another of the lawyers from London, a Mr Dallas this time. He has a very sharp manner and seems a bit of a bully, shaking his finger at her whenever she stumbles over her story or seems not to be saying the same thing as before.

'So Mrs Leigh-Perrot, her parcel in her basket, was just strolling past your shop like a lady with nothing on her mind after the supposed theft, is that what you are saying?

Miss Gregory does not reply.

'Come now,' he says, 'let's get the truth out of you. It's a simple question. Is the answer yes or no?'

'Answer the question, please,' says the judge.

'She was passing the shop, but she wasn't like a person with nothing on her mind and she didn't have her parcel in her basket either; she had it hidden under her cloak.' Miss Gregory stares at the lawyer triumphantly.

'That's a lie! She wasn't wearing a cloak. She was wearing a pelisse, the one that she has on now!' I can only admire Jane's courage. And her quick-wittedness! She stands up very straight, ignoring the faces of the rows in front of us that turn round to look at her. Her clear voice rings through the whole courtroom. Mrs Leigh-Perrot, of course, is not allowed to say anything in her own defence.

There is a murmur of sound as two thousand people turn to a neighbour and comment. Heads are craned, trying to see who has spoken.

'Silence in court!' The official almost yells it and the judge frowns. Mrs Austen, to my surprise, gives an approving grin and squeezes Jane's arm. Mr Dallas from London looks now like a hunting dog on the trail of something interesting. He gives a half-glance down at the table of lawyers, and in a moment Mr Pell – another of the London lawyers – is on his feet.

'With your lordship's permission . . . approach my client . . . a matter of ascertaining the facts . . .' Mr Dallas is almost breathless, and Mr Justice Lawrence gives a reluctant nod.

Mr Pell hardly waits for this. He is on his feet and up the steps to the platform almost before Mr Dallas begs permission. He bends over Mrs Leigh-Perrot, whispers a question, gets the reply and then gives a tiny nod in the direction of his superior.

'And so she had the parcel tucked under her cloak, did she?' asks Mr Dallas with the smiling expression of a cat looking at a mouse that thinks it can escape.

Miss Gregory nods, but her expression shows that she feels she has been trapped.

'But we have a witness who claims my client was not wearing a cloak that day,' says Mr Dallas gently, 'that she was wearing the very same pelisse that she wears today. What do you say to that?'

Miss Gregory looks uncomfortable. She looks around

the court. She looks at Mr Vicary Gibbs, who has a savage expression on his face; she looks at her lover, Mr Filby, but no one can help her.

'I may have been mistaken,' she says. 'Perhaps Mrs Leigh-Perrot wore a pelisse that day, but the parcel was under it.'

'Perhaps, my lord, I may ask Mrs Leigh-Perrot to stand up for the benefit of the jury?' Mr Dallas asks the question very carefully, very deferentially, but his expression shows that he scents victory.

The judge nods. Our aunt stands up straight and tall, looking magnificent. The pelisse had been made by the finest dressmaker in Bath and it fits her like a second skin, nipped in at the waist, tight across the stomach, well-fitted around the hips – there is no possibility that a parcel containing a gown could have been concealed under it.

'No further questions,' says Mr Dallas with a deep bow to the judge.

And then Mr Vicary Gibbs sums up for the prosecution – and does his best with the threads of evidence that have been left to him.

And Mr Bond sums up for the defence, making full use of all the uncertainty of Miss Gregory's evidence, of the improbability that the apprentice Sarah Raines was speaking the truth, and of the testimony that Mr Filby has tried the same trick on other customers. He hints vaguely at Mr Filby's character as the lover of an unmarried woman, but does not labour the point.

269

After that Mr Pell, the junior lawyer, reads out statements from many noble people and also from ordinary citizens of Bath, swearing that Mrs Leigh-Perrot's character is of the highest and that she has always been very strict about all money matters and has never left a bill unpaid or shown any moral laxity (that was from Lord Braybroke).

And then it was the turn of our aunt to read out her statement.

Surprisingly for a woman with a strong, clear voice, she begins in a very low, timid tone which we cannot hear. The judge, seeing everyone straining ears from the hall, sends the court official scurrying over to Mr Jekyll, the lawyer. He goes and stands protectively next to his client and repeats each sentence. It is a good speech, cleverly designed to appeal to the jury. It represents the strong-minded, authoritative Mrs Leigh-Perrot as a gentle, God-fearing, law-abiding woman (but of course blessed with all that could be desired in the way of riches) whose greatest concern is the injury that this false accusation, arrest and imprisonment has caused to her sick husband.

'How could I,' she says and Mr Jekyll repeats her words in his beautiful sonorous voice, 'lose all recollection of the situation I hold in society – to hazard, for this meanness, my character and reputation, or to endanger the health and peace of mind of a husband for whom I would die?'

Poor Mr Leigh-Perrot sobs loudly at this and so does Mr Pell, the junior lawyer. Mr Jekyll looks approvingly at his colleague and pats his own eyes with a very large, very white muslin handkerchief. The judge looks grave and the jury sympathetic. Jane nudges me but preserves a serious face, gazing intently at her aunt. Several sobs rise from the courtroom and I notice the journalist from *The Times* scribbling frantically in his notebook.

And then the judge sums up. I'm beginning to get a bit worried by all the long phrases about the law of the land being the same for a person of wealth as for the meanest wretch (the journalist from *The Times* wrote that one down) and how Miss Gregory's evidence is corroborated by Mr Filby whereas Mrs Leigh-Perrot has not been able to produce any witnesses to prove she did not take the lace.

'*However* . . .' When the judge says that word I begin to breathe again. He takes a long time to make his point but he does tell the jury that if anything makes them distrust the evidence of the shopkeeper then they should bear in mind the excellent character of the accused, a character that has been attested by some of the highest in the country, he goes on, no doubt having in mind Lord Braybroke.

And now the jury are retiring. There is a buzz of conversation when the twelve men file out.

'I give them fifteen minutes,' says the *Times* journalist to a colleague. He speaks just as the court official calls for order, and his voice sounds quite loudly through the courtroom. Mr Austen takes out his timepiece and Jane and I keep peering at it. Mr Leigh-Perrot sobs into his hands. Mrs Austen pats his shoulder. Jane told me last night that our uncle has resolved to sell all his property in England, his house in Bath as well as his estate in Berkshire, and move out to Australia if my aunt is convicted and deported. The thought of this brings tears to my eyes.

The time goes very slowly.

But less than ten minutes has gone by when a sudden bustle and a rising storm of whispers make every eye go to the door at the back of the platform. It opens, and the twelve men file in and take their places in the jury box. The silence is intense. Mrs Leigh-Perrot's face is like that of a statue carved from stone. I dare not look at her poor husband. It seems an eternity to me – what must it be like for them?

And then the judge asks the jury whether they have agreed on a verdict and the foreman tells him that they have. Another question, and then the magic words: '*Not Guilty*'.

And the whole courtroom erupts in clapping, exclaiming, laughing. Mrs Leigh-Perrot stays quite still, with her eyes fixed on the judge; the court official struggles to silence everyone. The judge tries to do the same, and manages to tell the prisoner that she is free to go. She makes a stately bow to him and another to the gentlemen of the jury, who all look as pleased as though she were their favourite aunt.

And then Mr Jekyll escorts her to where her husband sits. He is so overcome that he cannot move.

It seems as if the whole courtroom wishes to congratulate Mrs Leigh-Perrot. People throng around her –

even complete strangers are shaking her by the hand and patting her on the back. The wife of the prison governor comes to congratulate her and tells her how much they have felt for her in her troubles and advises her to 'wrap up warm and take a few glasses of port wine every day'.

It takes a good half-hour before we can make our way back to the coach. I fall asleep on the way home.

Wednesday, 11 May 1791

Today has been an odd day. Everyone is so relieved that the jury found Mrs Leigh-Perrot innocent, but it is almost as if some great weight is still over the household. Every time the doorbell rang Franklin seemed to jump, and even though it was invariably bunches of flowers or messages for Mrs Leigh-Perrot, he still did not relax. Augusta declared that she had a migraine and went off to bed, Edward-John went out for a walk and Mr Austen and James went to book tickets for the stagecoach home.

James had told some great news to the Leigh-Perrots over breakfast. He is engaged to be married to Anne Montgomery, General Montgomery's only child. 'Quite a fortune with her,' Mrs Austen had whispered to her sister-in-law and Mrs Leigh-Perrot smiled approvingly at James.

Jane and I wondered whether to go to the post inn with James, but then thought that might seem a bit heartless, so we hovered and didn't quite know what to do.

My aunt and uncle were restless too, moving from room to room, upstairs and downstairs, almost as if they could not believe that they now had the freedom to do what they wanted and to go where they wished.

It was Mrs Austen who put a stop to this. When we all sat down to dinner at three o'clock, she suddenly announced:

'My dear sister, what you must do is give a party. Allow all your friends to come and congratulate you. And hear of your experiences. Get it all over and done with in one evening. Invite everyone!'

'What a wonderful idea! Let's have it tomorrow.' Her brother beamed at Mrs Austen, and his wife was equally struck.

Everyone rushed through dinner. Eliza arrived just when it was finished and gave her enthusiastic support. Jane and I were seated at a small Pembroke table and set to work filling out invitation cards from a list that Mrs Leigh-Perrot produced from her desk. Two of the maids were employed in taking bundles of them all over the town while Mr Leigh-Perrot and Franklin decided on the menu and a long list of delicious food with pies of every description. Pastry-cooks, wine merchants, flower shops, musicians – all were pressed into the service of this impromptu party.

'No one will come at such short notice,' said Mrs Leigh-Perrot.

'Nonsense, everyone will come. They'll all want to tell their friends that they've seen you and heard your stories about the jail,' said Mrs Austen bluntly.

'*Chère madame*, you are a *cause célèbre*!' said Eliza fervently.

'Is there anyone you girls want to ask?' Mrs Leigh-Perrot is in very good humour with us. While pretending to berate Mrs Austen for taking two such 'innocent young women' into the courthouse, I think that she was touched by how the Austen family had rallied around her. Jane has become a great favourite with her — I think that both the Leigh-Perrots were amazed at her courage at speaking out at court. They both thanked her very earnestly. I noticed that they barely spoke to Augusta!

'What about Harry Digweed?' suggested Jane.

'Harry Digweed!' exclaimed her mother. 'Is he still in Bath? Goodness gracious, what on earth is he doing hanging around a place like this? I thought that boy was wedded to farming.'

She must have noticed something in Jane's tone because her eyes narrowed and she exchanged glances with Mrs Leigh-Perrot. And both of them stared at Jane, who looked unperturbed and started to fill out the next card on the list before her.

'Harry Digweed — of course, we must ask him! He was like a son to us during that terrible time!' Mr Leigh-Perrot was emphatic. Now James was the one to look put out. And Edward-John. Neither of them liked to hear such praise of Harry Digweed.

'He's a nice boy — a playmate of my boys,' said Mrs Austen, making it sound as if Harry was about ten years old.

'And what about you, my dear?' Mrs Leigh-Perrot looked across at me.

I felt a little hesitant, but I had promised Thomas to keep an eye on his sister so I asked her whether she would invite Admiral Williams and his niece, and she was very happy to do that, writing out the card herself instantly.

'Dear Aunt,' said Jane, after we had written for what seemed like hours, 'pray allow Jenny and me to deliver some of those cards.'

I was on my feet as soon as she said that. I could guess what she felt. After the tension of that terrible day in Taunton we just wanted to get back to normal again and to run down the hill streets of Bath and laugh and joke as usual.

'Why didn't you ask Newton Wallop?' I said to Jane as we walked through Queen's Square, neatly avoiding Phylly, whom we spotted on her way up to St Swithin's church. I was reminded of Newton because I could see him in the distance, coming up Barton Street.

'He's going . . .' began Jane and then stopped. Newton was waving violently at us, holding up a piece of paper. It looked like a letter.

'What are you up to, Jane?' he called when we came within speaking distance. 'Is this from one of your novels?'

Now I could see the paper. It was, indeed, a letter. The address:

THE HONOURABLE NEWTON WALLOP
YORK HOUSE INN
BATH

was written in large, straggling capital letters. Jane and I stared at it.

'And I had to pay postage on it,' continued Newton. 'Come on, Jane; don't pretend to be an innocent. Only you write letters like this.'

Jane took the letter and I peered over her shoulder. This is what we read – I've stuck it into my journal here.

Sir,

You are young and the young are often imprudent. Allow a person who admires your noble family to give you some advice. Pray shun the company of such young women as Miss Jane Austen. She may have some good qualities, but fidelity is not amongst them. I fear if you continue your acquaintance with her that you will abjectly degrade yourself.

Let me warn you against being swayed by the follies and vices of others.

A FRIEND AND WELL-WISHER

'An anonymous letter about me!' Jane breathed the words as though it was something she had looked for all her life. 'Pray, pray, Newton, let me keep it. Jenny can stick it into her journal and it will divert us during the long winter evenings.'

'Didn't you write it, then?' Newton sounded puzzled. 'I thought you were the only one who wrote in that sort of style. Are you sure that you didn't write it? I can remember you writing a play a little like this when I was at your father's place.'

'No, I didn't write this,' said Jane regretfully. 'But I wish I had. What fun to write letters about oneself! Though I would be sorry to make you pay postage, Newton. I would have trudged down to York House at dead of night and slipped the letter under the door.'

'You swear that you didn't write it, then?' Newton still sounded puzzled.

'Alas!' said Jane sadly, looking lovingly at the letter.

'It's all very well to think it funny, Jane,' I said hotly, 'but who is writing letters about you? It's a terrible thing to say. Whoever wrote it is implying that you are just a flirt.' I had a strong suspicion that it might be Lavinia, and yet it did not seem like her. I wouldn't have thought that she would use words like 'abjectly' and 'follies and vices'. They seemed to be rather old-fashioned expressions.

'Well, have it if you like,' said Newton in an off-hand way. 'Perhaps it is someone having a joke. I say, Jane, is Frank at home? I'm off back to Hampshire today and I wondered if we could get in some hunting.'

'I think he is still at Southampton,' said Jane absently. She gave her hand to Newton and we both wished him a goodbye and a good journey, but I could see that her mind was still on that stupid letter as we walked on towards Eliza's place. From time to time Jane gave a little giggle to herself and had another peep at the anonymous letter.

Harry was standing outside the door of number 13, Queen's Square. He often did that if he wanted to meet us, but this time there was something strange about his manner. He did not walk towards us, but waited until we had turned into the doorway and were under the arches before he moved.

And then I saw that he had a letter in his hand.

'Harry!' exclaimed Jane. And then suddenly she stopped. I saw a change come over her face. She took a step back. His face was white with fury.

'What does this mean?' he exploded. He didn't sound at all like the usual shy, slightly hesitant Harry.

'Let me see.' Jane held out a hand. Her voice shook and for a moment she looked as though she might cry. 'Harry, please give me that letter . . .' she said.

For a moment I thought he was going to refuse, but then he held it out, and when she took it he turned and walked away.

'Let me look,' I said. Jane wasn't looking at the letter but gazing after Harry; she looked quite upset. So I read through the letter myself. It was nastier than Newton's one and had things about Jane making a fool out of Harry and regarding him as the village idiot, but it was the same handwriting and also signed 'A FRIEND AND WELL-WISHER'.

'I didn't write it, Harry.' There was a funny quaver in Jane's voice when she said that, and Harry instantly turned on his heel and came back. He stood very still for a moment, looking down at Jane, and then snatched the letter out of my hand.

'Of course you didn't write it,' he said, and then I saw him looking closely into her face. I looked also. There were definitely tears in Jane's eyes. Harry put a hand on her arm and squeezed it and then he smiled. 'Of course you didn't write it,' he repeated, and now his tone lightened. 'Whoever wrote that could spell the word "friend", so it definitely wasn't you!'

And then he tore the piece of paper into forty or so pieces and thrust them into his pocket. 'There are a lot of very stupid people around,' he said.

And after that there was a minute's silence. They just stood there looking at each other. I remembered my thoughts the night after the ball at the Crescent when Jane said that the polished gentlemen were not quite real and that she could not imagine going for a walk in the woods with them, and I wondered again about her feelings for Harry. Was it just because he was a friend of her youth (as she put it) or did she have stronger feelings for him?

'We've an invitation for you, Harry,' said Jane eventually, taking the card from her reticule. 'It's a party tomorrow at the Leigh-Perrots'. Will you come?'

Harry took the card gently from her and smiled. He does have a nice smile!

'I'll come,' he said. 'I'll go straight back to my lodgings and write a polite acceptance.'

'Let's show the letter to Eliza,' I said after he had left.

'Let's not,' said Jane.' I know who wrote it, and it will only upset Eliza. Phylly wrote it. I knew I recognized the writing when Newton was showing it to me, but it was only when I saw the second one that I remembered.'

I felt annoyed about this and said that I thought we should tell Eliza. However, Jane insisted that she didn't want to. She seemed in a very good mood and was humming a little song to herself as we climbed the stairs.

Eliza was full of questions about Augusta, but she was not disappointed to hear that nothing had yet been said.

'Give her a day or two,' she advised. 'She's the sort of woman that tries to hold on to her spite. If nothing happens soon, then we might have to apply a little more pressure.' Her eyes met Jane's and they smiled at each other.

Augusta did not come down to supper this evening, and it seems nothing has yet been said to the Austens.

'Perhaps Mr Jerome Wilkins has abandoned her,' suggested Jane. 'She threw herself into his arms and spluttered, "*Damme, Jerome, I shall be married to you.*" And then he said, in a manner truly heroic, "*Damme, Augusta, you are too old for me.*" I've taken that from a story that I wrote when I was a twelve-year-old,' added Jane. She gave a melancholy sigh and said, 'I was so immature then; I could do better now.'

Jane always manages to make me laugh.

Thursday, 12 May 1791

And of course Eliza and Mrs Austen were right. Everyone did come to the party. The Leigh-Perrots' house was a large one, but it was thronged! There were even people sitting on the stairs to eat their supper since the crowds in the dining room were so enormous. In fact, that became the fashionable place to be for the younger crowd. When eventually Jane, Eliza, Harry and I squeezed our way downstairs and went in for supper the dining room had begun to clear.

The supper was delicious. Franklin, beaming from ear to ear, was serving every kind of exotic food. I filled my plate and went over to talk to Mr Austen, who was looking a little out of place among the smooth-talking Bath gentlemen.

'It's a wonderful party, sir, isn't it?' I began. 'I wish Thomas was here.' And then when he didn't reply, in desperation I asked the important question: 'Have Edward-John and Augusta said anything to you about me, sir?'

Mr Austen, however, was still not listening to me but gazing, with a puzzled frown, across the room, at Jane and Harry Digweed. They were standing with full plates, right in the centre of the room, and Jane was pointing directly across the room to where Augusta was demurely talking to Phylly while Edward-John hastened towards them with a couple of glasses of wine in his hands.

Her? I could see Jane's lips mime the word, while her face was filled with horror at some scandalous revelation about a cousin. Harry was looking embarrassed, his face very red, but that was all right. That almost helped the piece of play-acting that was going on. Now Eliza took part, stopping in the middle of the floor, staring at Jane — just as if she could hardly believe her ears — and then turning around to look with horror at Augusta. Augusta coloured up, made some excuse to Phylly, then moved away, only to be accosted by Eliza who, with the exaggerated gestures that would have looked good on the stage in Covent Garden Theatre in London, drew her into a corner and began to whisper in her ear, with many backward glances at Jane. Jane played her part well, rising on tiptoe to whisper into Harry's ear — her lip movements were so exaggerated that I, and probably the rest of the room, could almost make out the words *Are you sure it was really her?*

By now half the room was staring at Augusta. Mrs Leigh-Perrot looked puzzled and then decided to distract everyone. She moved to the centre of the room, called her husband to join her, and made a brief and quite moving speech thanking everyone for believing in her innocence and 'fortifying her' (that's what she said) with their constant messages, letters, cards and gifts of food. Then she spoke of how her husband had stood by her and of how she could never have lived through the experience without his steadfast support and belief in her. She smiled across at him then, and he smiled back, his eyes brimming with tears.

As for the horrors she had endured in prison – 'Well,' she said, 'one of these days, I shall write a book about my experiences and I shall expect all of you to put your names down for a copy. I shall ask for two guineas from each of you.' There was a great laugh at that. Someone began to clap, others joined in, and the Leigh-Perrots beamed at everyone.

Edward-John had now joined Augusta. Eliza moved away the moment he approached and gave me the suspicion of a quick wink as she approached Mr Austen and gaily greeted him.

'Whom will you dance with next?' he said with the indulgent smile that he keeps for his daughters and nieces.

'With you, if you will ask me, *mon oncle*,' she said in her most flirtatious way, and peeped at him over her fan.

I left Mr Austen in Eliza's capable hands – she would manage him much better than I could ever do. It was obvious that Augusta had still said nothing to him, but after Jane's performance she could be in no doubt that her reputation would be ruined unless she placated her husband's young cousin. Eliza would persuade Mr Austen to open the matter of my marriage once again.

I went across the room to greet the admiral and Elinor. Although Mrs Leigh-Perrot had politely invited them both with '& partner' after each name, the baronet, Sir Walter Montmorency, was not there. I tried to make conversation with Elinor, but although she gave me a very sweet smile she said very little, and once more she looked at the admiral before answering the simplest question and then mostly echoed what he had said. He seemed irritable with her and criticized her hair.

On the other hand, he was very friendly to me, chatting as if Thomas and I were properly engaged. I wondered whether Elinor had said something nice to him about me, but came to the conclusion that the rich surroundings and the motherly pat on the arm that Mrs Leigh-Perrot gave me a moment ago had impressed him. He asked me whether I had heard from Thomas yet, and told me that if I cared to write, a fellow officer was going to Southampton in two days' time and would be able to carry a letter to the ship that was scheduled to make contact with Thomas's at Madeira Island.

I thanked him fervently – thinking that by tomorrow morning, thanks to Jane and Eliza, my troubles with Augusta should be over. He smiled down at me, asked permission to admire my beautiful blue eyes and proposed himself as my partner for the next dance. I could see him looking around at all the evidence of wealth and splendour in the Leigh-Perrot household and I think it made a difference to him. After all, I might be a suitable bride for his nephew if my childless aunt and uncle were as affluent as this. I half smiled to myself, thinking of James and Edward-John eyeing each other like rival stags. Money was a terrible thing, I thought. It seemed almost as if it was the most important thing in the world for some people.

Suddenly I resolved not to worry any more. There were times when it felt as if everything was knotted up in my mind like a ball of wool, but now, bit by bit, the problems were unravelling. Eliza had given us a weapon against Augusta; Admiral Williams was cordial and welcoming and seemed to have accepted that I am engaged to marry his nephew; Thomas's sister Elinor was now quite friendly.

'Would you like to see my room?' I asked Elinor. 'I shall have to tidy myself before I can dance with a distinguished gentleman like your uncle.' I made him a curtsy and managed not to laugh at the surprised expression on his face. It was easy enough to do this sort of thing, I thought, if I imagined myself to be Eliza.

Elinor followed me upstairs without a word and I sat her in front of our looking glass and tried to tie up her rather limp blonde hair in the same style as my own. If I had seriously wanted to improve her appearance I would have asked Eliza to come with me, but I wanted the chance to talk to her. So I dampened some strands of hair and coiled them around my finger and then wound a warmed handkerchief over the hair and held it for a moment, chatting about Thomas until she relaxed.

'He's very love in with you,' she said after a minute. 'Do you think you will be able to get married when he returns?'

I told her that I thought we might, and she frowned slightly, and then heaved a sigh. 'You're lucky,' was all that she said.

And then I asked whether Sir Walter Montmorency had left Bath, and her very pale cheeks flushed red and then became white again. I pretended not to see and turned away to find a ribbon from my box.

'No, I don't think he has,' she said after a minute. And then there was another silence. I was hoping that the supper would last a good long time, as otherwise the admiral would be wondering what kept us.

'It's a pity that he couldn't come here this evening,' I said.

'My uncle has forbidden me to see him again. Apparently he has huge gambling debts.' Her voice was dry and hard when she said these words. I nodded. So the admiral had finally found out what half of Bath knew already.

'Are you sorry?' I asked her. 'Were you . . . ?' I hesitated a little, but then asked, 'were you fond of him?'

She did not reply. I found the ribbon and then came over towards her, but before I could thread it through her hair she jumped up and ran for the door.

'No, I hate him,' she said, but I could tell that she was crying. She slammed the door behind her, and when I went out, there was no sign of her.

The music had not yet begun again when I went downstairs. Most of the guests, the friends of the Leigh-Perrots, were middle-aged people who found gossiping, laughing and eating the delicious food more fun than dancing, so the supper break was much longer than usual. The admiral was chatting to Mr Leigh-Perrot so I went over to join my cousin, who was whispering to Harry Digweed and still staring at Augusta.

'Jane, how could you!' I murmured with an eye on Mrs Austen, who was looking suspiciously at her youngest daughter.

Jane neatly swallowed a tiny ham pie from the plate that she and Harry were sharing and looked at me with innocent eyes.

'Methinks she hath a guilty conscience,' she said sadly, slightly narrowing her eyes to make sure that Augusta knew she was still being looked at. 'But the woman is so hardened in sin that she needs more persuasion.'

I giggled. I couldn't help it, but I felt slightly sorry for Augusta when I saw her tuck her hand into Edward-John's arm, almost as though she were in need of protection.

When the music began she even joined the line, facing her husband, her thin lips compressed and her eyes aloof.

I had two dances with the admiral. Funnily enough I enjoyed them very much. I think that the last time

I danced with him, at the Assembly Rooms, I was so worried that he might feel I was unworthy of his nephew that I felt on edge and too anxious. Now I just asked him questions about Thomas when he was a boy and he told me lots of stories of how Thomas used to help him sail his yacht. I began to think that perhaps Thomas had misjudged his uncle, until he told me how he had whipped Thomas one day for taking the yacht out without permission in a howling gale.

'Mind you, he handled it well,' said the admiral with a chuckle, 'but discipline is discipline.' He frowned a little and looked around the room. 'Where's Elinor?' he asked.

'She's probably with my cousin Jane and Mr Harry Digweed,' I said hastily. I did not want Elinor to get into trouble with him. I didn't like the idea of his whipping Thomas – was Elinor still scared of her uncle? I wondered. Was that why she was so quiet and timid?

But the odd thing is that I did not see Elinor for most of the rest of the evening.

Not until the very end of it.

Towards midnight Jane and I went into the kitchen to have a quick chat with Franklin about how the party was going. Suddenly Jane exclaimed, 'A ghost!'

There was a shadow on the whitewashed wall of the steps outside the kitchen. A minute later the kitchen door opened and then hastily closed again. Franklin immediately dashed to the door and flung

it open. We followed
him. The shadow on
the wall had been that
of a young girl – just
like this sketch here.

'Elinor!' gasped
Jane.

Elinor's face was first
deadly white and then she
flushed a dark red.

'I was hot,' she said
quickly. 'I just slipped out
for some fresh air and the
door closed behind me.'

'You should have rung

the bell, ma'am,' said Franklin gravely. 'I would have
let you back in immediately. It's not fitting for a young
lady to be out in the night by herself.'

He insisted on escorting her back upstairs again,
leaving Jane and myself in the kitchen, eating up some
of the leftover pastries. When he came back he had
a worried look on his face and just shook his head
when Jane wondered aloud how long Elinor had been
outside.

Jane and I have just spent a long time talking about
Elinor. What was she doing? Why did she leave the
party?

Had she slipped out to meet Sir Walter?

Friday, 13 May 1791

I woke late this morning and told Jane to go down to breakfast without me. The house seemed very quiet, and I guessed that my aunt and uncle would sleep in after the excitement of the party.

When I came out of our bedroom my brother was sitting on the window seat at the bottom of the flight of stairs, staring out at the rain. He looked miserable.

I asked him whether he had had breakfast, but he just shook his head without speaking. I felt sorry for him and slipped my hand into his. The thought crossed my mind that he is my nearest relation in the world and yet we never seemed to talk. Jane chatters continually to all of her brothers; it would never even occur to her to stop and consider her words as I was doing now. What would Jane say, I wondered, if she were me?

'Edward-John, I want you to give permission for my marriage to Thomas.' The words popped out of my mouth almost as if it were Jane speaking.

He looked at me then with some surprise. It wasn't what I had said, I think, but the way that I said it, which had brought that look of astonishment to his face. I had not pleaded; my voice had not trembled; I didn't feel like crying; I said the words as if I were asking him to pass the salt.

'Are you sure?' He asked the question very slowly. His voice was leaden.

I nodded very firmly. 'Yes, I am quite sure,' I said.

And then their bedroom door opened and Augusta came out. She gave me a stately nod and a muttered answer to my polite 'Good morning, Augusta' and then took Edward-John's arm. Neither husband nor wife looked at the other on their way down the stairs to the breakfast parlour.

However, once in the room, Augusta exerted herself to be very charming, spilling out compliments about the wonderful party and so on, and under the cover of her enthusiasm I slipped into my place beside Jane.

Mr Austen, I noticed, was looking uncomfortable, but Mrs Austen wore her determined air, the one that she assumes when she has decided that something unpleasant has to be done and that it will be done that very morning. I had seen her look like that when the dairy needed to be scrubbed and lime-washed, when the creaking weathervane had to be mended, and when she wanted Mr Austen to speak to his bailiff about flirting with a village girl.

Mrs Leigh-Perrot seemed to be in on the secret also. She exchanged several glances with Mrs Austen and there was a faint air of a conspiracy between them. Both were being coldly polite to Augusta and warmly motherly towards me. Mr Leigh-Perrot was the only one who did not appear to be in the secret; he was wrapped in a cloud of happiness, making silly jokes to Franklin and laughing uproariously at his replies.

Augusta ate little and rose to her feet at the first opportunity. Edward-John got up obediently, but Mrs Leigh-Perrot intervened.

'Just a minute, Edward-John. Jenny and Jane, perhaps you would like to go for a little walk? We just want a talk with Mr and Mrs Cooper.'

'If it's about Jenny, shouldn't she stay?' I had already obediently got to my feet but Jane's words made me sit down again.

'Jane!' exclaimed Mrs Austen, but Mrs Leigh-Perrot nodded. 'The child is right,' she said. 'Jenny should stay.'

No one suggested that Jane should be present, but she tiptoed very gently after me as Mrs Leigh-Perrot led the way to the front parlour.

Although it was May, the fire had already been lit, and Mr Austen went straight to it and pretended to rub his hands in front of the flames, keeping his back turned to the rest of the room. Mr Leigh-Perrot immediately joined him; they both seemed to want to keep out of the discussion and allow their wives to speak for them.

Edward-John and Augusta sat down side by side on the sofa, facing their two aunts, who were sitting bolt upright on upholstered chairs. Jane crossed the room and perched on the window seat. I almost joined her, but thought that would be cowardly. In the end I went and sat beside my brother on the sofa.

Mrs Leigh-Perrot was the first to speak, and I was

glad of that as Mrs Austen was a bit blunt and had already quarrelled with Augusta and Edward-John.

'Obviously you want the best for Jenny,' she began, speaking quite mildly and looking enquiringly at them when no answer seemed to be coming.

'Obviously,' said Edward-John after a glance at Augusta.

'Your uncles and aunts all feel that this match with Captain Thomas Williams is a good one,' went on Mrs Leigh-Perrot. 'He is a fine young man, with a good career, a house of his own, a certain fortune and well connected. Who knows what the admiral will do for him! I have made enquiries, and he and his sister are the admiral's only near relations.'

'That's all very well . . .' began Augusta and then stopped. Jane had got up from her window seat sauntered over to the fireplace and picked up a two-handled pitcher in exquisite ruby-coloured glass. She held it up admiringly to the window, thoughtfully running her finger over the two large, ear-like handles, just as her mother did when checking that Sukey had done the dusting. I was glad that Eliza was not there as I would not have been able to stop myself giggling if I had met her glance and seen her lips form the words: '*Little pitchers have big ears.*'

'You were saying, Mrs Cooper . . . ?' Mrs Leigh-Perrot seemed a little bewildered, though Mrs Austen's glance had sharpened. Jane put the glass pitcher back on the mantelpiece and went to sit beside her father on the chaise longue.

'Oh, nothing, nothing; nobody wants to listen to me! I'm sure that I don't wish to interfere. Mr Cooper can make up his own mind about his sister's future.'

And then Augusta rose from the sofa, shook her elaborately trimmed gown, adjusted the lace at her neck and flounced out of the room.

There was a dead silence when the door closed behind her. I moved a little closer to my brother. I felt sorry for him with five pairs of eyes pointing in his direction.

In the end he handled it with dignity. He turned towards me, took my hand in his and said awkwardly, 'What do you feel about it, Jenny? We only want the best for you.'

'I am very much in love with Thomas and my happiness lies in marrying him.' I spoke just to him and did not once look at anyone else in the room. When I had finished he said nothing for half a minute, but then nodded and said quietly, 'In that case, I give my permission.'

And then everyone was hugging and kissing me.

And Mrs Leigh-Perrot started to discuss wedding presents . . .

And Mrs Austen declared that I had to be married at Steventon and began to plan a great whitewashing of all the rooms in the house before Christmas . . .

And Mr Austen told me that even if the Archbishop of Canterbury himself wanted to marry us he would insist on performing the service himself . . .

And Jane started to plan how she would decorate the church for the occasion . . .

When eventually we came out of the parlour, Augusta had just emerged from her room, with her bandbox in her hand. Behind her in the bedroom, I could see Rosalie busily packing gowns into the large trunk that they had brought with them.

'Dear Aunt and Uncle, we must, alas, leave you. We have recollected an urgent appointment, but did not like to spoil your pleasure last night by telling of our departure,' said Augusta. She did not look at me, but kept a false smile carefully pinned to her face as everyone bustled around, Mr Leigh-Perrot sending Franklin for a chaise to take them to the post-inn, Mrs Leigh-Perrot offering her lavender drops for the journey, Mr Austen falling over himself to assure Edward-John how much he valued his present of some sermons. Mrs Austen did not take much part in this, but rolled up her sleeves and set to work to assist Rosalie. Jane and I were called into the bedroom to help and I was glad to go, because I hated to see the look on my brother's face as he tried to pretend that he had known all about this sudden departure.

And now I have written to Thomas.

This is my first effort — full of crossings-outs and blots . . . I'm just so excited that I can't concentrate . . . can't think straight . . . I keep laughing and crying . . . Jane has already put on her bonnet and is telling me to stop writing and to hurry up – I think she can't wait to tell Eliza the whole story.

(She says that she has been like 'Patience on a monument' (Shakespeare) – she told me to be sure to write 'Shakespeare' in my journal.)

My dearest Thomas,

I love you . . . I love you . . . I love you . . . ~~I just can't believe it~~ . . . ~~you'll never believe what happened~~ . . . something wonderful has happened!!!

~~Edward-John has given permission to us to be married.~~

~~My brother is happy for us to get married.~~ We can be married! I want to write those four words a hundred times.

I love you so much and I am so happy that I almost feel that I can fly. I wish I could fly across the sea ~~and then I could be with you now just~~ so that I could stand beside you.

Last night I dreamed of you. I dreamed that we were standing together and looking up at the night sky ~~and the funny thing was that I was the star at the same time as being a girl.~~ One star seemed so beautiful and you said that I was your star.

I hope and pray that you will be able to

get back here for Christmas.

Jane and I are going to see your sister Elinor when I finish this letter. ~~I'm a bit worried about her. She seems~~ ░

With so much love, my darling, from your Jenny.

And now the house is quiet. Mr and Mrs Leigh-Perrot have taken the Austens sightseeing to visit a cathedral. Jane and I escaped by Jane's quick wits in recollecting an appointment with Eliza. When I have delivered my letter to the admiral so that it can be sent to Thomas's ship, we will walk to Queen's Square, get Eliza out of bed and tell her the whole story.

Elinor

Jane and I are running down the Paragon, along George Street, then hurtling down the steep incline of Gay Street and into Queen's Square.

We are going so fast that we almost crash into Harry, who is standing quite still in the middle of the pavement, his hat clasped against his broad chest, his blond hair shining in the sunshine and a tender smile on his lips as he watches Jane flying along, clutching at her bonnet.

'Come with us, Harry,' gasps Jane. 'We're going down to York Street to see whether Elinor Williams will come for a walk with us.'

'No, you two wait here,' I say hastily. 'I'll just give my letter to the admiral and then ask Elinor if she would like to come with us. She probably won't, but I'll ask anyway. I'll be back in five minutes.' There is something about the way Harry is looking at Jane and Jane is looking at Harry that makes me feel they would like a few minutes together.

Without giving them any time to voice objections I go on down the street without even looking back. I will probably take longer than five minutes as I am sure that the admiral will want to chat. That will be good. I will ask for him as soon as the manservant opens the door, I decide.

But when I knock at the lodgings in York Street it is the

governess who opens the door. She snatches it open the second my hand leaves the knocker – almost as though she has been standing just behind it.

'Where's Elinor?' she gasps.

'Elinor?' I'm puzzled. Miss Taylor's face is white and her eyes large and protruding.

'I thought she was with you.' Her voice is low, not much more than a whisper, and she looks over her shoulder in a worried way.

'Why?' I'm still puzzled.

'George said he saw her in the Greyhound Inn yard. She told him she was waiting for you – for Miss Cooper; he's sure she said that.' Miss Taylor's face changes. Her eyes look past me and she snaps, 'Thank you, George, that will be all,' at a manservant who had just emerged from a door beyond the staircase. She takes my arm, walks out through the hall door with me and shuts it behind us. We are outside. In the bright sunlight I see that her eyes are full of tears.

'Miss Taylor, what's wrong?'

'I'm afraid that she might be with Sir Walter Montmorency,' she whispers. 'She was supposed to be practising her music, but when I didn't hear the piano for ten minutes I came downstairs and found that she was gone. I started to search the house, to look for her. And then George came back from an errand and told me that he met Miss Williams outside the Greyhound Inn and she told him that she was waiting for you. You didn't...' Miss Taylor stops. She can see from my face how surprised

I am. She knows now that there was no arrangement between Elinor and me. 'I don't know what the admiral will say!' She sounds despairing and her eyes dart here and there, looking at the crowds of people in York Street.

'You go back inside. Give this letter to the admiral.' I'm thinking rapidly. Above all, the admiral must not suspect anything. 'Tell him that Elinor and I, and my cousin, Miss Jane Austen, escorted by Mr Harry Digweed, have gone for a walk. Don't worry. We will bring her back.'

Quickly I thrust my letter into Miss Taylor's hand and start to run as quickly as I can, back uphill, towards Queen's Square.

Harry and Jane are sitting on a bench laughing. Even in the middle of my worries about Elinor, I think that they look very nice together.

'What's the matter?' Jane sees me first.

I tell them about Elinor and they are both on their feet before I finish explaining.

'That fellow!' Harry is walking so fast that Jane and I have to run to keep up with him.

'They must be inside – I hope they are not in his bedroom,' Jane whispers when we reach the Greyhound Inn. The yard in front of it is quite empty except for a man grooming one of the horses.

'Have you seen Sir Walter Montmorency, John?' asks Harry. He seems to be well known here. The innkeeper's wife has just given a friendly wave at him from an upstairs window.

'Sir Walter has just left, Mr Digweed,' says John.

'By himself, or with friends?' Harry is no actor, and John gives him a sharp look.

'Just the young lady, Mr Digweed,' he says, keeping his eyes fixed on the horse's glossy back.

'Have your fastest horses put to a chaise. I won't need a post boy. You'll trust me, won't you? I'll bring it back safe to you. Fast as you can, John, please.'

'Why did they go off without us?' Jane is doing her best and her air is very casual. 'It was a blonde young lady, about my age, wasn't it?' she asks John, and he nods immediately.

'Yes, miss; Admiral Williams's niece,' he says obligingly, making a sign to the stableman.

'Which way did they go, John?' Harry's voice is grim.

'The Bristol road, sir, through Bristol, changing horses at Falfield, then going on to Gloucester; that's where the chaise is booked for,' says John, pocketing the piece of silver that Harry produces from his pocket. 'Thank you, sir. We'll harness up Dasher and his brother Dancer. They're the fastest horses in the stable. Much quicker than that showy Greylord and Greydawn that Sir Walter insisted on having. They've had a good fifteen minutes start on you though, and it won't be easy to make speed on the road to Bristol . . .'

Jane's eyes meet mine and she mouths, '*Gretna Green.*' I fear that she is right. I'm not very good at geography, but I know that London would have been the wrong way for Scotland. Gloucester is probably quite in line with Gretna Green.

'Be back in one minute,' says Harry, sprinting towards the door of the inn. We hear his boots clattering up the stairs.

John has everything ready by the time Harry is back. He stops at the sight of both of us sitting in the chaise, Jane looking innocently into the distance as if admiring the view.

'You're not going,' says Harry firmly.

'Yes, we are,' says Jane, and as he climbs up she hisses in his ear, 'We're chaperones. You can't bring Elinor back without a chaperone. She would be ruined!'

Harry's look of firm purpose melts and he looks indecisive. John shouts to a stable boy to open the gates a bit wider, Harry gathers up the reins, and then we shoot off through the gates and up Monmouth Street without another word.

'He's probably got a pistol in his pocket,' whispers Jane, nudging me. She looks blissfully happy and very excited. I don't reply. I feel so anxious about everything. What happens if we can't find Elinor and Sir Walter? How far will we have to follow them? Will someone miss us?

'Don't worry, Jenny; no one will miss us. They won't be back from Wells Cathedral until the evening – and Franklin will think that we are with cousin Eliza.' Jane has read my expression. She speaks in her normal voice. The wheels on the cobbled street are rumbling so loudly that no one but I could hear her.

Harry is a superb driver. The chaise swings around

corners without slackening speed. Dasher and his brother Dancer are living up to their names, hardly breaking into a sweat as we thunder along, avoiding all the gigs and carts on the road.

I'm going to take a short cut here,' says Harry over his shoulder. 'If I take the Nailsworth road and then cross over by Dursley, we'll cut out Bristol and be at Falfield before they arrive.'

Jane hugs herself gleefully as Harry swings off the Bristol pike road and sets the horses galloping up a narrow road overhung with beech trees. I guess what she is thinking. This is just like one of Mrs Charlotte Smith's novels.

But what about Elinor? I think. What is she feeling now? I wish I knew. Is she excited? Frightened? Guilty? Is she really in love? And if so, should we be going after her?

And then I remember her tears and her pale face and I know that we have to talk to her. 'I hate him,' she said, and her words stay in my mind.

The Huntsman's Inn at Falfield on the Bristol-to-Gloucester road is quite busy when we arrive. One of the ostlers takes the horses from Harry and promises to water them and allow them to rest.

'What do we do now?' asks Jane when Harry rejoins us.

'We wait,' says Harry. 'When they come we'll see if you can get her to come out of the chaise. In the meantime I'll go and order a parlour and some tea for you. I'll call you when I need you.' He strides across the yard and Jane looks after him thoughtfully.

'He's changed, hasn't he?' she says.

I know what she means. There was a time, not so long ago, when Harry would have asked Jane what he should do; now he makes up his own mind. When he returns with the news that the parlour is ready, she nods and follows me in through the door.

However, inside the dark hallway she pauses, puts a hand on my arm and whispers, 'Let's just stand here. I want to see what happens.'

We must have waited at least five minutes before anything important changed in the busy scene in the inn yard.

And then there is a clatter of horse hoofs. Two showy-looking grey horses, profusely covered in sweat, gallop in through the gates. The post boy jumps to the ground and holds the horses' bridles, and then Sir Walter Montmorency, elegantly dressed in a pair of skin-tight pantaloons and a greatcoat with three capes layered on the shoulders, climbs down. Within the chaise I see a pale blue bonnet.

'Change the horses – look sharp, my man, let's have a good driver and decent pair of horses this time.' The post boy glowers at this and exchanges a glance with the ostler from the Huntsman Inn.

'Sir Walter –' Harry taps him on the shoulder, '– a word with you, if you will be so good.'

I think for a moment Sir Walter does not recognize Harry. He frowns at him impatiently, but that seems to be his normal expression, and when Harry wheels round and leads the way towards the back of the yard he follows him.

'Quick,' says Jane, and in a moment we are both outside. A maidservant is passing with a jug of ale in her hand and Jane touches her on the arm.

'Could you ask the young lady in the chaise to come and join us in the parlour,' she says in a very grown-up way, and the girl bobs a curtsy. She instantly goes across, and a minute later Elinor's pale face appears. She doesn't lift her head, but follows the servant, the deep rim of her bonnet shielding her face.

'You take her into the parlour,' hisses Jane. 'I'm going to see what's happening.'

She slips away and I catch hold of Elinor's cold hand at the same moment. She starts when she sees me, but she does not resist when I draw her into the parlour.

Despite the May weather there is a fire burning in the grate and I sit Elinor in front of it. Her eyes are swollen and her pale face blotched with tearstains.

'Tea, ma'am,' says the landlady, following me in. I can see her glance with curiosity towards Elinor.

'Yes, please,' I say, moving to stand in front of the girl.

Neither of us says anything until the tea is brought in – just two cups, I notice, and some finely cut buttered pieces of bread.

When the landlady goes out I follow her to the door and then quietly and cautiously turn the key. I don't want to lose Elinor now that I have her safe. The lock makes a soft click, but she doesn't seem to notice. She has started to cry noisily, sniffing into a drenched handkerchief. I go over, kneel on the floor beside her, and take her hand.

'Did he force you to come away with him?' I ask softly.

She nods her head and then shakes it.

'You wanted him to love you – is that it?' I'm beginning to understand her. She just sobs without replying so I go on.

'He pretended to love you and no one has been so kind to you before . . . is that it?' I ask the question softly and put my arm around her.

'I thought he really loved me, but now I'm not sure.' The words are choked with sobs, but I can understand her.

'What made you change your mind?'

She looks at me with reddened eyes. I think that she might be quite pretty when she puts on some weight and is a bit happier. Perhaps Mrs Austen would have her to stay at Steventon and feed her up with cream from her Alderney cows.

'It was my governess,' she says after a moment. 'Miss Taylor told me that the admiral said that Sir Walter had huge gambling debts. My uncle told me that I must not see him again. I asked Sir Walter was it true and he got very angry. He . . . He hit me.'

'What?!' I stop myself saying any more. There is some great puzzle here. The girl wasn't abducted. She left the house of her own accord. I think she probably even met Sir Walter last night during the Leigh-Perrots' party. But why did she go with a man who treated her like that?

'But he was sorry afterwards. He kissed me. He was very nice to me then. I didn't know what to think. Sometimes he is kinder to me than anyone else . . .'

'Where is he taking you?' I am too puzzled by her to ask any more about her feelings for Sir Walter. If a man hit me, I would have nothing more to do with him – not ever!

'To Gretna Green.' She whispers the words, although it is only the two of us here in the room.

'Do you want to go? Do you want to marry him?'

Elinor shakes her head. 'No, but I have to because if I don't he will be ruined. He told me that when we were coming along in the chaise.'

'But you left the house to go with him!'

'I didn't know what we were doing.' Elinor's voice is dull. 'I thought we were just going to spend some time together. He forced me to go in the chaise. I kept asking him where we were going and eventually he told me. He said that I had to do it. I'm scared not to obey him.'

I get to my feet. I feel my cheeks burning with anger. This was abduction.

'Elinor, stay here. Try to drink some tea. I'll be back. Don't worry – Jane and I will take you home. No one will know. Your governess has already told the admiral that you have gone for a walk with us.'

Carefully I turn the key in the lock, and once outside I lock it again. Whatever happens, I won't allow Sir Walter to force her back into that chaise again.

'My friend is sleeping,' I say to the innkeeper's wife when I meet her in the dark passageway. 'You won't allow anyone to disturb her, will you?'

'No, ma'am, of course not.' Her voice is full of curiosity and, what is worse, she sounds amused.

I hurry outside and Jane comes rushing up towards me.

'Sir Walter has challenged Harry to a duel!' she gasps. 'But Harry just knocked the pistol out of his hand and punched him.'

The fight is still going on when we reach the backyard of the inn. There are several spectators, one of the stable boys even gives a slight cheer, but then the lad gets a severe glance from the innkeeper and turns it into a cough.

Sir Walter is getting the worst of it. Harry has a very red patch under one eye; otherwise he is unmarked, but the baronet's nose is bleeding profusely over his fancy waistcoat and his expensive greatcoat. Even his white pantaloons are smeared with blood. As Jane and I join the crowd, Harry's eyes go momentarily to us and then back to Sir Walter again. A slight smile comes over his lips, he draws his fist back and then it flies forward, lands on Sir Walter's jaw and with a crash the man is on the ground. Harry stands over him, and says in his nice country voice to the innkeeper, 'I think Sir Walter would wish to leave now. Could someone give me a hand to put him in his chaise?'

And with a stableman on one side, and Harry on the other, Sir Walter is dragged across the yard to the chaise.

Jane races ahead and politely opens the door. Harry heaves the baronet in, dusts his hands and says to the post boy, 'Drive him back to the Greyhound Inn in Bath.'

And Harry goes over to the pump, washes the blood from his hands and then splashes some water on his face.

'Come and have some tea, Harry,' I say.

'In a moment,' he says.

'You go back inside,' Jane says to me. 'We'll join you in a minute.'

I leave them and go back.

I can't help glancing over my shoulder though. Jane is in Harry's arms, her arms are around his neck and their lips are touching! I envy them, thinking of Thomas and myself.

Then I see one of the girls from the inn looking at me with a smile and I blush and move away. I wish they had somewhere to go so as to be private together, but neither seems to mind.

I've run out of conversation with Elinor by the time they come in. They are smiling and holding hands. They both refuse the tea and Harry offers his arm to Elinor and leads her out to the chaise.

Jane and I are alone in the dark cosy parlour of the inn. I look at her and she smiles at me.

'Did he kiss you?' I ask, pretending that I saw nothing, and she nods. The colour has rushed into her cheeks, and her hazel eyes are sparkling.

'And?' I put the question into my tone of voice.

'And . . .' she echoes teasingly. And then she suddenly hugs me.

'I love him, I love him, I love him, I've always loved him!' she says.

'What?!' I exclaim, but she just laughs.

'Perhaps we'll both get married at Christmas,' I say.

'Jenny,' said Jane seriously, 'don't even think of it. We are going to keep this a deadly secret. I can't imagine what my mother would say.'

Saturday, 14 May 1791

We are leaving Bath this morning so I haven't really got enough time to write down everything that happened yesterday. It's all a bit of blur: Sir Walter Montmorency eloping with (abducting, really) poor little Elinor. Harry being magnificent: hiring a chaise, overtaking them, then the great fight with Sir Walter, beating him to a pulp and sending him back to Bath like a whipped cur (that's Jane's expression). This morning when we met Harry he told us that Sir Walter Montmorency has left Bath, so Elinor is now safe from him.

We managed to get Elinor home before the admiral returned and the governess was so grateful. She whispered to me that the admiral took my letter and said he was delivering it to his friend whose ship is due to rendezvous with Thomas's.

But this is the big news.
    Jane is in love!

Really in love!

She wants to get married to Harry!!!!

Harry has a great plan, according to Jane. He hopes to rent a farm in Chawton, near Alton, where the land is good. He plans to brew beer. He says that the water in the river Wey is excellent for beer-making and he knows forty inns who will give him orders.

'And, of course,' added Jane, 'a brewer is a man of consequence; a baker is no one, but a brewer is a gentleman. I read that in *The Lady* – I had a quick look at it when we were waiting for Eliza in the lending library.'

'I hope your mother has read it also,' I said, laughing. 'Perhaps you could buy the magazine and put it under her nose. It's only sixpence.'

'But don't say a word,' warned Jane. 'This is a deadly secret. Mama must not know or she will fall into a state of apoplexy and then blame me for it. We will break the news to her once Harry becomes a man of fortune.'

And then she gave a little secret smile, hugged herself and then hugged me. It's lovely that we are both in love and both so happy. I'm sure that the Austens won't insist on her marrying a man of fortune.

Tuesday, 17 May 1791

Jane is trying to cheer me up, telling me that I should be the happiest girl in the world. I know I should, but somehow I can't believe it until I see Thomas.

There are another 14 days in May

30 days in June

31 days in July

31 days in August

30 days in September

31 days in October

30 days in November

That's 197 days to go before the first of December arrives!

How can I bear it?

I try to turn my thoughts away from myself and to Jane. I still can't believe how much in love she is with Harry Digweed, and I certainly can't believe that I never guessed that Jane – the girl who flirted with so many men in Bath – is now so in love with one man. She tells me that Harry has been talking to his father about renting the farm in Chawton. It's about seventeen miles from Steventon. That will be the first step towards setting up as a brewer. He has to grow a crop called hops. They grow up tall poles, joined together by wires. Jane says that Harry has told her that they grow so fast that you can almost see them grow. They have little flowers on them at the end of the summer – apparently you make beer with them.

For the rest of the evening we talk about Harry and his prospects, and somehow I do feel better. I think that tomorrow I will ask Mrs Austen whether we can buy some cotton so that I can make a start on my trousseau and sew myself some nightgowns and some chemises.

Wednesday, 25 May 1791

Why don't I hear from him?

I should have heard by now.

The ship carrying post should be back at South-ampton by now.

Perhaps tomorrow.

Thursday, 26 May 1791

Last night I had a terrible thought! Did Phylly write to Thomas? One of those horrible anonymous letters, full of spite and lies.

Perhaps she exaggerated Eliza's jokes about me and the French *comte*. Perhaps she even said that I was going to be married to that revolting slave merchant.

If Thomas heard that, perhaps he would be so disgusted that he would not want to have anything to do with me ever again.

I can't bear the thought.

I can't bear this unhappiness. Last night I did not sleep. I just tossed and turned all night.

It's too late to write a letter now.

By now Thomas's ship will have set out on the long journey to the West Indies.

And he won't be back until December.

Frank

It's bright outside, but I know it is still very early. The birds are singing in that special way they do at dawn, and the sun is still quite low in the sky, shining directly in through our window. There are no early-morning noises of cows being led into the milking parlour, or the clanking of the pump in the kitchen, or of Sukey slamming doors as she brings in wood for the stove.

But there is someone coming, someone on horseback, someone in a great hurry. There is a great scattering of gravel from the sweep, the sound of a horse's neigh and then a quick, sharp knock on the door.

At the sound of that knock I lie back on my pillow again. Only Frank knocks like that. For a moment, half asleep as I was, I had thought that it might be Thomas. I had been dreaming of him all night. Sleepily I wondered why Frank had come home. He had been with his ship at Southampton as the officers were supervising the men in its cleaning and repairing before a long voyage to the East Indies.

His footsteps are coming up the stairs now, noisy, clattering footsteps of someone in heavy boots running at full speed up the uncarpeted staircase. I smile to myself. Typical Frank! It would never occur to him, since he is up and about, that the rest of the house might be asleep.

But then there is a knock on our door. Jane jumps up

and pushes her nightcap off her forehead. She then lies down again and pulls the covers up over her ears.

I get out of bed and put on my wrapper. I go to the door and open it and there is Frank, all splashed with mud, his young face drawn and tired looking.

And only then do I think that Frank must have ridden through the night to get from Southampton and to arrive at Steventon at this early hour.

But why?

What is wrong?

And there is some expression on his face that makes me very afraid.

I say something . . . I don't know . . . perhaps I don't say anything . . . perhaps I just look at him.

A strange feeling comes over me . . . It seems as if some bizarre mist fills the air making me feel sick and weak.

I stare at him.

He takes me in his arms.

A half-sob breaks his breath for a moment.

I don't want him to say anything.

But I know that I can't stop it . . .

And I know what he is going to say . . .

'Oh, Jenny,' he says, 'there is some very bad news about Thomas's ship . . .'

I hear my voice – very strange, very far-off, and the voice is saying: 'He's dead.'

'No, no.' He holds me very tightly and he speaks into my ear, but still it takes a while to make sense of his words.

'The ship has been missing for two weeks,' he says. 'It

was lost in a great storm. Another ship nearby saw the mainsail torn down. But no trace of the ship has been found. Jenny, there's still hope . . . Jenny, Jenny . . .

And then I go down – into a deep, dark, bottomless well, where there is no light and no warmth . . .

'Mama! Jane! . . .'

. . . And now I am lying on my bed. Mrs Austen is sitting beside me, holding my hand; Mr Austen is standing at the bottom of the bed with an arm around Frank's shoulders.

Jane is lying beside me on the bed with her arms around me. She is crying.

But I am not crying.

Not even trying to stop crying.

There is nothing left in me. I'm just frozen.

Monday, 30 May 1791

I shall never write in this journal again. I think I will
burn it.

Bleak Midwinter

There was a storm overnight, and even now the wind keeps whistling and beating against the trees. The lawn is strewn with small pieces of twigs and strands of pale green lichen torn from the hawthorn bushes, and the sky is overcast, with black clouds scudding through the pale grey. Jane and I walk up the hill, side by side, towards Deane. We are going to fetch the letters from the inn. There was a time when this made my heart beat, when I hoped that there might be some news, though I knew that there could be none.

This terrible cruel hope that lingers when all hope should have ceased!

But even that has gone now, and nothing has taken its place.

Just a grey, sad loneliness.

But I make conversation. I talk. I try to laugh, to take an interest. I try to be there for Jane in her happiness as she was there for me during that brief spell of love and excitement, during that wonderful spring when all my dreams came true.

'Look, there's Harry by the church,' I say to her.

She laughs. She is very happy these days.

'He's soaking wet,' she says, making a face and pretending to shudder. 'And his dog too. Look at her!'

'You go and talk to him,' I say. I'm not fooled by her

words or her expression. No matter how wet Harry was, no matter how often the black pointer shook raindrops from her silky coat all over her, none of this mattered to Jane as long as she could be near him, could listen to his voice, could touch him, could feel his lips on hers.

I know all this because once I was like Jane.

Once I had someone who I loved more than the rest of the world. Someone that I thought I would marry.

'Go on,' I say. 'I'll fetch the letters. I'll only be ten minutes, and then we can walk back to the parsonage together.'

And so I turn away and leave her to run up the church path towards the man that she loves while I continue, drearily, walking up the steep and muddy road, pulling my cloak around me as the heavy mist begins to blow across the valley, dragging my hood over my curls, as the drips from the trees turn into rain.

The storm is increasing. I feel as though I am out at sea. The strength of the wind snatches the breath from between my lips. The roadside stream has turned into a raging torrent, its foaming waters are thundering down the hill and the branches overhead bend and creak.

I can see something on the top of the hill. Someone. A figure.

I push back the hood of my cloak and allow my blonde curls to whip around my face.

And at that moment the figure begins to run.

And the wind in my face feels like icy hands, one on each side, freezing my flesh and dulling my brain. Still I do not know; I cannot let myself hope.

'It's Frank,' I make myself say aloud, but I know it is not Frank. Frank is not tall; not broad-shouldered and long-legged like this man.

It's his ghost, I think then. A gentle loving ghost who has come back to earth to visit his wife-to-be.

And now he is beside me. His hands are on the sides of my face. Burning heat replacing icy cold. His mouth is on mine . . .

Thursday, I December 1791

I have just taken this poor journal from the trunk. Someday I will write the whole story of how Thomas's ship was caught in a terrible storm, how the sails broke, how they were driven on to a barren rocky island, how he and his sailors lived there for months repairing the ship, getting food . . .

But now I just want to write about my wedding.

It will take place in two weeks' time.

Thomas has gone to London. He has to give an account of the shipwreck to the Admiralty. There is talk that he might be decorated for bravery, Frank says, but Thomas says that's nonsense . . .

Mr Austen has written, this very night, to Edward-John and Augusta, inviting them both to Steventon to celebrate my wedding.

Mrs Austen has written to the Leigh-Perrots.

Jane and I have discussed my wedding dress.

Monday, 5 December 1791

We are in Bath! This is how it happened.

Mr and Mrs Leigh-Perrot arrived three days ago.

They brought a letter from the admiral. He hopes to see us in the Isle of Wight in the New Year. He spent a long time explaining why he can't come to Steventon at this time of the year (Thomas says that his uncle doesn't want to stir from Bath) and he sent a present of a beautiful cloak lined with swansdown.

But the big event was that Mr and Mrs Leigh-Perrot invited Jane and me to go to Bath for a week to choose my wedding dress, so here we are! We arrived last night and are now all ready for the great shopping trip.

The shop was as beautiful as I remembered it.

I rushed past all the colours though, past the rainbow shades of delicate flimsy muslins.

And there was the white satin!

It hung from a pillar in the darkest part of the shop.

There was just one lamp near to it, but that was enough. The material itself seemed to be full of light. It gleamed with a high gloss.

'That should drape beautifully,' said Mrs Leigh-Perrot with satisfaction.

Reverentially Eliza took it down and held it up against me.

'*Parfait!*' she said with a nod of approval.

'It's a bit plain though, isn't it? What about something over it? What would you think, madame?' Mrs Leigh-Perrot was determined that I should have the best possible dress in town, but I wasn't sure that I wanted anything other than that glorious white satin with its wonderful sheen.

'Not too much,' said Eliza. 'Let the material stand by itself. *C'est très beau.*' As always when discussing clothes, Eliza was decisive and confident. She trotted away – we could hear her high heels clicking as she moved from shelf to shelf. Jane followed her, but I just stood very still gazing at the wonderful white satin and thinking of the moment when Thomas would first see it.

'I have an idea.' Eliza was back, followed closely by the shopkeeper, a brown paper parcel in her hands. She waited patiently while Eliza explained how she thought the dress should be made. 'And then,' she concluded, 'the V-shaped centre of the bodice will be covered with this . . .'

And like a conjur0r she whipped off the brown paper and showed the most heavenly gauze, heavily embroidered with a gold thread.

'And the sleeves – long like this – they will be ending in a point so we must find something to draw attention to the hands, *n'est-ce pas?*'

'Eliza with clothes always reminds me of a little terrier on the scent of something tasty!' Jane whispered in my ear as Eliza went scurrying off, closely followed by the shopkeeper. Mrs Leigh-Perrot, I was glad to see, still wore an indulgent smile. I was hoping that Eliza would not involve the Leigh-Perrots in too much expense, but I knew that she would not be satisfied with anything less than perfection.

But when she came back with some lace, white embroidered on white, Mrs Leigh-Perrot gave a genuine cry of delight.

'Perfect! We'll take enough for a veil as well as wrist trimmings,' she enthused. 'And an ear-of-corn motif — most suitable for a wedding!'

'Fertility, she means,' murmured Jane in my ear, and I blushed and said hurriedly that we should now look for the material for Jane's gown.

'A nice pink satin,' suggested Mrs Leigh-Perrot, but Jane had already gone, striding confidently down the aisles, through the draped pillars.

'I've found it,' she called back.

It was a length of poppy-red satin that flamed in an explosion of colour. It was the brightest, most exuberant colour that I have ever seen. Eliza took it down and held it against Jane. With her dark eyes and dark hair, it looked wonderful!

'Red for a wedding, for a church — is that a little old-fashioned? They tell me that white is the latest fashion.' Mrs Leigh-Perrot sounded a little dubious, though I could see that she was unable to prevent a smile of pleasure at the beautiful picture Jane made.

'Dearest Aunt,' said Jane solemnly, 'I think red is so suitable for a church. In fact, I got the idea from the book of sermons written by Jenny's brother. As soon as I read the phrase: "*Though your sins be as scarlet, they shall be as white as snow,*" I suddenly thought that I would love a scarlet gown. Jenny will be in white satin, white as snow, and I will be in red,' explained Jane, her eyes wide and innocent.

'I see,' was all that her aunt could manage after that, while Eliza gazed at her young cousin with admiration. I hugged Jane and told her that the dresses would be beautiful together.

Today a letter came from Edward-John and Augusta. They fear they will be unable to attend my wedding. It is a very cold letter . . . no present . . . no wishes for my happiness . . .

Till death do us part . . .

Mrs Austen, Cassandra and Jane are all helping to dress me. I can see my reflection in the cheval looking glass: a small, slight figure in the most beautiful gown in the world. The dressmaker has done a wonderful job; the bodice fits like a glove, with the lovely V-shaped panel of gold-embroidered gauze in the front. The sleeves are bell-shaped, ending in a froth of white lace, and the skirt billows out from the narrow waist.

'Stand still,' says Cassandra as I twist to see the back. She is mounted on a small stool and is pinning a short veil of exquisite lace to the back of my head beneath the knot of curls.

'It's snowing,' screams Charles, bursting in through the door, and everyone except me – and Cassandra – moves to see.

'Stand still,' says Cassandra again, and now she arranges the swansdown cloak around my shoulders, leaving it open so that the gown can be clearly seen.

'Now walk slowly and keep your head up. Jane, you put back the hood when she reaches the church. Do it carefully. Don't dislodge the lace!'

When I reach the bottom of the stairs Thomas comes out from the parlour. I think he looks magnificent in his gold braid and navy-blue uniform. He has a sword by his side and so does Lieutenant Price.

Mr Austen had wanted to hire a post-chaise for me, but I refused and said that I would prefer to walk like everyone else.

And now I am so pleased that I said that.

We are a true bridal procession. Thomas and I first, Jane and Cassandra next, then Mrs Austen with her eldest son, James, Henry and Frank side by side, followed by the Leigh-Perrots and Eliza, with Charles racing between everyone. I hold Thomas's arm with one hand and with the other I hold up the satin gown. The ground is still crisp and frosty, and it's perfect for walking. My swansdown cloak makes me glow with warmth.

And the snow is falling gently, slowly, drifting down in pretty crisp flakes, settling lightly on the bare black branches of the elm trees and crystallizing on the small green shoots of the snowdrops.

Mr Austen, already dressed in his cassock and white surplice, meets us at the church porch door and he is the one that puts back my hood. He kisses me like a true father and then tells me to wait for a moment while the others take their places.

Jane and I wait in the little porch with James. It has been arranged that James will give me away; for a moment I am saddened that Edward-John has not bothered to make the journey from Bristol to Steventon, but I put it from me.

And then James opens the door to the church and I gasp.

Yesterday Jane and Cassandra had gone off to 'do the flower vases' in the church. Tom Fowle, Charles, Frank, Harry Digweed, Henry and even James had been with them when they came back in a merry shouting crowd and I was sorry not to have joined them. However, Mrs Austen had kept me busy with some sewing and now I see why.

The small bare church is filled with light from about twenty tall candles. The ledges in front of the six pointed windows have been piled high with branches of yew, the red berries sparkling in the candlelight. Trails of ivy decorate the pews, and here and there a small Christmas rose shows up wired against the smooth glossy green.

The altar table is like a tapestry of red, green and white. Every vase is filled with the mixture of the three colours: red-berried holly stands stiffly behind the delicate Christmas roses and great scrolls of ivy are stitched carefully to a cloth covering the front of the altar.

And then there is a touch on my shoulder. I look around. Edward-John is there. Gently he takes my arm and James falls back.

'You look beautiful,' whispers Edward-John. 'You are so like Mother.'

Slowly I pace the small aisle of the church, my hand on Edward-John's arm, and Jane holds up the train of my dress although the tiles have been scrubbed as clean as Mrs Austen's dairy. Everywhere I look, I can see the care and the love the Austen family have shown me. The small fireplace in the north aisle is blazing with pine logs and the church is so warm that I know Frank has been tending that fire since before dawn – he was chopping wood for most of yesterday and then bringing it to the church in wheelbarrow loads. Over the altar steps there is a large, rather unsteady arch that I've seen Charles hammering together in the barn. It is made from nailed-together elm branches decorated with strands of ivy. Beneath it are two brand-new kneeling cushions – I have had glimpses of Mrs Austen and Cassandra embroidering these over the last few days – and I recognize James's handwriting on the decorative order of service that Mr Austen handed me at the door. When we reach the chancel arch Jane nudges me and whispers in my ear, 'Harry climbed up there yesterday.'

I look up, and hanging down from the high roof beams is a large bunch of mistletoe, dangling from a long red ribbon. Mr Austen glances up too, but he just smiles.

And then the service begins.

Cassandra sobs, and I hear Mrs Austen whispering, 'Control yourself, girl,' but when I look sideways I can see tears sliding down my aunt's face.

The candles flicker, the fire crackles, words slide through my head and out from my lips . . .

'I take thee . . . lawful husband . . . for richer, for poorer . . . in health . . .'

And the awful solemnity of '. . . Till death do us part.'

And then Thomas slides the gold ring on to my finger . . .

And his lips meet mine and I stand encircled in his arms. And we are together and will never be parted.

Author's Note

Many readers of my first Jane book, *I Was Jane Austen's Best Friend*, have written to say how much they enjoyed the notes at the back where I record which parts of the novel are truly biographical, which parts I guessed from evidence and which parts I made up completely.

So now I want to do the same for the second book, *Jane Austen Stole My Boyfriend*.

I think that my inspiration for this book and for its jokey title was a quote from Mary Russell Mitford about Jane as a teenager: 'Mamma says that she was then the prettiest, silliest, most affected, husband-hunting butterfly she ever remembers.' I like that quote. I feel that it makes Jane stand out from the rather well-behaved genteel girls of the period and it was a great help to me when creating her character and describing the fun the girls had in Bath.

As I said in my author's note to Book 1, I have changed Jenny's name from Jane Cooper (couldn't have two Janes) and made her younger than she really was so that she could be nearer in age to Jane Austen.

So what is true? Well, Jane and Jenny truly were great friends. Jane's nephew and biographer, James's eldest son, talks of this. Jenny (Jane) did fall in love with a Captain Thomas Williams, he did propose marriage three weeks after they met and they did get married in

Steventon church in the month of December.

Mr and Mrs Leigh-Perrot did have a West Indian man acting as a servant or butler in their house. In reality he was called Frank, but I renamed him Franklin to distinguish him from Jane's brother. Mrs Leigh-Perrot was accused of shoplifting, put on trial in Taunton and acquitted in rather the manner that I suggest. The records of her trial still exist and I read through them very carefully.

I had a delightful visit to the beautifully preserved city of Bath before writing this book and I hope that I got the details right. You can visit the Assembly Rooms where Jane danced, look at the chandeliers, see the Pump Room and the baths which feature in her novel *Northanger Abbey*, walk past the house in Queen's Square where she stayed with her brother Edward (where I have lodged Eliza in my novel) and see the Leigh-Perrots' house in the Paragon.

Jane's cousin Eliza is a great favourite of mine. I feel that I know her generous, fun-loving character very well from her letters which have been preserved. Many of these letters were to her cousin Philadelphia Walter (Phylly). I'm afraid that I took a great dislike to Phylly from her letters (some of which have also been preserved). She was very rude about Jane when the poor thing was only twelve years old, calling her 'affected and prim' and 'not pretty', but I think the worst was the letter that she wrote to her brother when poor Eliza's mother died. Eliza had nursed her mother, who died of breast cancer, devotedly for months and months, but at the news of the woman's death Phylly seemed to gloat over the fact that Eliza would be left 'friendless and alone' and that it served her right after the 'gay and dissipated life' she had led.

I think that the most important piece of research that I did for this book was the story of Harry Digweed.

As I describe in the book, Harry was the son of the Austens' neighbour, literally the 'boy next door'. Though I feel sure that Jane's elder sister Cassandra burned the majority of the letters where she mentions Harry Digweed, one – which is mainly about how her writing desk was put on to the wrong coach – was rather revealing, as Jane alludes to Harry as 'my dear Harry'. In the eighteenth century this was most unusual. Jane normally, once she was grown up, talks of Mr Lyford, Mr Chute, etc. I think her use of those words might imply that Cassandra knew all about the love affair, but would not want to encourage Jane, as Harry had no money and Jane herself would be penniless.

I followed the career of Harry Digweed as best I could by looking up documents in the Hampshire Records Office and discovered that he rented two farms (from Jane's rich brother Edward) in Chawton and used them to grow hops. Hops were used in beer-making and were a very profitable crop at that time. It looks possible that Harry then went into the brewing business in Alton, a few miles from Chawton. The main brewery there was owned by an elderly lady and the chances are strong that she would have needed a young man as a general manager. Harry rented a house in Alton at the time.

However, even so, he would not have been considered a good match for Jane. And it looks as though her family conspired to part the two.

Fifty years later James's eldest son wrote about a letter written by Mrs Leigh-Perrot which expresses the opinion that the Austens moved to Bath in order to 'get Jane away from that Digweed man'.

Acknowledgements

Anyone writing a biographical novel is always conscious that their airy work of fiction is resting on the shoulders of those who have gone before – those wonderful people who spend years studying books, following up leads in archives, delving into dusty piles of handwritten letters, wandering through draughty graveyards, inspecting the sites of buildings that no longer exist, and always checking that every word they write can be substantiated.

Chief among this heroic band to whom I owe so much must be Deirdre de la Faye. She not only edited the definitive edition of Jane Austen's letters – tracking down every reference with that infinite capacity for taking pains which certainly amounted to genius – she did the same thing with Eliza de Feuillade, Jane's other first cousin, and allowed me to sense the personality of this fun-loving, brave, endearing woman. Deirdre de la Faye has also produced a book, *The World of Jane Austen*, which sat by my bedside during the months when I was writing these books and which proved of inestimable value to me.

The three great biographers Claire Tomalin, David Noakes and Park Honan have added to the picture that I had formed. Penelope Byrde and

Sarah Anne Dowling wrote informative and delectable books on fashion in the time of Jane Austen. Maggie Lane on Jane Austen's Bath and her world was another essential book to have at hand.

Lastly, I must thank Hampshire Archives for their prompt replies and photocopying of the documents relating to Harry Digweed and his life as a farmer in Chawton. It was fascinating to see all the details of the fields where he grew his hops and the rent that he paid for his two farms and to speculate on his possible career as a brewer.